Between Dog and Wolf

__Entre chien et loup__ The hour of metamorphoses, when people half hope, half fear that a dog will become a wolf. The hour that comes to us from at least as far back as the early Middle Ages, when country peopled believed that transformation might happen at any moment."

Jean Genet, Prisoner of Love

Joseph Phillip Natoli

ISBN: 978-0-578-72454-6
LCCN: 2019919745

CHAPTER ONE

"HANDSOME AND GRETA"

Okay. I confess.

I killed Greta's Handsome Johnny and my twin brother, Theo, took the rap for me.

The way Theo asked me to think about this was that he had accepted the burden of my guilt, more willingly, he said, than we had assumed Adam's guilt, although he said I showed no sign of assuming that guilt, my sins of my own originality.

Actually, Handsome Johnny killed Greta. I got a key to Greta's rat hole apartment in the Borough Park section of Brooklyn, right under the El on New Utrecht Avenue. I happen to have a *pied a terre* in the same neighborhood. "Rat hole" is Theo's description and the people living there were all traps for the clean living. He sounded like he had a religion, but he was what he called a nye alistick ate the yeast.

I walk into Greta's apartment and she's already dead, lying at the foot of a bed that Handsome is lying in, smoking. I give'em a What The Feeoak, the old WTF look and all he does is laugh.

"Are you the cleanup guy?" he says to me. "Mr. Wolf? Mr. Wolf. *Pulp Fiction.* Guy comes in and cleans up all the blood, removes the body and so on. He's like a Fixer specializing in body removal. Okay, get to it."

I'm on my knees feeling for a pulse. Greta's face is prune purple. With some small white teeth showing like she was nibbling on squirrel nut. It looks like she died of a too punched in face. My co-host on radio and the true North of my life, Evangeline Solly, advised me not to watch a movie or read a book that began with the naked body of a murdered woman. If she caught me, she'd put a bullet in one of my knees. I knew Eve wouldn't be walking in right now, but I got nervous anyway.

Greta looked better when I first met her at the *New Pompey* dive bar not too many blocks away. I had just heard my mother, my Hampton Bay mother who had inherited two fortunes, was going to marry the kid who cleaned all three swimming pools. That put my dining habits off but not my drinking. Bad news accelerates my drinking, which Sal, my therapist bartender, tells me is totally normal. He thought depression, anger, frustration and a sore throat were a virus best attacked with the brown whiskeys.

Sometimes things happen so fast I can't absorb them. Like now.

This kid punched my girlfriend's face till she died. Actually, I hadn't known her long. Actually, it was a one-night stand. I was on the rebound from another relationship that fired up and then fizzled and then fired up and then … Of course, I'm talking about Ms. Solly.

"I liked her," I said, looking up at this guy.

"Find another one," he said, adjusting a pillow behind his head.

I can't say I enjoyed this kid's attitude. But how did he know I had a real on and off again girlfriend, the one just mentioned. *Mon petit. La mia signora di taglia* special, *meine spezielle Dame.* All those foreign words Theo's parrot Cag, a Congo Africa grey parrot, screamed out when he saw Evangeline Solly. A Little Person. 4' 10" with high heels. He's a very smart bird. He avoids calling her Little Dove or Little Honeypot or any combination of "little." Eve carries a .38 Smith and Wesson Special someplace on her that she can pull out faster than Billy the Kid. She'd turn Cag into a pile of feathers.

So, at that moment I found Greta fascinating, my life with Eve had kind of separated. Our business relationship was melting. Eve said the relationship was emptying her life the way sap runs out of a tree. Terminal boredom had set in and it was my fault. I had a terrible lack of ambition; she had met someone else; I had taken a small amount of dollars out of her purse; I ate with my mouth open; she had been reduced to being a co-something of my failures as a human being; we were both cheating on each other in our open partnership, which she called Deep Cheating. I might have golfed or joined a health club. And so on. One, some or all of those. I'm denying I have faults and just don't have any interest in dealing with them.

I suspected Eve had gone to Atlantic City with some other

Handsome Johnny for the weekend. These handsome Johnnys were out there running like a school of mackerel in the North Sea.

So, when Greta came in the bar, I guess I was ready to meet someone new. She wasn't new but she wasn't old. She listened to the talk radio show Eve and I did, and she liked it. It's the kind of past midnight show that sadists, insomniacs, tweakers, and the entire depressed pre-carrot class enjoy. We mock, muck and mouth off indiscriminately is Eve's opening line on the show. We're unwoke but we're not sleeping. Eve told me all about the pre-carrot class which in letters is "precariat." You'll find out what a genius she is. Not the Bill Fates or Studebaker type of genius or stable like the president.

Greta had come into the bar looking for me. Not too many nice people come in looking for me. She wanted my autograph, fifty bucks for a blow job, and a hundred for a straight lay but I could go gratis if I interviewed her on my radio show. I told her that I'd talk to Eve about it. The interview not the sex.

"When you get an answer let me know," she told me and then I didn't see her again until tonight when she called and said she thought someone was going to kill her and could I come right over?

And so that thing with Greta got that kind of non-start.

Now, she's not alive but dead.

I stand up. Handsome tells me to get on with it and stop hovering over the bed like Frankensting.

"I'm taking a shower," he then informs me, ducking his cigarette out and getting up. He stands up. Naked. The pupils of his eyes are pin sized. He's flying. Punching her lights out was like a flight to the heavens for him, I guess. I don't use any drugs because I want to stay on the ball, which is what my twin brother Theo advised so I could see trouble coming clearly. And he said it always came when I was on the scene because I was the guy making it happen.

I look at Handsome Johnny. I could see why Greta would like him better than me.

Handsome is, as handsome does I heard the parrot say one time.

"You got blood on your hands," I tell Handsome.

He looks at his hands.

"What did she do?" I ask him.

"What?" he says, stupefied by the question. And then, he realizes he's entitled. That's what I saw. I see the Rolex on the night table. The Smartphone, probably latest version. I carry a flip phone myself. I don't like to see all those colorful apps staring at me. It puts me in a kind of zany, cartoon world, which makes some people feel connected and wanted but just makes me want to drink.

A lot that's buzzing around me puts me on edge. I transmit that on the radio, and it makes people laugh. The way Eve describes it, I have a fugue like thing, whatever that is, that people connect with. I don't really have any interest in the lives of others. It comes across in my voice. Eve thinks that "I don't give a fuck about you" tone in my voice is the draw.

Theo doesn't think that Eve Solly is a bright star of encouragement so I shouldn't think my overall nastiness is attractive to anybody. Theo has never liked Eve except for that one time and that goes back a long way, to the first time we met Eve and he wanted her and, big surprise to me, she didn't want him. She wanted me.

TWO

EVANGELINE SOLLY

I first met Eve Solly at the Gallery Players theatre on 14th St. in Park Slope. She was performing in some farce Theo was anxious to see. I suppose because one of the actresses, not Eve, had caught his eye. I went along because Theo said I needed an "airing." Hard to refuse a twin whose paying my *pied a terre* rent and who was the only family member who hadn't cut me off totally.

I had a flask of Jim Beam rye and a ham and swiss on a Kaiser roll, so I settled in nicely along with Theo in the middle of the small theatre. I ate the sandwich, pulled on my flask of rye, dozed off, snored. Theo elbowed me awake. I think I missed the farce part.

Eve had a kid's role, a kind of nasty brat that shot zingers at her mother's boyfriends and pulled snot out of her nose. I don't know where the father was. He wasn't in the play. Theo's lady, whom he had never met, had most of the lines. She was somebody's neighbor or maybe she was the brat's aunt. She could have been the mother. Eve was billed as Evangeline Solly. Lot of name for a kid.

I didn't find out that she wasn't a kid until later, when Theo and I went around to what he called the backdoor and Eve comes out and I see right away that she's not a kid. Just small. Anyway, she comes out this back door of the theatre with the other actress, the one Theo wants to meet.

So, he goes up to her and introduces himself. I lay back and watch. Theo's an imposing kind of guy. My height but not my weight. He keeps what he calls his ideal weight. Good for him. He's not fat faced and has a kind of old movie star thing going on, pencil mustache, receding hairline, bulgy red lined eyeballs. He has a hard time sleeping. I have a hard time not sleeping.

Would the actress want to get a drink? And her friend too. They were both sensational he tells them. Or we could get something to eat, he tells them.

"My brother, Dirk." He points to me. "He's hungry."

Eve looks over at me. "That's your brother?" she asks, right off with a dosage of scorn. "No thanks. I'm going home. There's less shade in my apartment."

That goes over my head.

Theo is not one to take any No's, so he tells her we're okay. We both went to Princeton. We're twins, he tells her.

"What species?" is what Eve tells him.

Theo laughs but not like he was.

"Your twin's got crumbs on his coat," Eve tells him pointing to me.

"Hey, we are knights, my lady," Theo says, still laughing. "Noble, gentle knights."

"I could go for something to eat," Theo's actress says to Eve.

"How about it?" Theo says. "I have a standing reservation at *Fausto's*, a refined ristorante with rustic setting for rustic, seasonal Italian dishes plus biodynamic & rustic reserve wines."

Eve stares at him. "You are the classic stage door Rustic Wanker, aren't you? And he looks like Pant and cruel," she says, once again pointing to me.

And I'm wondering how come I look like that?

"Ah! Tiny, beautiful and well read!" Theo shouts and then in a flash Eve slaps him hard in the face, a kind of tennis player up on your toes swing.

Don't use the diminutive or something like that she tells him. I break out laughing. Theo rubs his cheek, but I can see he's not mad. Theo doesn't get mad. He went to a Taoist preparatory school after Princeton. He tells me what he does is put anger in reserve some place in his mind and pulls it out when he's driving.

"Now we all know where we're at," Theo says." Let's go to *Fausto's* and really get raucous."

I don't know how he did it, but the actresses went for it.

I ordered a few of the most expensive items on the menu: pasta with wild boar sauce, a whole roast chicken with cippolini onions followed by a formaggio plate and tiramisu. We drank three or four bottles of Barolo. Theo was always flush. The family money.

Eve told me one time that she figured he had his inheritance plus mine, but I didn't think it was true.

I'm knife and forking it at a steady pace and I look up and Eve is staring.

"What's what?" I ask.

"I only saw somebody eating like that in a documentary about hogs, "she tells me. "Brindled hogs."

"Probably Berkshire," Theo says.

It's amazing the shit Theo knows. I could have spent fifty years at Princeton and Taoist Prep, and I wouldn't come out knowing half of what he knows.

"Excuse my brother's table manners," Theo tells the two of them. "He has tissues. Issues."

"Mental and physical?" Eve asks and Theo laughs.

"He's gotten most of his social interaction from his hand puppets. Nurse Handjob and Doctor Snotface. He was nine when The Mater took them away from him."

"Nurse Handkerchief and Doctor Meniscus," I said, correcting my brother, who got some pleasure out of mocking my puppets. "Mother didn't take them away. Nurse Handkerchief died."

"Your puppet died? Is he serious? That is so funny. He's funny too. Is he your twin? I mean you look alike, except you kind of look different and talk different?"

"Don't mind her," Eve said, pointing to Theo's once upon a second love. "She's got a bad case of puppet brain. Tell me, how does a puppet die?"

"Her wool unraveled," I told her, remembering that sadness.

"Of course," Eve said. "What might I ask do you do for a living?

"I haven't had much success with anything," I say to Eve who's giving me an appraising look. "I'm looking for work though" is what I say.

"With puppets?"

"Not exactly," I mumbled. "But Theo's got a chain of launderettes in Paris. I just use the one on 55th."

Theo laughs." I just have that one to meet the lovelies of Paris. I'm a venturesome capitalist."

"Let's have some champagne then," Eve tells him. "I don't always get a chance to squeeze the wallet of a venturesome capitalist. I get wet just thinking about it. Me and Ayn Rand."

"So, I take it you are anxious to redistrict the wealth?" Theo asks her.

"Don't say `so'," Eve orders.

"You don't say so?" Theo asks her, puzzled. "Is there a problem?"

Eve tell us she doesn't like it when somebody says something to somebody and then that somebody says the word `So.'

"Really?" Theo asks. "How fascinating."

"Eve's funny like that, not liking this word or that and all, just like they were clothes or jewelry," the chosen actress says. "She's got a thing with words."

Theo gives her a look and I see right off that he thought she was dumb. I know the look and Theo doesn't like dumb in ladies. He likes dumb dogs though. He finds them more loving than smart dogs. He likes his parrot, Cag, the best. She has a 150 IQ and is a MENSA member.

Theo looked at Eve.

I only like a conchacello or something like that kind of 'so' Eve tells him. "I don't like a dismissive whatever so."

"I say whatever all the time," her friend says. "Or 'as if' as if I were listening to them."

"I also have this thing with words," Eve told us, "where people don't put enough space between their brains and their mouth."

"I think that's hilarious," her friend said, laughing. "As if."

Theo sighs and then looks back at Eve.

"I agree. No one really listens to anyone anymore," he tells her, nodding and I can see he's now attracted to Eve because she slapped him and is witty and quick with the quips. Plus, I see she has eyes that kind of magnetize you. I mean they drew me from my plate more than once. Theo says she's caustic and she tells him she's like acid on copper with people she thinks are assholes and he fits the bill. That makes me laugh too so Theo gives me that be quiet look.

So, … is that a conchacello `so'?

I don't know but Theo was excited like he gets when we're searching tide pools and he finds what he calls a pricey chard from the past

Seemed to me that Eve was not as excited by meeting Theo as he was meeting her. She seemed to be having a lot of fun turning what he said to her around, like he says, "Going forward I see some toney awards for you ladies" and Eve tells him he should go forward to a great mishaps. She told me later it was perhaps not mishaps she had said though what I said had worked too.

Then the other actress, the taller one, the one Theo took us to see, gets really pissy and drunk and Theo tells her there's nothing worse than a bad actress who's obviously also an idiot who can't hold her liquor. He goes on like this about what a really bad actress who's also an idiot and can't hold her liquor. The farce sucked.

Eve was the only one good in it.

So ... I mean, and then, Eve reaches across the table, half her body on the tablecloth and gives Theo another hard slap. It looks like he's not going to save his anger until later but then all he says is "You're a shitty actress too" and she right away tells him that at least she's not a shitty human being which he is.

Then she tells her friend, Debbie or Peggy or Maggie, who's crying, let's get the fuck out of here to which her friend Jenny says these guys are jerks and she grabs Theo's coat and heads for the door and Theo jumps up, goes after his coat and they both go outside, leaving me alone at the table with Eve. I'm a little worried she's going haul off on me for using the word `so.'"

"Wanna take me home, Pants and Cruel?' Eve says to me.

I'm putting the finishing fork to my tiramisu but I'm surprised.

"Me? I thought you told Susie you wanted to go home?"

"Shut up and come on."

She tells the waiter that Theo is outside and if he grabs him, Theo will pay up. I follow her to the kitchen, through it and then out a door where a guy is bringing out a pail of garbage.

"Can you afford an uber?" she asks me when we're out on the street. I look to the front of the place, but I don't see Theo or the actress.

"Theo pays," I tell her. "What's an uba?"

"Let's walk. We can catch the bus."

She walks fast even though she's kicking it with high heels.

"I live on New Utrecht. 55th," I tell her.

She stops and gives me a WTF look and asks me if I know *The New Pompey Bar* and I shake my head and she says good because that's where we're going, and she doesn't want to go to any bar where I hang out. She said she didn't have the patience for it.

On the B9 bus we sit side by side and she says I take up one seat and a half and she takes up a half so we're all good. We're made for each other she tells me, but she's got this I don't think so look.

"You didn't like Theo," I ask her after about ten blocks of silence between us. I feel a large intestine eruption coming on and try to wish it away. Wild boar is hell on the innards.

"What's to like," she tells me. "I mean he likes himself enough so he doesn't need me to like him."

I laugh.

"Theo says I'm a walking farce."

"That you should believe," she tells me. "What happened to Dr. Maniscus?"

"He's at the pied a terre with his friends. He's kind of worn out now but he still gives good medical advice."

"You know you're on a spectrum? You didn't really go to Princeton, did you? You should have. They need somebody like you. The whole fucking education system needs a guy who lives with puppets and gets medical advice from a puppet."

"I don't really listen to that. Why did you smack Theo? Women usually really like him."

"Your brother thinks everybody but him is simple. You know how I would describe me?"

I thought of saying tiny but beautiful but I didn't say anything.

"I'm caked with a salty humor, rough with splinters of disillusion, and tarred with a bright black authenticity."

"Wow! But you're not black."

"Don't say wow," she told me. "You get a dumber look on your face when you say Wow! Anyway, somebody said that about a great lady, not me but it fits."

She studies my profile, which my mater had said was decent when I was nine.

"You've got some strong facial lines there," she told me, "but the face overall needs more guidance from your brain. I don't think it's getting it. But there's definitely something latent."

I rubbed my jaw. Forgot to shave.

"You able to drink some more, big guy, because that's what I intend to do when we get to *The Pompey*. I need to hang one on. Meeting your brother requires an antidote."

I nodded.

"Yeah, take a lot of booze to soak through that bulk," she told me, pinching my forearm.

"I guess it is what it is," I said, realizing that she wasn't exactly attracted to me the way I felt attracted to her.

"That's bullshit," Eve said, this time slapping me, but lightly on the face. "It is what somebody tells you what it is. Somebody towering over you, think they have all the power. Your brother, right? You listen to him?"

"Our father. He's a scientist. Says with identical twins, there's only so much brains and I got some, but Theo got most."

"I don't know what kind of scientist your old man is but next time you see him tell him to go fuck himself. Okay?"

I didn't nod or do anything.

"Listen to me. You're not that guy's twin. Theo. The guy I just sat at table with? He's his own twin.

He's got the whole twin thing wrapped in himself. No room for you. He's eating you up. That's what those fucking to the manor born narcissists do. He's the whole twinship in himself. He's a fucking twin without pity. Wake up."

I didn't think she knew Theo very well, that he paid the rent at my *pied a terre* and helped me plan my life.

Yeah, the first time we met, Theo got to like her but she slapped him, couple of times, hard, and she liked me, which I didn't expect, but we stayed at her bar, *The Pompey* until it closed and then she wanted to see my *pied a terre* so I took her there.

She said she wanted to see my retchings. Kind of strange. Right off the bat, I didn't follow half of what she said.

"I'm never going to be the bottom with you," is what she told me when she climbed on me, naked. "I want the sex but not the crush. And don't swallow me. I'm Eve. Not Jonah. And pace the friction."

A lot of crazy went on from there and then we had a radio show and I went into the future for the first time and my brother didn't plan it.

CHAPTER THREE

MR. SPINALZO

The first question Eve puts to every caller is "How tall are you?"

Depending upon the answer to that, it can go very bad for the caller.

I start with a thank you so much for calling and not a question about how tall you are or why don't you go fuck yourself which is what Cag ... Theo's parrot ... uses when I come into a room. Every time. Without fail. But I'm not the kind of person who will take lines from a parrot, even if he's the smartest of his lot.

Right now, in Greta's apartment, this naked entitled murderer of my one night postponed stand girlfriend Greta was working on my one remaining nerve-end devoted to the Seven Virtues. You keep your eye on the ball and stay devoted to the Seven Virtues and you'll be alright. That's Theo, not his parrot.

"I know she could be annoying as hell," I tell Handsome Johnny. "Pissed me off a lot that one time I was with her. I didn't text her the next day. I had no friends on Faceship or Instacram. Only losers had flip phones. You don't know how to answer this woman. I can see that."

He's now giving me an amazed look, like the kind of look a Queen would give a butler for chatting her up at a royal dinner. But then too he's looking at me the way my tutor Mr. Spinalzo ...

Mr. Spinalzo?

Head of hair piled up like a haystack, grease spotted ties, worn out shoes, high pitched voice that cracks and he coughs a lot.

We're nine and Mr. Spinalzo weighs what one of our thighs

weighs. Our father, an inventor scientist registered genius something, can't afford to pay a tutor so we have Mr. Spinalzo, M.A., who takes five dollars an hour. Theo says the M.A. stands for Missing Aorta.

"I need the money," Mr. Spinalzo told us as we sat in the kitchen, our composition books in front of us. He said he was teaching us the hidden wisdom of people like Herman Twisthiswristoff. He taught Theo and me to be good card magicians is all I remember. And we memorized: "This visible world is something or other that's invisible and is full of other somethings besides humans, like crayons, angles, and Ellie Mendals, who we never met.

"I need family support here in order to do my job," Mr. Spinalzo explained. "And I'm not getting it."

"Mother and father are getting a divorce," Theo told him, still drawing amazingly lifelike pictures of naked women. I suspected he was posing a couple of the upstairs maids naked for practice. Theo threw his underwear under the bed just so he could see Ooh Anna, for instance, bend over, looking for them.

The divorce seemed to cheer Mr. Spinalzo up and he nodded knowingly.

"Your mother will be free of her burden," he told us. "And I think both of you will be also. Your father is very cold in regard to human empathy. In short, your father is a terrible human being."

"Won't father be free of his burden also?" Theo said, cheerily.

That made Mr. Spinalzo sad.

"Your father ... and I say this because I think you boys need to know this. Your father is lunatic. Mad, actually."

"Besides being a dick?" Theo asks.

"That also. He is out of whack with the movements of the planets. I'm sorry to have to tell you this."

Theo nodded. He had that thoughtful look on his face that like his cheeriness was totally phony. For Theo, Mr. Spinalzo was a great source of fun. I think because he had to work for what Theo called wages. Theo thought the very idea of wages very, very funny. Meanwhile, I was confusing "mad" with "angry." Father was never angry, being always in the Lab.

"You think our father is mad?" Theo queries.

Actually, Theo's passion to torture our tutors didn't trouble me as I didn't like being tutored. I had no talent for it.

"I don't believe he thinks so," Theo says, holding up a drawing of a naked woman. "She's purposely not anatomically correct. Ooh Anna's breasts are bigger and her legs thinner.

I claim artistic license."

I saw she had enormous breasts and fat thighs.

"That is so very sad," Mr. Spinalzo said, shaking his head, taking the drawing and staring at it.

Then he quoted some Latin, which he always did when looking at the pictures Theo drew, though he wasn't Latin.

It sounded like "In Sid's sinus omelets and Amish fairies create roses."

"Every madman thinks everybody else mad," Theo translated, as he always did although he wasn't Latin either. My father said we were of a more ancient stock than the warps, whoever they were.

"And that is so unfortunate," Theo concluded.

I was still stunned by the news that our father was mad.

"Don't they say all great scientists are crazy?" I said, wanting to defend my father from the charge.

Mr. Spinalzo gave me that pitying look I had gotten used to in my nine years.

"Your father, P.T. Bratter, thinks your origin is that lump of earth he keeps in a fish tank. Neither the Macaronism nor Micronomism is that."

"You mean the shit rock?" I asked, stunned. "The one that smells awful?"

"Precisely," Mr. Spinalzo replied, nodding.

"And how sane is a man who dresses in our mother's underwear?" Theo asked him, beginning another drawing that looked a lot like our mother. She spent as much time in her bedroom as father spent in the Lab.

Mr. Spinalzo got angry.

"Young people should be like creatures without speech," he whispered to Theo. "Or things will go bad for him."

He attempted to run a hand through the stuff on top of his head and then he gave up.

"You boys should know that we are all slaves to our limitations. Sex and sleep."

"And food," Theo added, winking at me.

Theo didn't tell anyone about Mr. Spinalzo dressing in our mother's underwear. Not then. He liked having Mr. Spinalzo around teaching us card tricks and how to disappear under a table, and how to read the stars and name the constellations and how to pick out an evil spirit in a crowd. But mostly he liked to bust his bollocks, as Theo put it.

Mr. Spinalzo tutored us until, as Theo put it, "they came for him."

CHAPTER FOUR

THEO TAKES THE RAP

I looked around the room and I only saw Handsome Johnny. No Theo. No Mr. Spinalzo. I do a lot of mind travelling during the day.

"Shut up, jerk, and get this done," Handsome ordered, working his way through what I might be to what he knew he was.

"I never slapped her," I told him, looking down at Greta's naked body, her arms somehow hugging her head, and poked the body with the tip of my all weather Timbos.

"But you, you're a different kind of guy. You literally punched her … "

"Who the hell are you?"

"Her brain into one of her ears is what it looks like."

I'm leaning down, studying the body again like one of those medical examiners on TV.

I guess everything for Handsome Johnny had gone beyond knowing and into funny because he starts laughing, not a good laugh but like one of those asylum laughs you hear in the movies, the kind a sane person can't figure out. Something shorted out and something else cross wired and overloaded a tottering mind was the way Theo explained human behavior to me, myself always his example.

I block HJ from the door to the john. His head reached my shoulder. He's not short but I'm door frame size. I start to tell him I don't see the humor when he makes a rush at me so it's my turn to laugh because he's so small and feisty but I don't get a chance because Johnny sweeps one leg fast and high and kicks me in the boys.

I bend over to grab them protectively and then he does some kind of ballerina twirl and lands me another kick right square into my nose. I reach out blindly, holding my nose with one hand, feeling and seeing the blood rush, and then something shorted out and something else cross wired and overloaded a mind tottering on the edge and I grab the next leg he throws at me and swing him off the floor, one handed. I let him go like a shot put and his head, the really vulnerable part, finds a home in the wall.

When I come out of the bathroom with a wash cloth to my bloodied nose, I see that Handsome Johnny is not moving, his eyes are open and popping and his neck doesn't look good. He lost his good lucks with one throw. I do the CSI thing again and feel for a pulse.

I sit on the bed and call Eve.

"I'm away from my phone" is what I hear, which is a lie because she never is. Away from her phone. She carries it alongside her .38.

That's when I called Theo. He came over right away.

Mr. Spinalzo said Theo was a problem solver of problems he created. He skipped high school or maybe it was grammar school. It didn't take him long to figure out what my problem was here, unloop the knots, find the trail, see it all clear.

Then he went through all the reasons why I should get the hell out of there and he should call the cops. He should say he came over to talk Greta into giving me one more chance and he found these two dead bodies. He'd get Eve Solly's lawyer friend, very good and very solid, Summer Arpeggio, to defend him if it came down to an arrest.

I know he was lying about Summer Arpeggio. She wasn't solid and she wasn't good. But she did have what people called a way about her. She could run at you like you were holding up a red cape. Sal the bartender at *The New Pompey* told me. He knew because he had gone out with her in the 8th grade. It was a hard relationship for me to imagine, home tutored as I was, though I think I did the 8th grade twice. Or maybe it was the 4th I did twice and the 8th once.

"She throws every word in the dictionary at you until you give up" is the way Sal described Summer Arpeggio.

I didn't know until much later that Theo knew Summer Arpeggio got herself locked up for disorderly conduct more than she kept any client out of jail. Sal wasn't sure if she ever had a client.

Whatever and so on. You see, the thing was, and it took me a long time to figure out the why of it, Theo wanted to go to prison. It was at that moment the only safe spot for him. He had been a bad boy and how bad I didn't find out until much later.

Instead of saying they were both dead when he arrived, Theo had to confess to finding Greta dead, getting angry and taking it out on Handsome Johnny. It was an accident. He just went too far. Johnny was attacking him. He was standing his ground. Self-defense. He doubted that the case would ever appear before a judge, especially in Texas. But we were in Brooklyn. And right then he knew it would go to trial and that Summer Arpeggio would fuck up and he knew he'd go to jail. Huge mystery to me at the time.

Okay, I said, agreeing to his plan.

He had reasons. I had none. I've always been short on reasons. I borrow.

You want to know why I would allow my brother to take the rap?

Well, I did. The way Theo put it if he were locked away, he wouldn't go climbing walls because he had a rich and deep inner life to sustain him. He was self-partnered, so he didn't have to worry about his sex life. He could think in several languages. I barely had American. I also had a paper thin inner life. In truth if I had one, I wouldn't know where to find it. A prison term or execution wouldn't expand it. I'd go bananas in a week. Either that or turn vegetable, which may have been true because Eve Solly said that if I had been born with five points less unused IQ, I'd have to be watered. I recall hearing someone say that in a movie.

This was all explained clearly to me by Theo.

Actually, prison sounded like *my pied a terre New Pompey* life.

You wake up, you go to Ernie's Luncheonette, you have breakfast, you listen to last night's adventures told by the neighborhood adventurers, you go to the *Pompey*, you listen to last night's adventures told to you by maybe different guys, you go back to the *pied a terre*, take a nap, get up and eat the dinner Mrs. A, my landlady has made, you go back to the *Pompey*, you hear moans and groans, shouts and threats, you come home, you sleep.

In prison, you wake up, you eat, you sleep, you eat, you go into the yard, you sleep, you eat, you sleep. You could lift weights if you wanted or visit the library. You could go out on a road gang or make license plates or sew garments or work in the laundry or make cold calls to old people and pitch a wealth management or reverse mortgage scheme. You could call old people and tell them their identity had been stolen, get all their identity details and then steal their identity. Entrap manure ial stuff like that.

Theo could catch up on all his reading in several languages. I on the other hand couldn't get into words on a page like I could if they were spoken. In fact, I had a hard time seeing the connection.

But then again, the way Theo figured it, neither he nor I would be serving any time.

We came from an elite lineage, though I was the family discard. Lots of reasons there. Theo said he had the kind of police record that Rev. Billy Gravehand and Evangelist Billy Sunray had. I had a lot of citations: failure to piss in properly designated locations, felony loitering in the Hamptons, a couple or three bar fights that went viral on *YouTube*, some jay walking smoking a jay, failure to yield while driving without a license, disturbing the peace in private compounds, shooting air fowls in city parks, contempt of Morgan Stanley and a few other banks, causing emotional distress to the mail lady, a Section 8 from the military.

I enlisted right after I got thrown out of Princeton. I don't know how I got in. Oh, yeah. Theo took the SAT's for me. Identical twins have a lot of benefits.

CHAPTER FIVE

WILLIAMS AND MORAN

I wasn't the only one who didn't get through boot camp at Fort Bragg, N.C., the largest military installation in the world, 50,000 active duty personnel. That number included the three of us who were being held on bad conduct charges pending on compliance with Section 8 review.

Nick Williams, who was called Nicky Sweetheart, reminded me a lot of Theo because he could repeat things he read but he was kind of lost in some kind of dream world with some lady he called his sweetheart in his head and nowhere else. That wasn't Theo. Theo had three feet on solid ground and liked his sweethearts on a bed.

Williams, though, got the very highest score on the Armed Services Vocational Aptitude Battery Test but was failing the shrink exam. I was borderline something, going through a couple of rounds of shrink interrogation. I was they said a low functioning Asperger fully able to fire a weapon. Theo said they'd put me in the Cannon Father brigade or something like that.

My mother's third husband, Jabba the Hut, a gazillionaire, arranged for Theo to begin work immediately at one of his firms when he graduated Princeton. But when I got thrown out of Princeton, he arranged for me to go into the military. He thought a tour in Iraq would be a wakeup call and possibly trigger my will to power. If that didn't happen, I might disappear into the desert or, better yet, step on an IED.

Dennis Moran was a buddy of Williams but they weren't much alike. He got into trouble right off and got Williams and me into trouble too. He had a juvenile record but the Court had sealed it is what he told me.

Moran started a fire in C Barracks, stood in the middle of it yelling "Burn baby, Burn!," Williams dashed into the flames to save his diary where all his poems and pleas and whatnots to his sweetheart were being threatened by the flames, which is what he was screaming, and I went in to carry them both out, which I did but my Zippo lighter fluid, which I had given to Moran, was found at the scene and I went with Moran and Williams into the Stockade.

I told Major Sweatscough that Moran had started the fire and Moran told the Major that I had started the fire and Williams told the Major he may have started the fire but it may have been in a dream.

So, the three of us got Sectioned 8 out of the service after spending six months in the Stockade. We were destined to become good friends.

I remember it was Christmas when we got out and I took Moran and Williams to the family Farnsworth Estate out on East Egg. This family compound had been built in a potato field, but the potatoes had gone because only the Irish ate potatoes and we weren't Irish.

I didn't know where else to go and they didn't have any place to go. Moran did want to see if he could, in his words, pay the monthly nut without working. Williams wanted to find his sweetheart and seemed confident that he could though he didn't have the vitals as Moran put it. Long Island seemed like a good place to look for her.

So, they came along with me. Williams was about my age, 23, and Moran looked older but said he too was 23. My mother had divorced P.T., claiming that he had gone off the deep end, abaft the beam, although he didn't sail. There were other reasons. I remembered Mr. Spinalzo saying that my father was nuts, which was possibly something my mother agreed with.

She had divorced P.T. and married a Wall Street investor named Fartsworth, called "Gunner" on the stock exchange, who had made millions starting up something, maybe a car or a lawn mower.

The guy who greeted us wasn't Fartsworth, who had stroked and died, but the Fartsworth financial advisor, Jabba the Hut. I had forgotten his real name. I mostly remember the made up names Theo gave people. Theo claimed years later that he was the linguistic filter of my past. Anywho, the Mater had married Jabba, who dropped his own name and took the name Fartsworth.

Despite all these fathers, the only face I fixed the word father to was P.T.'s holding a lump of primordial rock which he said was what had really fathered me long, long ago. Never made any sense to me but that shit rock, as Theo referred to it, was destined to play a big part in my life, like Vesuvio and Pomp Bay. That rock seemed to me then a big part of his mad side.

My mother had married Jabba for what she called "fiscal and bodily security, warmth, understanding, and digestive and mental relief." Theo said Jabba was big enough to cover all of that. Unlike Theo and I who Theo said were of Rabble Lays Pants and Grulio size, or something like that, Jabba was what he called just a fat fuck.

"So your hitch is over," Jabba said as we three newly released Stockade prisoners leaned on the massive bar in his living room.

My mother sat on a sofa by a fireplace big enough for me to lie down in it, which I had on occasion during Fartsworth's tenure. This was my first time in the house under Jabba's regime.

He was behind the bar happily tending to our needs. His belly pushed against the bar and his shirt buttons were popping.

I was surprised he had let us in. I wondered if he was disappointed I hadn't stepped on an IED in Iraq.

"Yes, sir, Colonel," Moran told him, sitting on one of the high stools, his eyes on the array of bottles displayed in front of a thirty square foot mirror that we could see our faces in as well as Jabba's fat ass.

Moran had one blazing red eye and one calming blue eye. He spoke with what Williams said was a more than slightly vulgar accent of American English tinted with Gullah. Williams claimed that Moran's speech was a violation of Midwestern Standard English, which Williams, who spoke as if he was born and raised in London among the Irish, held to be a peachable offense.

Moran had slapped the battered leather briefcase he always had with him on the bar. I don't know what was in it, but he carried it everywhere. He took it out of a locker at Penn Station when we got out of the Stockade.

"Me and the Army got along like a hooker at High Mass."

Jabba giggled.

"Well, water under the bridge. The horse is already out of that barn. Too late for tears. And so on. What are you drinking, Mr. Moran?"

"I'll have a Robert E. Lee High-Ball," Moran said, nodding. "Yeah, that's what I'll have. Call me Dent. That's what friends call me. I've got a slight dent over here. You can feel it."

He leaned over and parted the thin hair on his head with one hand so Jabba could see and feel the dent.

Jabba declined.

"I don't know that one," Jabba said. "Robert E. Lee High-Ball. Sounds feisty."

"Dickel sour mash," I said, out of my mental warehouse of mixed drinks.

"I don't either, Colonel," Moran said. "I just remember the name. Change that to a Millionaire Sour. Serve it in a clean glass."

"Don't know that one. How about my favorite, a Scotch High-Ball?"

"Yeah," Moran said, visibly annoyed. "Hold the Scotch and give me a shot of any bourbon. Just make sure it's not a High-Ball."

He laughed and broke into song:

"Drink a high-ball at nightfall,

Be good fellows while you may,

For tomorrow may bring sorrow;

So tonight let's all be gay."

"My sentiments exactly," Jabba sang out and he poured himself another shot out of an unmarked crock.

"Don't you drink too much," my mother whispered into my back.

I jumped. I thought she was sitting over there on the sofa.

"I need to talk to you alone. Seriously."

"Drink, Sarah?" Jabba cried out jovially to her. She shook her head and walked out of the room. It looked like she had jumped when he spoke to her.

"And what will you have ... Nicholas?"

Williams ignored him. He was staring at a couple of ivory carved elephants behind the bar.

"You like those?" Jabba asked, following Williams' gaze to the elephants.

"We'll tak'em," Moran said. "Wrap'em up."

"The elephant must be a symbol," Williams said in a very low voice. "But of what? They're like survivors of another age. Before we humans."

"Fair enough," Moran said, and knocked back his bourbon.

Williams wandered away from the bar.

"Hey, Nick," Moran called out to him. "You need to have something in your hand. Have a tonic water."

He broke out in song again, which he had a habit of doing when he drank.

In time of trouble and lousy strife,
You have still got a darlint plan,
You still can turn to a brighter life –
A pint of plain is your only man!

Williams turned and looked at him. He had a pale, thin face, thin, sandy hair and his eyes when he focused them on you were like weak headlights lost in a thick fog.

"Flann O'Brien," is all he said.

Then he shook his head.

"How about letting go of some of that elixir you're drinking?" Moran asked Jabba. "How come a millionaire like you ain't drinking a Millionaire Sour?"

Jabba laughed.

He poured Moran a shot and another for himself. I picked up my shot and the three of us saluted our health and good fortune.

"So what's the New Year's resolution, young gentlemen?"

"Lower the flag!" Moran yelled out and then farted, loud and long.

"Cheers," I said.

"Sláinte!" Jabba shouted.

Whatever was in his mystery crock probably had a radioactive alcohol content.

I saw Williams in the bar mirror walking toward us. He stopped two inches from Jabba's face.

"From childhood's hour I have not been
As others were -- I have not seen
As others saw."

Jabba gave him a surprised WTF look.

"So there is something of a poet in you, Nicholas," Jabba said, backing away from Williams.

"Edgar Allan Poe," Moran told us, nodding.

I gave him a quizzical look. I don't think Moran could read. I mean I never saw him read anything all the time we were in the stockade. He liked to watch my card magic. He picked it up easily and gotten way better than me.

"He told me," Moran told me.

"I was a captain," Williams said.

"A decent occupation," Jabba replied, hesitantly.

"If men live decently, Colonel," Moran said, "it is because discipline saves their very lives for them. Sophocles said that. My friend Williams was a captain. No offense meant, Colonel."

"And then I knew I couldn't be a captain," Williams went on.

"If there is no God or any gods at all, how can I be a captain?"

Jabba took to rubbing his hands as he thought about that one.

I knew how to let deep stuff like that fly off so none of this troubled me. When Moran and Williams went back and forth with each other from what Moran said was the Hatter's picnic table, I kind of tuned out.

"Well, I find that it's best to encourage your fellow man to believe in something," Jabba said, kind of nervous like. He was probably beginning to wonder why he let us into the house. I didn't know why.

"Exactly," Moran replied, enthusiastically. "Like Williams here believes in his sweetheart. Like Don Cricket. To dream the impossible dream, to go blah, lala."

"And what belief have you, Mr. Moran?"

"I'm a Sweat and Pourgian."

"Not quite sure what that is. Christian denomination?"

"Scientist," Moran said, nodding, pouring from the special crock.

"If you cut me, don't I bleed?" he cried out. "But don't call a doctor."

His own words put him into a fit of laughing.

"Sickness is an illusion, right?" Jabba said. "Prayer is the cure."

"It's a mental error," Williams shouted, bending over, eyes closed. "That's what they say about the sweetheart."

"And so on," Moran said, nodding. "Getting back to the Sweat and Pourgian. It's a Swedish cult. We spend a few hours in a hot sauna and then jump into the Baltic Sea. It's an eye opener I can tell you. You should try it sometime. Got a yacht? We could sail there. Better yet, how about loaning me the yacht so I can do a test run?"

Jabba laughed, but it had a tinge of fear in it.

I could see Moran and Williams were beginning to rock Jabba back on his heels. I had seen this routine in Barracks C. any number of times. It always ended badly.

"I see I am drinking with erudite young men," Jabba said. "I compliment you, Dirk. I see a bright future ahead for all of you. Genius wears well in this world."

"It's better to wear out than rust out," Moran told him. "Did I tell you that genius is commonplace where Williams and I are from."

"And where might that be?"

"A place where genius is more often found in a cracked pot than in a whole one," Moran shot back and slapped Jabba on the back. "Where joy ruled the day and love the night."

"I need to set my GPS to get there," Jabba shot back, trying to get into the swing of madness.

"You don't need that," Williams told him. "Take any road we've already paved, you can't go wrong. The whole country is one vast asylum. I can't find my sweetheart there. Long Island is a severe disappointment to me."

"That's a bit too pessimistic for such a young man, isn't it, Mr. Williams?" Jabba asked him.

"What is?" Williams replied.

Jabba took a deep breath but said nothing.

"Dirk's a pessimist," Moran said, pointing to me the way a prosecutor does, "but he doesn't let it get in the way of his appetite. Right, big guy?"

I could see Jabba kind of tottering behind the bar. Might have been the secret mash in the crock or Moran and Williams. Probably all three.

I figured it was time I went in search of my mother.

CHAPTER SIX

MOM & THE MOB

I got lost looking for her. I had pretty much grown up in P.T.'s Lab compound in an off campus abandoned lot and hadn't spent much time here in the manor house.

There was a fragrance. My mother's perfume or toilet water or whatever. I followed it. Knocked on a door.

She was sitting at a small writing table writing. When I came in, she jumped up. She rushed to me and put her arms around me. She was a tall lady, well over six feet, who had, as they say, kept up her gangly appearance. She didn't seem to have trouble finding husbands. I think money drew them in.

"What are you writing?"

"I'm writing something to be left to you and your brother. There's so much you both need to know about … "

She began to cry and I led her over to a small couch she had in the room. I glanced at the bed. Jabba would crush the whole length of her if he slept in that with her.

"About what?"

"Gunner didn't have a natural death," she said, sobbing. "He was killed. Murdered by his partner."

"Jabba?"

"Who? Maybe. I don't know why. Yes, I know why. They were both gangsters. Criminals. They laundered money for The Mob."

"The Mob? What Mob?"

It came to me then that she was the whacko one and of course being whacko she had accused P.T. of being whacko.

"Who knows? That's the way The Mob works. Nobody knows who they are or if they are. The staff here say The Mob is the Deep State. Whatever could that be? The President says they're at the southern border. They dig tunnels under toilets. They travel in caravans. But we have drones. Oh, it makes me sick."

She glanced toward her own in suite WC.

"The Mob is on *Facebook*," she said, grabbing my sleeve. "They might be visitors. From another planet. Or Chinese. They make furniture. And minds. They want to hurt the rich. It takes a whole village to make one of them and yet there's enough of them to travel in caravans. Who does that? I tell you, I can't stand it. I'm disoriented and possibly a wreck. "

I got the impression The Mob was everybody, which meant nobody.

"Did I say someone killed Mr. Farnsworth?"

Kind of strange that she called her second husband Mister. She leaned toward me and whispered in my ear.

"And Port is part of it."

"Jabba?"

Jolly, fat rolls Jabba? He himself could be the whole mob.

"He handles the details of the laundering operation," my mother said, nodding, her eyes darting round the room as if it were filled with spies. The Mob's spies.

For a second, I was tempted to get the details on what the hell this operation was, but I didn't want to fuel her nuttiness.

"I'm frightened," she told me and I could feel her shaking. "My life is in danger."

"Tell me, was P.T in this laundry business?"

She shook her head.

"No. He's in his own ring in Hell. He's not at all stable. Only when he's in his Lab. His Lab associates are co-dependents. That terrible woman with the purple hair. She's was a Nazi. She told me. She did awful things to innocent Jews. Yes, your father is so awful. Not really human. But he's not a gangster. No Mob would take him. I've told you before. He's a liability."

I think the Nazi she was referring to was Madame Uberalles, one of P.T.'s Lab associates.

I looked over at the bedside tables to see if there were any drug bottles. Opioids.

"You don't believe me?" she said, suddenly, angrily, pushing away from me.

"You know what I think?" I said. "I think you need to talk to Theo about this."

She shook her head.

"Theo's working for them in Paris."

"Laundering?"

"He's working for Richard ... "

"Who's Richard?"

"Richard Port. Jabba. You idiot. You're out there drinking with him along with those two lost souls you brought here with you. Oh, I wish you had more of a brain in your head. The best lack brains and the worst are very ballsy. I wish I could trust Theo. I can trust you but that's like trusting Winston Churchill."

"The British guy?"

"No, silly. My pug."

"You think Theo is in The Mob laundering for Jabba in Paris?"

"I'm afraid so," she said, shaking again.

I stood up.

"I got to get back. Jabba might think you're telling me about The Mob. You wouldn't want that, would you?"

I know I sounded like the guy who was trying to get around a mad dog and find an escape window.

"You don't believe a word I've said, do you?"

"What? That you married one insane guy and two gangsters? That The Mob is going to kill you? And that my brother is in Paris laundering shirts? And The Mob is everybody but Jesus and his epistles. What's not to believe?"

That comment made her angry.

"I wish to God, if there was a God, you'd have some religion in you. You could have picked any of the gods to believe in. P.T. always said you have limited understanding of quadruple equations or something like that. Now I can see you have limited compassion also. It's probably my own fault. I should not have left P.T. in charge of your education."

"I guess so. Did you know Mr. Spinalzo used to dress in your underwear and Mr. Patawala didn't know as much English as Theo's parrot."

She gave me a "I am so disgusted by you" look.

"No chance of you learning anything the twenty years after all that," she mocked. "I've listened to that radio show you have with your little paramour. Nieve Jolly. You both sound low and vulgar. Selfish. Nasty. Very small. So small for such a large, over large man. You could have been a god of Wall Street.

And that tiny, nasty woman? She sounds vile. Odious. Very, very odious and lecherous."

"I'd tell you to call in but we got cancelled."

"I'm surprised. It seems like the world is full of people who would enjoy the filth you two spewed over the airwaves. Who doesn't want to be mocked by a vicious, little woman with a deep, lecherous voice?"

Spew. The word triggered a rhyme that was Theo's favorite:

"The only man that e'er I knew who did not make me almost spew was Fuseli: he was both Turk and Jew—And so, dear Christian friends, how do you do?"

I did as previously instructed and left her boudoir.

CHAPTER SEVEN

MUCH FURTHER OUT

When I got back to the merry band at the bar, I saw right off everything had gone sour, not like it happens after everyone has smoked too much righteous weed and fallen into their own mindscapes but more like children all grown up had returned home for the festive holidays and wrung their aged parents out with all the wrongs they had done to them when they were growing up and now both camps sat wary of each other.

Jabba was sitting sprawled on a couch and Williams and Moran were on a couch facing him. Jabba seemed pretty drunk. Moran and Williams seemed sober. If they weren't, they hid it well. I had been present when both drank mythic levels of jars.

I went to the bar and poured myself another Dickel.

Jabba was giving me a steely eyed look.

"Did your mother tell you I was trying to kill her?" he said to me in a new voice, the voice hidden under the other. The voice I figured was your inner life voice when your inner life was Dark Vegas.

"Something like that," I said.

"What is life without the radiance of love?" Williams then cried out, his back to us.

Jabba turned his attention to Williams and then back to me.

"What's your intention with this little visit with these gentlemen?"

"They had no place to go. I brought them along."

"I intend to find my sweetheart," Williams told Jabba, as he walked back to the bar.

"Put a little Satan in that," Moran said, getting up and going to the bar where he poured from the magic crock into Williams's glass and then his own.

Williams knocked it back quickly.

"Don't you just love that word. Sweetheart," Moran said. "It reminds me of when I was like 22 in Port Urine, Michigan and knocking up the ladies like pins falling in a bowling alley. Pardon my image. I was at that time blind to the predicament of women in a patriarchal society."

I began to image an even smaller, young Moran with one blazing red eye throwing a bowling ball and the pins screaming for help. Williams behind him, waiting for his turn.

Moran poured a shot of crock elixir in Jabba's glass.

"We're two shots ahead of you," Moran told him, bringing the drink over to him. "That's the trouble with the world. It's always two shots ahead of us."

"I'm going to bed," Jabba said, flatly. "You and your friends can make your own way out. Just don't be here in the morning."

He got up and faced Moran who was blocking his way.

"Do you know that there is a moment in each day Satan cannot find?" Moran asked Jabba.

"Have the drink," Moran said to Jabba, hand in Jabba's waistband and yanking him back toward the bar where Moran pulled a .45 out of that worn briefcase.

Jabba looked at it and instead of shivering, his eyes just narrowed into tiny slits.

"What's the gun for, Mr. Moran?"

"You know about guns? Delta is now using 9mm Glock 17s, 19s and 34s. The 75th teams mostly use the Sig Sauer 226.DEVGRU, or SEAL Team 6, does use Heckler & Koch .45 for special occasions when they need a suppressed capability. I bought this one black market when we were in Stockade."

He laid the gun on the bar.

"Two G's and it's yours"

Jabba poured himself another shot and knocked it back.

He turned to me.

"Did you know your friend Moran here told me that he plans on stealing all he can in one night's work and then setting the house on fire? What do you think of that? Extraordinary man. Will you be going to prison with him and this other lunatic?"

He motioned to Williams who paid no attention to the gesture.

I looked at Moran. He winked at me.

"I think you should take him seriously," I said. "Can we have a few words Moran?"

"As many as you want," Moran said, slapping me at the waistline.

I got him into the entrance hall. That's a foyer castle size.

"I didn't bring you here to rob the place and burn it down."

Moran laughed.

"I wouldn't do that. Come on. You know us better than that."

"My mother tells me this fat guy in there is connected to what she calls The Mob. They had her previous husband, Fartsworth, the man who built this castle, killed. So, if you rob and burn, this Mob will probably come after you. That's what they do in the movies."

Moran whistled.

"Noise of the fly," Moran told me, eyes on high torch. "But mice to know. I'll keep it down to the silverware and like that."

When we got back to the living room, Jabba was hefting the Glock and Williams was standing in front of a painting. It was that painting with the blonde walking out of a clamshell.

"All good?" I asked, stupidly. The Dickel was dickling my brain pan.

"Your other lunatic friend was talking about the noise of a fly."

"Yeah?" I said. "What was that?"

"I neglect God and his Angels for the noise of a fly," Williams recited.

"Donne," Moran told me.

Coincidence? Telepathy? It tired me out thinking about what was going on with these two. I need a background of the pure normal to live my life.

"May I ask, sir, why you have a picture of my sweetheart naked hanging on your wall?"

"What's that?" Jabba snapped, looking over at Williams who was pointing to the clamshell lady.

"That's Botticelli's *Birth of Venus* you idiot. That's not your sweetheart."

"Goddamn you to hell, you fat degenerate!" Williams screamed, suddenly jumping toward Jabba and grabbing him by the throat. "Where have you hidden her?"

"Let him go, Nicky," Moran said, and Williams did.

"I'm calling the police!" Jabba screamed picking up one of several cell phones on the bar.

"Better not," Moran warned him. "Williams packs a pistol.

Probably not loaded though."

I left them to sort it out and went to bed. I had gotten used to the games Williams and Moran played while I was in the Stockade with them. I kind of got into Williams' yearning for this sweetheart. It helped pass the time that yearning for this beautiful lady. And Moran always kept things lively, summating with burning half the place down.

The staff reported some stuff missing the next morning, including the painting and the elephant statuettes. Nothing had been burned and Moran and Williams were gone.

"You committed an act of aggression coming here with those miscreants" Jabba told me as I was ushered out the door. "I'll let it pass. Only once."

"She's afraid of you," I told him.

He kind of laughed and then he didn't.

"Your mother has been seeing a psychiatrist. A Dr. Growth or Grew. She's bi-polar. Emotionally dysfunctional. She says things that aren't true. Or real. It's a serious psychotic disorder."

"She said my father had it."

"So, whatever she might have said to you, you need to consider very unreliable. And very dangerous to repeat."

I was halfway down the driveway when one of Jabba's minions rushed up to me and handed me a note. It was from Williams.

"I was much further out than you thought

And not waving but drowning."

[Stevie Smith]

We all shall meet anon.

Nick Williams

CHAPTER EIGHT

I WASN'T THE GUY

Bottom line was, I looked like a malcontent aggressor at the time of Greta's and Handsome Johnny's deaths and I still look like one. Theo looked like a guy who would turn the other cheek, no matter what, although he called The Beateatatudes the Bunkatudes.

Anyway, Theo said he had the genes for self-sacrifice. All he had to do was follow them through, put them into action. While poor me, I had the genes to dismantle my life. The parrot heard that and yelled "He's a fuck up!"

"That parrot has to treat me better if I have to watch him if you go to jail."

Theo laughed.

"He loves you. He does. You won't have to worry. He's working on a dictionary, so he'll be out of your way. Just feed him and keep the cage clean. And download his Dictaphone every three days."

I nodded agreement but he could see how sad I was. None of this seemed to me to be fair. I mean what is a Dictaphone and how do you load it down?

Theo told me it was only fair that he compensate me for the gene injustice. It wasn't my fault I got the wrong end of the egg yolk.

"Yeah," I said, not sure what he was getting at. It's the stick isn't it? The wrong end of the stick? Why would anyone but a caveman want a stick anyway?

We all went into deep shock when the judge gave Theo two to five, out in one for good behavior.

Summer claimed this as a great victory but Sal, Gee, Angelo and Pico and a couple of other savvy regulars at the *Pompey* thought it was a harsh sentence for three reasons:

1. Theo manslaughtered the guy unpremeditated;

2. Theo had been defending himself and standing his ground;

3. Theo had accidentally killed a guy who had just murdered his girlfriend, so allowances had to be made;

4. Theo was the Grand Knight in the Oddfellow Masons Society of Judaic-Christian Brotherhood, a Fourth Stage Cabalist, a Rosey Croton, a Golden Door and a Republican;

At one point in the trial, the representing attorney, Summer Arpeggio had pointed to me and said that even though as the jury looked at me and thought I was obviously the one who had smashed Handsome Johnny against the wall because I was the same kind of low life douche bag who would do that kind of thing and not my twin brother who had already been sainted by the Theo Soapistic Society, I wasn't the guy.

I thought it was an odd tactic, but I just sat that and ate the jury's hard looks.

Based on all those reasons, which sounded all the same to me, that sprung from the choir of guys a whole lot smarter than me at the bar, I went cranky on Summer and told her that Sal the bartender said that if she had been on O.J.'s Scream Team, O.J. would have gotten the chair, the rope and the needle. In short, she sucked as a trial lawyer. She told me to shut the fuck up and make some allowances for her launch effort in the courtroom.

Gee, who owned the bar made me feel better about the whole thing.

" I figure your brother, rich guy like he is, is gonna get Martha Stewpot's old digs including pots and pans and live a life for a year better than the bottom 40% of the U.S. population. Am I wrong here?"

Everyone at the bar shook his and her head and I did too. He wasn't wrong here although something was really fucked which was what the parrot, Cag, named by the way after Theo's favorite old actor, Cody Jarrett, perched on the bar in front of me, told us at that point in time.

Cag's last words to Theo brought tears to my eyes.

"I didn't want this for you, Michael."

Of course, I didn't know who the fugawee Michael was but a bird can't be judged for whatever shit he says.

I mean she says. Parrot set me straight on that right off.

"I'm all woman, shithead!"

CHAPTER NINE

BONNE FETE

This all happened super-fast. I'll slow it down.

Back story.

Theo is paying me a visit in my under the New Utrecht El digs, my *pied a terre*, sitting here looking at me in disgust.

We're celebrating our 31st birthday. There's a cheap cake from Under the El Second Hand Baked Goods Delivery on the multi-purpose kitchen/dining room/parlor/bedroom area table.

The cake looked like a cat had walked through it and as Mrs. A had about a dozen cats roaming the building like Ninja warriors, chances were this is what happened to the cake. She never spayed her cats, saying it was domestic cruelty.

I watched as Cag, the parrot Theo had taught to talk, in more than one language, as I was to find out, picked at the cake crumbs.

"You want a sandwich or something?" I ask Theo, wanting one myself. "Mrs. A can bring up a couple of Reubens. She's good with them."

My landlady, Mrs. Angeloni, took a special interest in me. She was nosey. She had seen my picture in some tabloid, read my black sheep connection to the Fartsworth billions -- I had been cut off totally for sporrick reasons associated with bad behavior and piss poor attitude -- and from that moment, Mrs. A decided to turn me into a legitimate heir. She said all I had to be was developed and brought to scale.

I didn't tell her that I would never be allowed back into the family fold and she wasn't thinking straight if she thought I would be. Regardless of this confusion, she was a fantastic cook. You don't have to think straight to make a great Bolognese sauce.

"Don't bring that witch up here," Theo said, shaking his head and sighing. "She upsets Cag. You know she carries a gun. Small .25 caliber. I thought Eve Solly would be here for your birthday. Cag digs her."

"He does?" I asked, noticing that the bird was now wolfing down the cake in a way that scared me.

"I'm kidding, dear brother. He hates her. She's twisted. Only you don't see that. But your landlady does carry a gun. She's very twisted too. Killed her husband, kill you. You know the old saying."

I didn't. I didn't ever know any of Theo's old sayings. I also thought by twisted he meant Eve was small.

"She's not a dwarf," I told him.

"I don't denigrate height. Let the gold pile up I always say. Besides, your girlfriend just looks small because we're huge. Mythically huge but you know that. Did you ever wonder why we are so huge when our father was jockey size?"

"The Mater is very tall?"

He laughed.

"You don't really think she's our mother, do you? What did she ever do that was motherly?"

I was thinking about that when Cag jerked his head up and eyed us. A crumb dropped from his beak. I thought he was the huge, mythic kind of thing and not us. When he was pissed off, he would flutter his whole wingspan, which was impressive I can tell you. And what bird speaks several languages?

He belched loudly.

"Are you eyeballing me, shithead?"

"He doesn't like Mummy. He knows she's a mockery of a mother. You know what words are spoken in a parliament of fowl? Your mother just flew off and left you."

"Is she listening to us? Does she have to call me shithead?"

"Certainly. You would deny her freedom of speech? The right to bear arms, join a posse, practice heathen bird rituals? Bird cackle is more a form of speech than a ten dollar bill, don't you agree, brother? What do you think of my brother, Cag?"

"Do you know Hugh DuBartas, shithead?" the parrot asked me.

"Do I know who departed?" I repeated, shaking my head. "What's he saying?"

Theo laughed.

"I believe he said you too departed.

Although it could be *vous departez*. He knows some serviceable French."

"None of that makes any sense," I told the bird.

"Douche bag!" he squawked.

"It's good advice though, isn't it? " Theo said.

"You mean douche bag?"

I didn't know what that advice was but I let it go.

Theo began to give me one of his state of the union addresses.

I ate cake Cag had left and listened. Somebody had put big, colorful LOL letters on the cake and they were now lying among the crumbs. I picked one up and licked it.

"This derangement of American life we are witnessing," Theo was saying, "is a visitation upon us because someone we all know has killed the King of Denmark."

"Dump this guy in the toilet!" Cag screeched.

"Makes sense," I said, picking up the letter "O" and licking it. As usual, I had no clue as to what my genius brother was saying. And his yes man, the parrot, didn't help.

"Your sense is in your feet," Cag said, looking at me, and yawning. "Where your brains are."

I used to not know why Theo put up with this parrot who was mythically big, scraggly and smelly but I have to admit that he said some stuff that made you say "What?" or "Whatever" or "So?" and some other stuff that made me say WTF and then want to feather and fry him.

I got up and went to my portable fridge for a beer. Theo drank wine. He not only drank it, he gave you a lecture before, during and after he drank it. Every grape had a story. He could give you what he called the provolone of a pair of shoes. I couldn't give that much attention to a grape. Or shoes. Theo, as usual, had brought his own wine. Two bottles. French. Bordello. He had named them Jules and Jim.

"Our king is our Constitutional democracy," Theo went on. "And the god of money has assassinated him. And that god has put the false idol of a mad usurper before us. I ask you, dear brother, what keeps you from saving this planet? I mean you personally. What keeps you from getting off your fat ass and saving the lower orders?"

I told him I didn't know. I mean I didn't know it was up to me. I didn't know the lower order personally. I also didn't know what the fugawee he was talking about.

"Tell that to this precariat parrot," Theo said, pointing to the bird, who now had one eye cocked at me, his head tilted. He looked angry, as if he was going to fly into my face. It was a big, glassy, angry one eye.

"Tell the last parrot flying why you have not saved her planet."

The parrot and I were staring hard at each other.

"You twizzle dick!"

"He hates you for that," Theo told me. "You need to apologize. Of course, he spends too much time on Tweaker where vile bodies exchange vileness."

I was about to say something when Theo jumped up.

"Is your bathroom usable decent? No logs floating in the sink? I think that second hand cake has given me the rampant shits."

He rushed out of the room but not really because the WC was almost at our knees. The thing about a *pied a terre* is that everything is very pied.

Theo was in there for quite a while. When he came out, he poured himself some wine and sat down on my overstuffed once again.

"Did you notice that your neighborhood here is being infiltrated by all manner of shops where the products have names and provenance?"

I shook my head. I didn't really shop. Mrs. Angeloni shopped and cooked. I got beer, wine and booze at Pablo's Bodega around the corner.

"The old sweat your ass off gym is now a yoga studio," Theo told me. "Our childhood rabid mongrels roaming the streets in packs have been vacuumed up and exterminated and now what you see are purse size designer dogs fops on phones carry around and diaper. The good old salmonella greasy spoons where a greasy thumb went into everything served are now fusion joints, dive bars are being driven out by mixology and mayonnaise emporiums. What in God's name is a coffee based beer and an artisanal cocktail?"

I couldn't answer any of that, which was usual with Theo's questions.

"Yes, indeed," he told me, dusting the arms of my overstuffed with two hyper-extended fingers. I had picked it up at The Salvation Army. Theo was a cleanliness nut. He owned three vacuums with various talents plus a robotic one that was constantly moving throughout his apartment, which was about a gazillion times bigger than my *pied a terre*. It was a whole body a terre. He was the fortunate one who sucked on the teat of a family trust.

We each have our destiny is how he explained it to me, some to rule, others to drool.

"Our tutors put a lot of crapulous idiocy out there," Theo went on. He liked to hear himself talk. And after I had some whiskeys and some beers, I didn't mind.

"You, my stolid brother, absorbed it all. I threw it back in her face. I mean Mommy. And Mr. Patawala, who called himself a tutor, in Hindi, was a heathen. We should never have been exposed to him, although I do not regret the Sanskrit he taught me. It comes in very handy in my line of work."

I didn't ask. I mean he owns launderettes in Paris.

"I did enjoy the card manipulation, Mr. Spinalzo taught us," Theo said, while flipping a poker deck in his left hand, cutting the cards one handed, flipping a card out and then catching it in a fanned out deck. It was what he called his default career. I had the same talent but didn't think of it as any kind of career.

"I suppose Mr. Rectum was the most intelligent and most damaged of our tutors."

"I don't remember him. Mister Rector?"

"Rectum. It was interesting the way his theories fit his surname. That often happens, I suppose. Our name for instance. Bratter from the Greek for breakage. It makes perfect sense."

"I don't remember him or his theories."

"Well, he would be sad to hear that. If he's now in a place where hearing can go on. He instilled in us what he called the Trivium. Sex, violence, and money. They were, according to Mr. Rectum, grounded in friction. Transparent connections really, when you think about it, but no one had observed this before our tutor Mr. Rectum."

"I don't see them."

"What? The transparent connections? Well, you agree that sex is the friction created by two bodies? Or, in your case, one hand. I joke, dear brother. I'm sure you and your petite engage in heavy friction in low places. And violence is no more than the friction between life forms, humans included."

"And money?"

"The hot friction of competition, Dirk. I learned a great deal from Mr. Rectum."

"How come I don't? I don't remember him at all? What did he look like?"

"Before or after he went up his own rectum? Just some birthday humor, dear brother."

"So, what happened to him?"

"He was caught in a heavy friction state with one of the maids. She went and he went. I was sorry to see him go. But it was really his own fault for putting his theories into practice. He should have known that theories stand the test of time when they are neither tested or practiced."

"I don't remember any of that."

"I'm surprised but only partially. You were at that time sending *billet doux* to that maid. Johanna I think her name was. Pronounced 'Ooh Anna!' She certainly could turn an eight year old boy's attention to friction."

"I don't remember her at all and I doubt if any of this is true."

"That's because there are good reasons why you have blocked all of this out of your mind. Nevertheless, it dwells in the deepest recesses of an overtaxed mind such as yours. Eight-year-olds cannot deal with the trauma of childhood abuse."

"What?"

"Or friction abuse as Mr. Rectum would say."

"Are you saying he abused me? Sexually?"

"No one knows. He was only caught flagrante delicto with Ooh Anna."

"But you knew? And you didn't stop him?"

"Alright. Don't go into a fit state. He didn't abuse you. I just made the charge. I didn't want Ooh Anna to be fired. She had a decidedly more friction rich effect on me than you, being as I am a far more sentient being than yourself. I convinced father that Mr. Rectum was forcing himself on Ooh Anna after she had come to your defense. He went and she stayed."

"But that still doesn't explain why I don't remember any of it? I mean, there wasn't any abuse for me to … "

"To repress? No. Not of a sexual abuse nature. It was Mr. Patawala, our next tutor who was instructed to memory wipe you as part of our path to enlightenment lessons. He had great success as you now demonstrate. He said it was as easy to erase your memories as to erase chalk from a blackboard. You have what's called a permanent *tabula rasa*."

I was in a kind of dumbfounded state, not knowing if anything Theo had told me was true. I mean, I didn't have a memory before and now I did but it was false but maybe it wasn't. Fucking with my mind made Theo happy on his birthday. And I kind of understood. He always had to prove I wasn't him and he wasn't me.

Theo reached out with his right hand and put the card on my knee.

"Don't be sad, brother. The half-life of that childhood exposure has already passed. We're here to celebrate our birthday. Cag, give us a poem!"

That made me smile. The bird giving us a poem.

But he did. Really, he did.

"Twaddle had a hovel,
Twiddle had a palace;
Twaddle said "'I'll grovel
Or he'll think I bear him malice."

"Do you know why I went to fat?" I asked him an hour or so later as I shook the last drops of Jim Beam rye out of the bottle.

"Your landlady stuffs you like goose destined for patè?"

"No. Because you were thin. I went for any difference I could. I didn't like looking in the mirror and seeing you."

"Right back at you, brother. I look at your face and I see what I was attached to for nine months during our gestation, where obviously all the good nutrients and such went to me. Anyway, fat is a cheap difference. Like proper nouns, bottom shelf liquors, and whores in Amsterdam's Red Light district."

He yawned. The parrot was sleeping in the cake box, her head tucked under a wing.

"This descent into the bowels of our birth has gotten me very depressed, brother."

Theo got up and punched me in the face.

Or tried to. I ducked and came up with a right to his chin. He fell back on the bed; the parrot woke up and screamed. I thrust a Timbo into his boys and then he sprang up and wrestled me to the scatter tattered rug. He laid some incisors into my cheek. I howled but at the same time managed to get a thumb in his eye.

It was a birthday ritual, done since childhood.

We went at it like this until one of us said Uncle! For years now, it was always me who had to say uncle. He was quicker and more nimble. But now I had about fifty pounds or so on him and he said "Uncle!"

He stood up, gave me a dark look which turned to a smile and a wink.

"Where did you throw my coat?" he asked, looking around for it.

Theo didn't like to lose at anything.

The parrot flew to his shoulder and turned to look at me as Theo opened the door.

"Lock and load! Rock and roll!" Cag shouted at me.

"*Bonne fete,* mon frère," Theo said and they left me sorting through cake crumbs.

CHAPTER TEN

HOT SPARKS OVER THE RADIO

Eve Solly and I used to have a talk show, a talk radio show here in the New Brooklyn.

At first, we did it at a studio. Our ratings went from low to lower with the Dividend Class, and higher with the no money to shop dregs who still listened to radio. Thus, we lost advertisers but at the same time picked up some really odd product endorsements. Of course, we had the whole gun lobby behind us. Eve Solly reminded our listeners that you needed one carry for certain occasions, and two for other, besides the hidden you always carried. She said what Karl Marx meant by "close at hand" was a gun.

Things changed on the show when Cag, the parrot joined us. Up until then, I was only a kind of a prop that Eve used when she wanted to do what she called a three way with the caller. She said when I spoke I sucked up most of the oxygen out of the caller's brain, which was limited in the first place.

Eve and I hated going too far from a bar stool at *The New Pompey* on New Utrecht Ave so eventually we left the studio and ran the show at the bar.

That lady could drink straight shots of Jim Beam rye in a legendary way. And reach what she called a High Plateau of Celeste's observation. Celeste who? I asked but she just kicked me.

Anyway, that all ended. Not the lifestyle but the paying job.

Our chat radio show, while it lasted, was called *Shut Up!*

but it's a command nobody takes personally. It's always the other guy who needs to shut up.

One thing our producer had to admit about Eve: she was always ready to interview clowns, none of whom actually have a circus job, but they fit her requirements.

When you say a clown is on the line, Cag gets really excited. I figured there's more clowns in a parrot's world than probably in mine. This isn't an issue either because clowns don't enjoy Eve or the parrot telling them they're clowns.

In brief, after people got used to us, we pissed them off in our different ways.

The podcast we retreated to after we lost the radio show was different. The title was the same though. No salary but believe it or not there were enough loonies in cyberspace to keep Eve, me and the parrot as well as our two person staff solvent.

Here's the funding chart I was given to study:

$18 per 1,000 downloads for a 15 second pre–roll

$25 per 1,000 downloads for a 60 second mid–roll slot

If the podcast gets 3,000 downloads per episode, you'll get $54 for a 15–second pre–roll and $75 for a mid–roll slot.

When The Mater dies, everything goes to Theo is what I expect. Theo will give me half. Cag told me that sometimes Theo promised him a melon feast that never happened so I should get everything in writing.

CHAPTER ELEVEN

IT'S A PROCESS

Before Eve and I got fired from the radio show, the three of us did have a meeting with The Concerned Producer of the show, Brad something or other, Eve called him Broad because that's the way he pronounced his name. He pronounced a lot of words funny as if his vocal chords ran through his nose.

People, Broad had told us, were dying to call in their tweets and hear their own voices crushing other tweeting voices. I tried to make a thing in my mind of that crushing but I couldn't get a handle on it. I kept seeing sparrows yelling at each other.

Broad didn't look bright and shiny sitting across from us.

Right now, Broad was telling us how disappointed he was in us, as if I had at some point in time had some ambition not to disappoint him. I wanted to have ambition the way somebody wants to have cancer. It was Eve Solly who had gotten me into this line of work, pointing out one morning as I lay in bed enjoying my coffee that her boyfriend had to have a job.

"Lucky guy," I had told her before she punched my head into an awareness that the guy was me.

Anywho, Broad was summing up.

"You think telling a caller to shut the eff up is a winning ticket?" Broad asked, looking at me.

"So, the thing of it is that the show's not about thinking," Eve tells The Broadster, dryly before I can open my mouth. "We reveal what minds do without having to think. Mouths too."

Eve's seated to my right, a petit towering inferno.

"You should both be interviewing à la mode," Broad tells us.

"I told you. Shut up and go home!" the parrot shouts and then retreats under his wing, leaving us to handle the afterglow.

I note that Broad doesn't seem to have heard. Eve was right. The bird wasn't in this guy's reality bubble. He thinks we have a third partner on the show, a young guy from L.A. called Cag.

"Then who is it we're supposed to be interviewing?" I ask, thinking of pie à la mode and at the same time multi-tasking a wink at Eve who ignores me.

"Remember. It's the year of the woman," Broad tells us, flicking his pen about a foot upward and then pinky catching it. "Men are obsolete. Mansplaining over the airwaves is extinct."

"We don't have any men on the show. Just this guy."

I ignored Eve's taunt, as was my habit.

"We've got 54 different genders and men aren't on it," Broad went on. "The only men that draw are the ones hashtag metooed or apologizing. You've got to find a Harvey Wadstink to interview. Get some schmuck to apologize."

"Very nice to know," Eve tells him dryly, eyes not opened I think. "For what, exactly?"

"What?"

"I told you to shut the fuck up!," Cag screams and flies onto Broad's desk, causing him to push away from the desk and knock his chair to the ground.

"Who's the ventriloquist?" Broad asks, picking up his chair. He sits back down.

"He is."

"She is."

"Actually, the parrot does his own talking."

"Are you serious?"

"No," Eve tells him, flatly.

Broad looks at me and then he looks at Eve and then he looks at Cag and then he looks at Eve again and then he looks at me and then again a Cag, who is still on his desk absorbed in turning pages on the desk calendar with his beak. He seems interested in what he's finding there. Then he starts pecking at the cellphone lying there on Broad's desk. I'm wondering whether he can call up for sandwiches?

"I've got an idea that may save us," Broad says

"That'll work," Eve tells him.

"I haven't presented it yet."

"Even better."

"Hashtag Me-too him," Broad says, pointing at me with his pen. "Testify on the air that Dick here. ... "

"Dirk."

"Even better. Dirk abused you. With the power of his position. He dropped his pants. Went full harassment. Exposed his dirk. Grabbed you by the pussy, as the president advises. And so on. Capitalize on the dynamic you two generate on air."

I'm about to ask him if he can send out for sandwiches at this point in our meet when Eve begins a line that once cast ends badly.

"So, I suggest we change the narrative, Broad," she tells him. "Going forward, that is."

These words brings him to life like a shot of adrenaline and he starts the pen juggling again. The word makes him comfortable again; it makes him happy. I know Eve does not like certain words.

"So, right now they own the narrative," Eve goes on. "We need to take it back. The narrative. Should I say narrative a couple three more times?"

"Yes, of course," Broad says, leaning across his desk and peering into Eve's big, luminous, Mad Hatter eyeballs.

"So, it's a process is what it is," Eve tells him.

"Yes, of course a process."

"A process going forward. So, we can give them The People's narrative as the process goes forward. At this point in time."

"Exactly," Broad says, nodding.

"So, we can multi-task on the way there. Mindful and woke is what it is."

I see the shifting winds blowing across Broad's face. Easterly, he's drawn to the magic words. Westerly, he detects mockery.

"Anybody hungry?" I ask.

I didn't even want to look at Broad's face. I felt sorry for the guy. He wasn't a bad guy, just a victim of having met Eve and me. We were like reminders that personal choice really doesn't come into the picture as long as we're alive.

"Our listeners do not want to hear you two anymore." Broad finally snaps, teased to anger.

No sandwiches. I see it written on his face.

"That's it. Change your script. Get with the program or you're done. "

"So, yeah, we can't do anything different," Eve tells him, turning to me in response to hearing the loud noises my stomach was making.

"You two are already too different. In any business difference is doing what most people aren't doing. Two people listening in instead of two million. Difference is death in marketing."

"How about we get a couple three pizzas delivered," I volunteer.

"Your ratings stink," he yells at us. "They not only suck but we get more requests to fire your ass. My shareholders want to throw you both under the bus. Or kill you. And the Feds? They want to lock us all up. Look, it is what it is."

"Didn't I tell you to shut the fuck up and get out of here!" the parrot croaks, head turned, one eye only on Broad.

"You can't put him on the air," Brad tells us. "He's profane."

I guess Broad missed the last three hundred shows in which Cag ran his mouth. I looked at Eve. I feel a threat to our national security in the room.

Broad suddenly jumps up, big smile on his face. He's not a bad kid. He just doesn't see his victimhood in his future, like Theo advised me to see.

"I can't believe we've missed the low hanging fruit!" he yells at us.

At that, Eve does pull out the .38 and points it at Broad. She never shoots to kill. She'll probably go for an ear lobe. It was like the words "low hanging fruit" set up a target.

"What you want to know, Broad," I said quickly, "is that you're close to the bleeding edge. She shoots and then hides the bodies."

"That's it!" Broad yells. "What optics! How did I miss it. You two don't belong on smash mouth radio. You belong on a podcast where everybody can see you."

"I think Broad has something here, Eve. You could power through any screen like a Helen Muck rocket."

She had put the gun away.

"We'll take it to the next level," Broad told us, his enthusiasm moving that pen in gravity defying ways. "We'll tee it up. Take the power sitting right in front of me online."

I snapped my fingers.

"Let's do lunch!" I shouted.

I had two eyes on two fried egg sandwiches and one eye on Eve. She was in some kind of metamorphoragic state that I had read about or Sal had told me about, transitioning to another place in that multi-plex brain of hers.

"So, you know," she began as I watched Broad's pen spin laterally toward me and then shoot back into his fingers.

"When it comes to power we need to go back to the Old Testament for a woman with power. Eve in the Garden is the first porn star; did she just hold out an apple to Adam and say `Eat this.' No, the lady is naked and she had to be a perfect ten because she's in Eden, a perfect location. No blemishes, no body stank, no fly away hair, no fungus toes, no squinty look, no weight problem, no crack pipe, no housewife blues, no nagging, no trouble getting up in the morning, no sagging breasts, no football field butt, no una-brow, no pre-mature ejaculating sex partner. Everything is Edenic. Look it up. Check it out. She's a knock out. A naked goddess in a beautiful garden holding out an apple to the first guy with the first hard on. She's 5' 10" at least. How can he resist? He never had a choice. Or a chance. How can he be blamed? He's got a Garden of Eden sized hard on in place of brains. He's an idiot and she's irresistible. Where's the original sin in that?"

"I like it," Broad said. "It will mean a whole paradigm shift in the way you do your show. You two will be moving the needle. You'll be changing the paradigm."

"I told you to shut up and go home!" Cag shouts.

"I don't think he likes me. Well, I hope we've reached an understanding here," Broad replies, eyes on Eve. "Look, I'll have to run it up the flagpole and you might have to bite the bullet in regard to compensation, but I think I can say at this point in time that we're talking six figures here."

"Run it up a flag pole. We'll be around."

I nodded an affirmative. Her rye flask materialized. She saluted us, took a pull and then passed it to me. I did the same, passed it to The Broad

He smiled sheepishly, took the flask and knocked a swallow back.

I was impressed. I kind of figured that Eve had sent his head so far up his ass that he wouldn't be able to swallow.

I made another plea for lunch on Broad's dime which didn't fly, and Eve and I walked out, dreaming of new optics, moving the needle and changing a pair of dimes.

"Remember to flush!" Cag shouted on the way out.

Nothing came of that optics project, although we did launch a podcast down the road on our own, without The Broad on something called The Dark Web that Eve figured we were made for.

At the end of the day, I think some honchos ran The Broad up the flagpole. The process had a bad end. The narrative had a bad end. Broad got crushed. The process didn't process.

Unemployment was par for the course for Eve and me.

As the gods designed was the way she put it. I didn't have the inclination or the strength to ask her about self-empowerment and the original Eve and all that.

CHAPTER TWELVE

NEUROTYPICAL

Eve Solly and I were five weeks into collecting unemployment and five weeks into sitting at the bar at *The New Pompey* half in the bag discussing world events and how many ways the world could go wronger if an orange faced guy assumed the throne of the presidency for life. I asked her who she had in mind but her head dropped to the bar and she began to snore.

I happened to be watching Sal massage a whiskey glass into a thing of beauty when he made a nod with his head toward the door.

A guy who was a stranger to me walked up to the bar and instead of standing in the balconies he nudged his way through, getting some looks he ignored.

"I'm looking for a Dirk Bratter," he said to Sal. "I was told Mr. Bratter has his slippers under this bar, which means somebody here must know him. I'm an emissary from Mr. Sulmondson's law office."

"Drop dead over there in the corner!" Cag screamed, and he was looking at the guy who was now looking for me.

We all could hear Eve snoring.

The Emissary made a magician's move with one hand and a card appeared. He laid it on the bar and wrote something then handed it to Sal.

"Give this to him."

He was looking at me when he said this. I had finally come into view. I couldn't look small even if I wanted to and I didn't want to. I saw that sneer on his face.

"Tell Dirk Bratter," he said, coming up to me and looking me straight in the face, "that his brother was stabbed to death in Rikers and Mr. Mitchell Sulmondson wants to talk to him about the estate. Right away."

"What did you say?"

"He said he stabbed your brother."

My vision kind of blurred right then and I lunged at this guy, grappled him and flung us both across the bar into one of the booths. I felt his fingers in my eyes as I smashed a fist into his face and pulled him up to my chest and then smashed him down on the side of the booth.

He wasn't getting up when they pulled me off him.

"What the hell is going on?"

"Guy came in and said he stabbed Bratter's brother."

"He was just the messenger, Gee. He said somebody stabbed…"

"This is supposed to be an emotion free safe space!"

"Shut that fucking parrot up. Drag that guy out back and throw him in the dumpster. Comes in here and shows no goddamn respect. Throw Bratter in a cab. Goddamn it, Sal, I don't want guys coming in here and showing no goddamn respect to me, this place and my customers."

"Okay, Gee."

"Why that piece of shit stab in his brother?"

"I don't think he did Gee."

"It was in Rikers."

"Rikers. That place has it all. Explosive violence, staff brutality, rape galore, abuse of the uncertifiable mentally ill, and one of the nation's highest rates of solitary confinement. I was a witness to all of it. And I will testify for one shot of Johnny Red."

"Ego te absolve vos omnes self-abusers!"

"Can it, Padre. His brother just died."

I was being led to the door.

"I am sorry for your loss, my son. But I shall quote Flann on this occasion of unexpected sorrow. 'Not everybody understands the far from scrutable periculums of the intricate world. Death is not an experience we can have in life thus I say little on the topic.'"

Since I knew that Theo was immortal, I knew his death wasn't a topic. Fake news. Identical twins always know when their twin dies. So, I didn't know and so Theo wasn't dead. Besides, weren't there enough people dead already to satisfy the celestial quota?

"I have found God, but he is insufficient!"

"Put that fucking parrot in the cab with Bratter!"

There were two reasons I was in Rikers.

I mean Princeton.

Theo had taken the entrance exam for me and I was a legacy. The Farnsworth name. I was a legacy is what they called it riding in on Theo's coattails. I slid off after a term.

For me the past is like a stone and you can't swim holding a stone.

But I remembered. Imagination was the womb of things, Theo once told me, quoting somebody, but memory was a graveyard. And when you were at the end of your destiny, you began again, unless your imagination failed you. Some of that was parrot wisdom.

Theo and I were crossing the Quad heading toward Prospect Avenue, Theo stops and gives me one of his eyeball to eyeball looks.

"Do yourself a favor and enlist in the Army. Or the Navy. Or any of it. Just get out of the city. Something's come up and I don't want you messing it up."

"I wouldn't do that," I told him, truthfully.

"You've got my face, right? But you don't think straight. You could run into somebody who thinks you're me and that might complicate things for me. And tragically for you."

"I won't," I promised him. "I've got plans. I'm following my own destiny. Not yours."

"They might not take you on account of your Asperger."

"My what?"

"Mr. Rectum said you had it. Not remembering that is part of the syndrome."

"The friction guy? And I still have it?"

"Not Asperger. It got bought out by Autism. You're a very low functioning autist."

"Like an artist? Is that better?"

"Than an artist? Worse. You remember when your piggy bank broke and you looked at all the pennies on the floor and said $4.83 without counting them?"

"No. Was I right?"

"That never happened. You didn't even have a piggy bank."

"Look, if I had this, why wouldn't the military take me?"

"Well, you might have an aspie meltdown during a special forces mission. You would jeopardize the whole mission. We would never have gotten Ben Louden. Then again, if they thought you were a high functioning aspie, the military might be able to use you.

You might have quantum level computer skills or master sniper shooting skills or desert survival skills. You might be able to get to Mars without aging."

"I don't think I have any of those."

"Well, not to worry. Dr. Fraud said Mr. Rectum was talking out of his surname. You're just NT."

"What?"

"Neurotypical.

I did join up as a neurotypical.

CHAPTER THIRTEEN

PIED A TERRE

You know my place right under the El on New Utrecht Avenue. A one bedroom *pied a terre* with a kitchenette off an area Mrs. A called a parlor, small table, couple of chairs, tiny bathroom, shower stall I couldn't swing my arms around in, big, old overstuffed chair in the parlor that had boxes of tapes from our radio shows all around. Hand puppets with various facial expressions drooped over the top crates.

The BMT West End Line rumbles past shaking all my two dishes and assorted three cutlery pieces every quarter hour. It used to be my *pied-a-terre* in the flush days when I had a more commodious place near Sunset Park but now it was my one and only home sweet home. Affordable. For old times' sake, I still call it my *pied-a-terre*.

You know about my landlady. Mrs Angeloni. She was what they call in Brooklyn "The Super." She was also the owner of the place. Mr. Angeloni had died in his sleep and left her with the building. That way of dying in this neighborhood was always code for "his old lady snuffed him out with a pillow."

Eve had a crib on Colonial Rd. She couldn't afford it now. She'd have to get out. And move in with me. Again. It never turned out. The place had too many high-end, luxury features, including a nosey landlady, that hampered our true romance. Eve's words. There was an absence of a gooseneck in the toilet that made the place uninhabitable in her view.

I was almost back at my *pied a terre*, just doing a normal jay walk when one of those tank size SUVS makes a fast turn on 55th and comes at me.

I make a quick run to the curb but I'm in slo mo, actually still frozen in place. A guy my size can drink a lot of rye but brain and body communication slow down after the first three or four shots.

That's who got out of the car. Three or four. Went straight at me. I decide to stand my ground given the reality that my running is actually a freeze in place. I got two fists the size of catcher's mitts up but one guy, little guy, runs up and saps me on one knee cap and then he does the other, surgically.

I go down like a steer hammered to the head on the hamburger line. Then I'm dragged to the back of the SUV and humped in like a five hundred pound lumpy bag of unroasted coffee beans.

My assailants and abductors are cursing. In Russian. Maybe Ukrainian. Maybe Polish. Definitely not Hungarian. Could be Romanian.

My culinary memory kicks in. These guys smell like chicken Kiev. Ukrainian. Coulibiac. Russian. Herring and vodka. I've got a gag on my mouth, hands banded in those plastic bands you can never release, and my knees feel like they're broken.

Sleepy time.

When I opened my dream world eyes, Theo was there, sitting across from me at a table in The Lab. Our father's research posse sat around the table.

Our father's gang of weirdos, so loyal to him, The Principal Investigator. The Leader of the Lab Pack. I wasn't a fan. One of PT's Lab posse one time told me it was unfortunate my brains had been scrambled while Theo's brain would be closely studied after his death.

There were plates of sandwiches and bottles of pop. Theo didn't look happy. He also looked about eleven years old, which meant I was eleven years old.

"Elbows off the table, Dirk," someone at the table ordered.

I became aware of my father, PT Bratter at the head of the table. He was holding up what looked like a lump of something, a rock, a chunk of dirt, maybe what Theo called a shard, but it didn't look Swiss.

I looked at Theo who was pinching his nose and making a bad stank face.

"So that is it," the forensic Professor Crumblerumple sitting to my father's right said.

I don't have to tell you that Theo gave everybody who came to the house names he said possessed their flesh and blood. I instantly understood that. A bone thin man with a cane, the shakes and wearing a rumpled suit was naturally Crumblerumple.

"Yes," PT said, solemnly, dropping the shard lump in his soup dish. "Primordial, prelapsarian, primeval. It begat Adam. We are to publish this discovery in *Nature.*"

He looked down the table at Theo and then at me.

"It begat the twins."

All eyes were on us now and I heard the words "remarkable," "so big for their age," "a magnificent discovery," "amazing proteomic application."

"Can we leave now, father?" Theo piped up. "I have a train to catch."

"I don't believe you do, Theo," PT told him solemnly. "Eleven-year-old do not have trains to catch. Also, there is no train. Why do you lie?"

At that question, Theo smashed his head into his dish where his sandwich lay, then jerked it up, tears streaming out of his eyes, a chunk of sandwich in his mouth.

"But why don't you believe me?" he sputtered. "There is a train, isn't there, Dirk?"

PT looked at me.

"Where?" I asked.

That one word made PT very sad.

What courage Theo had I thought as I smuggled another edible into my school jacket. We had required dress wear, home, school, play, sleep, prayer, parties, waterboarding and so on. The Mater thought a school uniform was protection against a sudden assault by the failing Government Schools. Meanwhile, we were home tutored. Mr Patawala had designed and made our uniforms. Tunics with beads, baggy trousers, and Krishna blue vests.

"I don't think you appreciate the significance of your father's discovery," my father's magician whom Theo called Cranialhemorrhage told Theo. He had a thin, ashen face and dark rings under his eyes and his thin lips were blue.

He had a habit of dancing the fingers of one hand on his temple, as if he were trying to soothe a headache or keep time to a musical beat in his head.

"I do," Theo told him, "but Dirk said it looked like a lump of shit. And smelled like it."

I saw many disappointed faces looking at me.

"Young man, do you know what impact aliens have already had on our human development?"

Theo called him Professor Gruppenfuhrer, Brazilian with a heavy Germany accent, who wore a military uniform underneath his lab coat. He spoke a great deal about jeans, but I never saw him wearing any. Madame Uberalles, sitting right beside me whispered to me that she could tell an alien from a human according to what jeans they wore. Theo said that she and Gruppenfuhrer had frequent sex in the lab. He had drawn several pictures he hung on the wall of our bedroom.

"I have a poem!" Theo shouted, jumping up from his chair.

Whether the weather be fine,
Or whether the weather be not,
Whether the weather be cold,
Or whether the weather be hot,
We'll weather the weather,
Whatever the whether,
Whether we like it or not.

"Sit down, Theo," our father ordered him, although I could see he was amused. He often told Theo that if he could turn his energies toward looking into a microscope thirty three hours a day in a lab, he'd find great success.

"I think your Theo is something of de Wiseguy," Gruppenfuhrer said, giving Theo a threatening look.

Theo sat down, pulled a paperback copy of *Lolita* in French out of a pocket and began to read. Theo like to read novels in French for what he called the greater pornographic intensity. I swiped the sandwich from Madame Uberalles's plate.

"Dirk has more of the mud clinging to him than Theo does," PT now told the table. "Time will tell how that works out."

Now all the eyes were back on me, but I kept on chewing. My mother didn't dine with us because of what she called our filthy behavior. She also didn't like P.T.'s Lab associates either because they encouraged an ungodly pursuit of what she called shabby living and lunacy they called science.

"Time will tell us how what works out, Poppa?" Theo asked doing his best imitation of PT's voice. It was uncannily good. All his mimicry was good.

"Time will run out," Cranialhemorrhage said and I saw he was casting his eye spell on Theo. "People suddenly stroke and die. You'll find, young man, that there is very little time to make something of yourself. I fear it may already be too late."

"What if time is a wrinkle, Father?" Theo asked, eyes opened brightly.

"Time produces wrinkles, young man," Madame Uberalles told him. "Time is not a wrinkle. Adjust your thinking."

"Mr. Spinalzo thinks you are Carmina Burana, Father," Theo told father, happily as if this was good news everyone was waiting to hear. "One hundred per cent certifiable."

"And who is Mr. Spinalzo?"

"The five dollar hooker … I mean tutor Dirk and I had until you said he was redundant, which he was. Many, many times."

"Ah, yes, Mr. Spinalzo. He had an online degree he received from a twelve year old cyber prodigy living in his basement."

"Poor fools inevitably wind up in a perpetual recursive mental collapse," Gruppenfuhrer told us. "Autodidacts especially. They map the route to the death of their own mind. Deficiency in the jeans."

"Also, father, he dressed up in mother's underwear," Theo chirped, happily yet again.

That seemed to be news to father.

"And how is Dr. Patawala, your new tutor?"

"We have to learn Hindi," Theo told him. "He doesn't speak or write English. He's taught Dirk alternative facts and Dirk believed him."

"That can't be true," P.T. said, turning to me.

I didn't know I believed in alternative facts.

"Water is H20," I said, nervously, in my own defense.

Theo had a habit of accusing me of stuff that wasn't true, but a lot of people believed it. He had the upstairs maid he did nude drawings of convinced I was buy polar at the border and she should run when she saw me. At the border, I supposed.

"In alternative realities there are alternative facts," Theo went on. "Dirk believes in those also."

"There are no alternative realities, young man," Gruppenfuhrer said, angrily. "The strong crush the weak."

"Dirk thinks his hand puppets live in one. That's where he goes to talk to them."

"That can't be true," P.T. said, turning to me.

"It's true to Mr. Patawala," Theo told him. "He says there are multiple universes and multiple realities and they run parallel to each other and they're all different and if you prayed to an elephant, you'd see them. That's why Dirk has an elephant puppet. Fatgut."

"Frank," I said, correcting him.

"Hogwash," Gruppenfuhrer spit out. "It's all nonsense."

"I said that to Mr. Patawala and he said I was chaos."

"Did he tell your brother that, Dirk?" P.T. asked me. "No. I don't want to know."

"So, your puppets are in one of these different realities, my dear?" Madame Uberalles said to me, gently.

"I don't know. They know when I'm sad though. And they get happy with me. And frightened too."

"These are two very sick tutors you have exposed us to, Father," Theo said to P.T. "I know I shall not been damaged by them but as you can see, Dirk's mind has already been totally fucked by them. He would be schizophrenic if it weren't for the drugs he takes."

"What drugs are you taking, Dirk? Never mind. I don't want to know. Never use profanity, Theodore. It signifies an unscientific mind."

"Yes, but don't you feel guilty, Father?"

"You're just a punk, Theodore," Gruppenfuhrer said.

"A punk in chaos," Madame Uberalles said, sadly.

"A punk in chaos!" Theo yelled, and threw a portion of his sandwich in Madame Uberalles' face.

"Yes, I think you are right, Gruppenfuhrer. Theo is a punk, heading for trouble I think. He believes he's wiser than he is."

"Every young man thinks he is wise, my dear P.T., until he is punched in the face," Madame Uberalles said, stretching across the table and taking a swing at Theo but missing.

"But Dirk I'm afraid is attracted to bloviations of reality," P.T went on. Oblivious to Madame Uberalles who was sprawled across the table and trying to right herself.

"You should definitely take those puppets out of his life," Cranialhemorrhage said. "It makes me nervous thinking about a human/puppet molecular interchange."

"Trouble ahead!" Theo yelled and I clapped.

And then Theo and I were wrestling under the table and having a good time of it because my father had excused us from the table *but not from underneath the table.* Theo and I were laughing our heads off.

I saw dust motes in the air and then Theo rising out of them.
Pass me the sweet earthenware jug,
Made of the earth that bore me,
The earth that someday I shall bear.

Sunlight woke me up, those lines of poetry Theo had recited still in my head.

And now Theo was dead.

CHAPTER FOURTEEN

THREE GUYS IN ONE

I was in bed. Not my bed.

Then I recalled being run over, sapped in head and knees, and hitting the pavement like Kong off a roof.

I had just sat up, hand to my aching head when a guy with a big smile comes in. No knock.

"Dobroye utra, Dmitri!"

"Okay. Who's Dmitri? Me? I'm not Dimitri."

"Of course, you are Dmitri. And you are here. And I am Ivan. And it's a wonderful morning. Get dressed. Mr. Pavlovich wants to speak to you."

I was about to ask who Mr. Spav a loaf witch was or is but instead I croaked:

"Coffee."

The sun was really shining as I was led, coffee cup in hand, out to what turned out to be the boardwalk, Atlantic Ocean glistening in the distance.

I scanned the boardwalk up and down. Yeah, Brighton Beach. Little Odessa. Coney Island. My retreat in hot summers from *my pied a terre* without AC.

Eve and I had done a broadcast about these ocean loving Russians: Sheepshead Bay, Bath Beach, South Beach on Staten Island, that other travesty of destruction, accomplished mostly by cement loving Italians.

I even knew the bistro I had come out of, after climbing down two flights of stairs. *The Sea Bird* is what it was called in English.

I didn't know the guy who looked like that director Scorecchi, plastered back silver hair and dark glasses half the size of his head. He was wearing a black cassock. A priest.

"Dobroye utro," he said cheerfully.

He motioned for me to sit down.

There were blini, hardboiled eggs, pickles, jam and more coffee. And a bottle of Zubrowka. Ice cold bottle to the touch. You got to love the Russians, as the President of the United States says.

I poured myself a couple of inches, knocked it back and then put knife and fork to the eats.

He seemed to enjoy watching me.

"Your appetite is blessed," he told me. "Go, eat your food with gladness, and drink your wine with a joyful heart, for God has already approved what you do. Ecclesiastes 9.7."

"Okay," I said and stuffed another hard-boiled egg in my face.

I finally got enough of my mouth free to question.

"Who are you and what do you want? Beside break my knees, shanghai me and give me breakfast. "

He laughed.

"I'm Fyodor Pavlovich but everyone calls me Patriarch Victor. He has saved us and called us to a holy life."

I didn't question any of that but poured some of the vodka into my coffee.

"I will hear your confession now," he said to me, bowing his head.

"No, thanks. I guess I'm finished," I said, pushing away from the table and standing up. Time to leave.

"I'm gonna stroll over to the Aquarium now. I like to look at the octopoi."

"Sit down," the Patriarch told me, putting a hand on my shoulder. "We can put a bullet in your head right here on the boardwalk. But the decision is yours."

I settled back down.

"You killed Niky Grigory," The Patriarch said in almost a whisper. "Our Niky. He set off for a distant world and squandered all his wealth in wild living."

"Your Niky?" I repeated, wondering who Niky Griggy Or Wee was. "Wild living? Did he confess?"

"Listen to him," Ivan ordered, poking something in my shoulder.

I listened.

It turned out Niky whoever was Handsome Johnny. The guy I had plastered into the wall with too heavy a hand. Actually, I had just sent him flying, one hand holding my injured boys and he had piloted himself into the wall.

And then Theo had been stabbed in Rikers. Shanked is what Sal called it. Shivved. Shanked. Stabbed. Dead.

"You had Theo killed ..." I muttered as I made a grab for the vodka bottle, not to drink but to break over The Patriarch's head. I didn't think he was a real Patriarch anyway, whatever that was.

Before I could follow through somebody hit me with something.

When I woke up this time, I was on that bed in that room with the colorful paintings and The Patriarch was sitting next to me.

"You killed Theo," I muttered.

"I will hear your confession now," The Patriarch said.

Ivan was behind him holding an icepack to his nose. His eyes were almost closed. I remembered doing some wild arm swinging before I hit the ground.

"Lippen up, flats bah. Fodder Vic dinneit snow yer brudder waspkilp and lippen up we dinit kill him snow get oven dat."

His nasal had gone so far up his vocal cords, I didn't know what the hell he was saying.

"The Lord says it is mine to revenge," The Patriarch told me in a very quiet, calming voice. "No one is going to kill you for killing our Niky Grigory. He was lost and also, like you, what we call a rastochitel."

"Is that good?"

He laughed.

"A wastrel. Not so good. You need only seek absolution."

"He killed Greta," I told him. "Your Nicky did. Punched her ears into her head. That wasn't an accident. So, you didn't have Theo killed?"

I guess the fact that I hadn't yet absorbed his answer to that question set him off because he jumped up, arms out, eyes flashing and began to scream.

"Even at Horeb you provoked the LORD to wrath, and the LORD was so angry with you that He would have destroyed you!"

He came at me like a rush of hot fire balling up out of dry grass. I put both arms up for defense and closed my eyes.

"Giv'em somdin," Ivan whispered in my ear. "Convess."

""I told some lies," I began. "Profanity. Some minor theft.

Public space urination. Accessory after the fact a few times. Mistaken stalking. Shop lifting. Failure to yield. Loitering with intent. I put my hand up Lois Lane's dress in the fifth grade … "

"What about gluttony?" The Patriarch asked me, settling back down.

"Yeah. I drink too much too."

That admission got The Patriarch screaming.

"**They** shall say to the elders, 'This son of ours is stubborn and rebellious. He will not obey us. He is a glutton and a drunkard.'"

I had a glass of vodka in my hand and so did The Patriarch.

Then once again he calmed down in a flash and was all kindly and soft spoken. He reminded me of a guy who had called into our *Shut Up!* broadcast and after he went through an emotional swing like this, Eve says: "Take any gun, yours or a neighbor's, put it in your mouth and pull the trigger. Do it for us."

"And you have killed no one," The Patriarch was going on. "You shall not murder. Exodus 20:13."

I hesitated. I accidently killed … man slaughtered Nicky whatever. How could I confess to that to this lunatic? But Theo's death was different. I deliberately sent him into that prison. I was ready to confess to that.

"I cannot absolve you of sins you do not confess," The Patriarch told me gently.

Ivan leaned over and whispered in my ear.

"If he doesn't absolf ya, hill kill ya."

I felt the sweat rolling down my face.

"I killed your nephew, Nicky Wastrel. It was a fight. He wanted to kill me. I let my twin brother take the rap and … he went to prison and they killed him in prison, so it was me that really killed him."

I think I began to cry.

The Patriarch made the sign of the cross.

"Et ego te absolvo a peccatis tuis. In nomine Patris, et Filii, et Spiritus Sancti."

I saw Ivan put his gun away and I breathe a sigh of relief.

The Patriarch got up, patted me on the shoulder and left me.

When he came back, he found me drinking.

He was wearing a suit and tie. He was still wearing shades so I couldn't see his eyes. I wasn't even sure this guy was the other guy. The guy behind the guy. The Patriarch. Maybe he was a twin, the one who didn't quote the Bible.

""I express my sympathy for the loss of your brother. Your twin. But just maybe he had his own enemies?"

"You didn't know him so maybe you should shut up, Mister The Patriarch."

Once again Ivan leaned over and whispered … or slobbered in my ear.

"Dis one is da real deal. He's an ate he ist. Don't crack wise. He'll kill ya."

"You can call me Mr. Victor. This could be the start of a beautiful friendship, Dirk. We didn't kill your brother. I'm telling you this for the last time. But just maybe we can find out who did. If there's something in it for me. I'm not in the charity business, you have to understand."

"Why would you want to help me?"

"I know who you are. No one who listens to me is going to kill you. I'll see to your safety."

"I think you already busted up my knees."

He smiled as if my pain made him happy.

"I'm a man who likes to talk straight. Let's say I need your help to get some influence with the connection your family has with The Mob."

The Mob. No, really? The Mob again? Had The Patriarch been talking to The Mater?

I really felt the need to call Eve. I took out the phone and held it out. He nodded. But it was the same deal. She was away from her phone. She wasn't. She just saw my name and gave me the finger.

"What I'm after is a letter of introduction into the Farnsworth holdings."

"The Farnsworths? I'm not in that family. You didn't read my life story very closely. I got spit out."

He laughed.

"The only people I know are the ones who have gotten spit out, as you say. We'll do fine."

I remember what Eve told me when I talked about my regaining my proper place in the family.

"You'd have to go half way up the Devil's ass," is what Eve said. She didn't recommend it. Eve didn't like people who she called overly tall and she didn't like people who were overly rich. Or for that matter, overly stupid, fawning, annoying, gentrified, and red haired. I had been two of those but now I was just nothing. Thing is, Eve didn't like people period. Theo was enough people for me. I just couldn't get attached to them. I had more of a relationship with Eve's octopus, Harry. Not really, though. Harry went out of his tank when I was sleeping and tried to take my right foot back to his tank.

The fuck is a predator big time but Eve thinks he's loveable and besides she'll shoot him if he goes rogue. He's another one who knows a lot of languages. What do you do when all the lower orders you know are higher, much higher than you?

This new version of The Patriarch, Mr. Victor, excused himself.

I was ready for the new transformation when he showed up. He was wearing a black velvet jacket and sporting a large, flowery neck scarf. He smelled like something the Mater called Toilet Water.

"Cheer up, mon semblable," he said to me, smiling, slight lisp. "Your time for joy will come, believe me. It's what Pushkin said."

"Is that what he said? Push Pin?" I said and laughed. The name was funny.

I heard Ivan clicking some nix that behind me.

"You don't have any issues, my dear, Dirk. Your issues are paper thin. You should be happy."

"Really? Do you know about my girlfriend? Evangeline Solly. She's the one I've been calling. We live together. I mean we can't live together more than we can."

I poured another vodka.

"Sometimes I got my hands on her throat. If she didn't stick that gun in my ribs ... Forgive me for my violent nature, Patriarch."

"Oh, not him. How funny. I'm Victoire."

The guy just looked at me the way the shrink, Dr. Fraud, who talked to Theo and me a couple times a week for a couple of years used to look at me. Reaction was what Theo said he was looking for so don't give it to him and he'll go away. That was Theo's strategy for me. For himself, a different strategy.

Theo called him Dr. Fraud and told him a different pack of lies every week, all in different accents. Dr. Fraud wanted Theo to stop reading too far above grade until Theo's word and world links could be re-adjusted. He wanted me to spend a couple of hours a day listening to Gregorian chant. I didn't mind the sessions. Dr. Fraud had a wall to wall fish tank with about a gazillion colorful fish of all sizes as active as shopkeepers in Istanbul. There were some wastrels too who just hung out in the rocks, peeping out at you as you stared at them. Dr. Fraud called them parasite fish, living off the creative genius of heroic fish. I thought he was nuts and I remember I didn't feel any different when he hung himself in a closet. Theo thought I might have gotten to him when he got a closer look into my mind.

VicWha was screaming. That brought me back.

"I told you that you are too hard on yourself!"

At that, this guy jumps out of his chair and grabs me by the shoulder.

"You need to fight back! *So he dashes, like a demon, - proud, black demon of the tempest, - and he's laughing and he's weeping . . . it is at the clouds he's laughing, it is with his joy he's weeping!*" That's *The Song of the Stormy Petrel* by Gorki."

Wow! He recited poetry like Theo did.

"You will inherit the Farnsworth fortune."

"The pool boy she married will," I told him. "He's a boy toy."

"The pool toy boy husband is nothing I tell you. The lawyer Sulmondson will keep sucking the blood of that fortune, your fortune, unless you do something."

"You think so? I mean you know about Sulmondson and the kid my mother married? How's that?"

"What I know is that you will inherit something of great value. And I can help you."

I leaned back in the chair. My knees, in spite of the vodka, were drumming, like each one had a tiny drummer right at the head of the kneecap, doing a steady shuffle with sharp hits on the snare. I was thinking of getting one of those saps they had used on me but maybe I should carry one or two of the guns Eve had given me last birthday. In fact, she gave me one on every birthday. I had them in their boxes under my bed.

Afterward, that very night when I finally got a sit down with Eve and told her everything I remembered about being with the Russians, she twirled the shot glass in front of her and summed it all up:

"I take it you think that one of that crowd of douche bags in your family or the shyster lawyer got Theo stuck with a shiv? Not your Russians killing him because he killed a favorite son ... Prince Nicky ... although he was a douche bag ... and they killed your brother on their way to killing you but they don't kill you because you can connect them to the douche bags in your family and some business between them and your Russian with three personalities can happen. Wait, The Patriarch. And Mr. Victor. And the one who recited poetry? The guy is three guys, you say. Right? And then after all that they'll kill you for killing Prince Nicky. Is that it?"

"Well, he was The Patriarch for a while. I had to confess and he gave me absolution."

"Shut up."

"Probably not real because then he came back as Mr. Victor who was really scary. And then he was a guy who quoted a lot of Push Pin. Vic Wha. And he mentioned The Mob.""

Eve gave me one of her close scrutinizing looks.

"Listen. Stay clear of that guy. He's three guys in one and none of them are him. That is never good. Except for sex. Believe me."

I nodded in agreement.

"He gave me some good advice though. He said I can tell my mother that Theo's murder has made me realize that I need to step up and be a better man. Convince her of my redemption. No one sees a bad man without thinking of redemption. This is specially so with mothers. or something like that. *Thy long career of war and crime.*"

"Push Pin again?"

I nodded.

"Maybe it was Poochkin," I told her.

"Yeah, he isn't real either. I think this Russkie sized you up as a ball of dough with an amyloid brain he can shape anyway he wants. Kind of like the way I see you."

"Vengeance cannot be clouded was the last thing Vic Wha told me. He stood up reciting Poochkin again.

"For there is no worse punishment to Man, then to want to avenge and not being able to."

"What the hell does that mean?"

She laughed.

"That just means he's going to kill you next. It's all about revenge with those Russkies. You been all day with that whacko?"

"No, I just strolled down the boardwalk putting pieces together and lining up the ducks and tracing the ins and outs and following the trail of blood, gloves and prints. I didn't get anywhere."

"No surprise. Thinking is not your thing. Just don't say it's a process is all I ask."

"I stopped in at the Aquarium and got surrounded by school kids on a field day trip to see the fish. I sat in front of an underwater world and watched the inhabitants swim by."

"Kids probably thought you were a whale got out of a tank. Shut up now and let me think. Get that Bison grass vodka out of the freezer. I need some grey cell lubricant."

CHAPTER FIFTEEN

LIKE A PARADOCKS

Eve was petite and lovely to look at was the way Eve described herself to her listeners and she wasn't wrong.

That first night we met and she chose me and not Theo, we wound up at *The New Pompey,* bar and grill I had never been in before. There was a restaurant in the back where one night we had dinner. She said I studied the menu the way a Hard Shell Born Again studies the Bible.

We didn't move forward and I didn't change shape except for a couple of pounds. Eve said it felt like I put eight arms around her. And I met Harry, her octopus. He was Harry the Eighth because they didn't live long.

And then Theo, my better me, was shivved in Rikers.

"The memorial service is at the compound on East Egg," I told Eve.

"Okay. You know, getting back to reality. Did you ever think that schizoid Russkie killed Theo just to have you sweat it out until they come and stick a shiv in your fallowness?"

She put a cold bottle to her forehead. She needed to straighten herself out. She was a terrible alcoholic.

"Right now, your fear's got you manageable. The Patriarch and all his other personae obviously want something from the Farnsworth empire, and he figures you're his way in. You know, your family's connection with The Mob. To me The Mob is the Boogey Man in the closet. Comes out, I shoot him."

Eve opened her eyes and stared at me.

"You know, I change my thought. It can't be that. You're not manageable. And no chance of frightening you. You're before fright, fire and toilet training."

"No, I'm not."

I don't know where it came from but the .38 was in her hand and it was pointing at me.

"Say you're scared."

"I'm scared."

She shook her head.

"But you're not. Even though I'm drunk enough to shoot you. And I have many reasons. Since you came into my life, my life has turned mosh pit. And, alcoholics have more reasons than anyone else. That's the thing. Everybody has their reasons that's why the human race is heading for extinction on *Twitter*. But I've got one reason that holds up. You've wasted eleven decades of my life so far."

"Nicky Gregmorey was a wastrel is what The Patriarch said."

"Okay," she said, and the .38 vanished. "Yeah, you're too obtuse to scare. Awareness is required. And memory. You know, Theo told me to take care of his parrot when they sent him up. He thought your landlady, Mrs. Anna Magenema would kill him one day when you were out of the place. Your brother didn't trust you to feed a parrot."

"Mrs. A?"

Eve had closed her eyes again, going deep into thought.

I liked watching her when she was thinking. She was the only person besides Theo who I found myself interested in. The parrot could be very interesting too, come to think of it. Kind of mystifying though. I mean how could Theo have taught him The Sentence? And then string another sentence to that? And The Sentence Diagram? And how could a bird compile a dictionary from his point of view? Which is what Theo had told me. A bird's eye view, he said, would shake up the world. Mystifying but interesting.

"Okay, here's where I'm at," Eve told me, pointing to the ceiling. "Your Patriarch probably didn't kill just to scare you. Pointless since you're not thinking you're next, are you?"

"Next what?"

"Exactly. Now, where does that leave us? Probability is that someone did want to get a Richard III thing going. You know, kill off the contenders to the throne one by one. The Coney Island Patriarch wants you to inherit the Farnsworth trove, right?"

"He wants me to talk to her. Talk to my mother."

"I'll have to write that script," Eve said in her usual smartass.

"You know I went to Princeton."

"That one term wore you out. Just shut up and listen."

"I don't want to be a contender to the throne. It's The Mob money anyway. That's what my mother told me."

"And another mob, a Russkie one, wants you to inherit that money. They could kill you and get you out of the way. Or you could inherit."

She pointed to her glass and the always at hand Sal poured her another. He was as always listening, but he never butted in on Eve's conversations. She put the fear of the Lord in the whole bar.

"Wait. Did you say kill me?"

"What have I been talking about?"

"If Cag comes back are you going to shoot him?" Sal asked.

"You're invading my drinking space. Sal. Step back."

"Sal told me you went out with Picca Piccalini or something like that."

"Sal should mind his own business. Anyway, that guy's not around anymore And I didn't. Not recently. Years ago. He's a wasted shell in my life."

"You shot him already?"

Suddenly the thought of Theo dead and his pupil, which is what he called Cag, made me very sad.

Theo was dead and Cag was out there lost someplace in Brooklyn. The old Brooklyn would shoot her off a fire escape and the new Brooklyn would give her a cage with Bluetooth.

I took out of a pants' pocket the card The Earmissary had left here at the *Pompey*. I handed it to Eve.

"That's the lawyer," I told her.

"If he wants to see you, I think this means you're in your brother's will. Did your brother have anything worth anything?"

"I don't know," I said. "Just the parrot. He didn't have a car. Or a house. I don't know whether he left his laundry in Paris or he owned a laundry in Paris. He never said. He's been living in Paris for a long time."

"Okay. Go see the lawyer. If you do inherit anything from anybody, I want what you owe me. I can put a price tag on the days and nights you've taken from me."

"I'm sorry," I told her, feeling on the border of tears

"Fuck me," she yelled. "Concentrate on this. You need to get one of those businessmen's haircuts. The Prodigal Son Returns haircut.

Make your mother proud she didn't abort your ass. Get reinstated on that Death List."

"Death list?"

"Or maybe, just maybe, it's a list where your name is first on inheriting the Fartworth fortune."

"I told you. I'm off that list. Disowned and such."

"Sweet," she said, ignoring my words. "You know just maybe one of the three guys says he's The Patriarch can help you. Be like Putin helping the President."

I was lost.

"I want to meet him. If he's conning you, I'll know it."

It didn't sound like a very good idea to me. I shook my head.

"You'll have to confess," I told her. "Before The Patriarch can give you absolution."

"I take my absolution in a bottle."

"You going to shoot him then? Do you think Cag told the lawyer, Sulmondson, anything?'"

She gave me a WTF look.

"Like what? Who stabbed your brother? Who killed cock robin? Who pissed on the president in Moscow? Where's your brain? He's a fucking parrot. What does he know? What's he got to pass on?"

"Theo said he was ... you know, the parrot was working on a dictionary."

"Get yourself together, Big Boy. You're in a meltdown."

She was off her barstool and at the door when I felt I had to tell her something.

"I just thought The Patriarch was a good person."

"So, he's a good guy because he gave you ... what did you say for breakfast?"

"Blini and vodka."

"And he absolved you of all the fuckups in your life? Your sins of commission, omission remission, submission and being a big slug who let his twin go to prison where he was murdered?"

She laughed and I had nothing.

"Get up, wash your armpits and let's get some fresh air."

I thought about doing that, but I didn't move.

"What's the matter? Can't be conscience. You're hungry, right?"

"Everything, I guess. Theo's dead."

But I had to admit, I was also hungry. You can be sad and hungry at the same time. It's like a Paradocks.

CHAPTER SIXTEEN

AT THE SEA BIRD

Eve wanted to make a night of it and as usual she got her way.

We didn't go to The Patriarch's place until around ten. *The Sea Bird.*

I called and made a reservation. We took the N train and walked Surf Avenue to West 8th and then down to the boardwalk.

It was one of those early Spring evenings when the sky, the ocean, the air, that sea salty smell, and your hunger added up to something if you weren't too hungry to notice.

The Sea Bird was lit up out front like a carny big tent act was going on inside. Occupancy sign said 250 but there was about 500 in the place. No smoking but no one was not smoking. There was music and cannonade coming over speakers.

"You think the new Brooklyn Gentrifiers are going to find their gluten free blini, dairy free ryazhenka and vegan Stroganoff in here," Eve asked me.

I studied her face.

She looked a bit hung over. Of course, when you look through bleary red eyes everybody looks hung over. Theo once quoted some guy from another century who said if you looked through the eye and not with the eye, something something.

Eve had a skirt so tight I think you could bounce nickels off her ass. And she was rocking her customary high heels. She wasn't 5'10" but she had a 5' 10 presence.

Table for two. Not far from the bar, not far from the musicians: soft, easy jazz trio. The piano player looked a lot like The Patriarch.

I guess because it was The Patriarch's other guy. Mr. Victor. Or the other guy, Vic Wha.

When I had called up, I had said that my date was petite so could they have a couple of cushions in a chair for her. No, not a child. No high chair. I could just see Eve pull out that .38 and let fly. Then the hostess or whoever was on the phone says something that sounds like "garlic." I hung up. Freak it. I didn't want to have this meet anyway.

When the waiter pulled out a chair that somehow perched Eve perfectly over the table without fanfare, I had to smile.

As the waiter ran down the specials that evening, explaining all the culinary augmentations and drizzles and ganashes and garnishes and unexpected flavors until you lost your fucking appetite, I remembered the garlic.

"We're not in fear of garlic breath," I told him, "so you can lay that on."

The waiter gave me a puzzled look but jotted it down on his pad.

"Any allergies?" he asked us.

"Yeah, soup with nasal floaters," Eve tells him and he says "Of course" and takes off.

I ordered us a couple of Smirnoffs straight up but they didn't come as timely as two alcoholics would wish.

"Get off your lazy ass and go to the bar and get'em," Eve told me, picking up a stalk of celery, then throwing it down.

"I hate limp dick celery."

I was at the bar, which was two layers thick with customers when Vic Wha suddenly appeared at my elbow.

"How did you like my piano playing?" he asked. "Monk."

"Monk? That reminds me. Are you really a Russian monk?"

"One of us, not me, has multiple personality disorder," he said, in a low voice. "I request that you keep that between us. And please don't mention it to The Patriarch or Mr. Victor. They're not totally aware of the situation. They repress."

"Okay," I replied, slowly, realizing that there was no sane place to rest in The Patriarch's head.

"I'll have drinks sent over to you. What does she like?"

"Anything. Absolute. Smirnoff, Zubrowka. Vodka really any kind. Ice cold. No ice. Neat, ice cold in tumblers."

I looked over at Eve.

"Ah, the garlic. She has a stunning face. Gorgeous in fact."

"The Garlic?"

"Midget is I think what it is in English."

"Oh, fuck," I said, looking at the shining, lustrous set up of bottles behind the bar. "Don't call her a midget. Or a dwarf. Or small. She'll shoot you in the head. I don't care how big a Putin you are around here. She'll shoot you on the spot. She's just below average height. She's 5′ 2″."

"Really?" he replied, startled, amused, wondering. He had it all written on his face. He was fascinated with the fact that Eve would shoot him dead.

"And so, what does she think she is?"

"A fucking goddess, okay?"

"Khorosho," he said, now a big smile on his face.

"Yeah," I said, not knowing what core ash go meant. "And she drinks like a fish. A whale. Not a fish. So, I can come back to that table with carrot juice, but I got to have a double vod in hand for her."

"I'll arrange it. Come. Introduce me."

"And get some celery stalk that holds an erection."

As he took my arm, I felt my flip vibrating. It was a call from Mitchell Sulmondson.

"I gotta take this. Go over and introduce yourself. She's here to meet you. Or one of you."

I made a quick exit to the boardwalk.

"What's up, Mitch?" I said, like he was an old buddy.

Actually, I had met him years before when I was still a welcomed member of the family and Jabba, my mother's third husband, had introduced Sulmondson as the guy taking over the family legal shit.

"Why didn't you come and see me as Rechert advised you?"

"Wreck it? Who's she?"

I had my flask out by this time and took a long pull.

"The emissary you beat up. Listen. Your mother doesn't want you at the memorial service."

"Okay. Tell her to expect me."

"Hey, I'm in your corner, buddy. I'll see what I can do."

"You knew Theo, right?"

"I am his lawyer."

"He's dead."

Long pause.

"You shouldn't show up at the memorial drunk. You'd be disrespecting your brother."

That didn't go down well with me.

"He wouldn't feel that was disrespect. He'd laugh. You know …

You don't know anything really about me or my brother. We had a private language."

I once told Eve that and she sneered.

"Yeah, you said Cag. He said Cag. The parrot said Cag."

I felt like throwing the cell over the railing into the sand, probably hit a tourist got himself lost wandering around looking for the old trashy, smelly, vulgar, noisy, rude Coney Island used to be when everybody fucked under the boardwalk and the sand was rich with condoms. That was what Eve had told me.

"Don't bring that little bitch. Your mother doesn't like her."

"Don't call her that. Or, call her that to her face and see if your bodyguard protects you."

"My apologies. By the way, your brother didn't leave you anything. He had nothing to leave. He had a lot of debts. His business went belly up."

"The laundering in Paris?"

"What's that? Oh, yes. The laundering in Paris."

"My brother left me with a lot of great memories," I told the prick.

"You know, Dirk, this could be your chance to get back into your mother's good graces. She says she once asked you for protection and you told her you had your own problems."

I snapped the bitch shut which was the only thing I liked about the old phones that flipped. You could slap'em shut. I liked slamming a receiver down a lot better though.

I went back into the restaurant.

I expected to find Vic Wha either beet red and crying for mercy or bed sheet white and dead. Those were two usual side effects from dealing with Eve.

I was wrong about Eve's effect on Vic Wha. She hadn't fucked him up. He had made a quick change into his Patriarch personality. I guess she drove him to it. Seeking to be saved.

I sat down.

"The lawyer Sulmondson says I can go to Theo's memorial. He arranged it because … "

"Shut up. Can't you see he's hearing my confession?"

I looked at The Patriarch. He had one arm resting on the table and his head was down, resting in one hand, and his eyes closed. He was listening to her sins.

"Where's was I?" Eve said, as I picked up the vodka and poured myself a drink.

Eve tapped her glass and I refilled it.

"Oh, yeah. I was the daughter of a Russian Jew who emigrated to the U.S. I was born and raised in Uglich. I used to speak Russian but I forgot it. I got to be about 5'10". I had a couple three boyfriends. One of them died and the gendarmes ... "

"Politsiya in Russian," The Patriarch told her.

"The politsiya came after me but I got out of the country just in time."

"I thought you were born on New Utrecht Ave in Brooklyn?" I said. "Went to school in Brooklyn. Brought up in an orphanage? Sisters of Little Cruelty or something."

"Shut up. Who's confession is this? Little Sisters of Much Cruelty."

"If you lie in confession, God will not forgive you."

That comment of The Patriarch's didn't go down well with Eve.

"Who believes in God? Who's looking for forgiveness? I'm just waiting until you've had enough of playing games and you tell us why you're really interested in the slob over here."

"Proceed with your confession," The Patriarch said, closing his eyes and going into his confessional listening crouch.

I had a thought that Eve might pop him out of whatever crazy hole he was in.

"I committed bigamy."

"How many times?"

"Bi. Twice. One guy got shot. Then again, I've never been married. You can fuck without marrying, you know? I'm self-partnered. He doesn't count."

I knew she was lying through her teeth ,but The Patriarch seemed to be taking it all in as Gospel. Why wouldn't he? He couldn't tell a handbag from a slice.

"Is that all, my child?"

"There's more but it's a matter of remembering. I usually put shit like this out of mind. Oh, yeah, the guy who was fatally shot? I shot him. He called me my child."

"This is a very grievous admission, my dear," The Patriarch told her.

"Okay. Now you tell me. Did you have his brother killed in Rikers?"

It seemed like he was taking a long time to answer.

"Perhaps a personality I'm not on speaking terms with, did kill somebody's brother someplace. I wouldn't know. Is this large man who lied in his confession, your new husband?"

"Him? Pantagruel? Do I look stupid? Besides I told you. I didn't have any husbands. Just domestic partners. A couple.

The others were long motel stays. I've been popular my whole life."

"You cannot lose favor with the gods for that. Being popular. Your president is very popular and look how wonderful that is for populace."

"The gods?" I couldn't help saying.

He opened his eyes and looked at me.

"Of course. One begat another. A celestial begatting."

Then he stood up, spread his arms out and shouted:

"Adam begat Seth, and Seth, Enos, Kenan, Mahalaleel, Jered, Henoch, Methusaleh, Lamech, Noe, Shem, Ham, and Japheth. The songs of Japheth were Gomer, Magog, Madai, and Javan, Tubal, Meschech … "

I don't know how much longer he would have gone on with the names, some I recognized from old movies, the begats, but Ivan and another guy came alongside him and whispered in his ear and then he walked away docilely with them. Looked more like they were frog marching him. Probably time for his meds.

I looked at Eve.

"What's with Uglich?"

"Uglich is famous.," she told me, her eyes on the dragging away of the owner. "And quaint. And scenic. Ivan the Terrible's 10-year-old son was found with his throat cut there. The death was ruled accidental, however, and the bells that reported the news were 'exiled' to Tobolsk, Siberia."

I shook my head in amazement.

"It's awesome what you know Eve," I told her.

"Right back at you, Duckie. Awesome what you don't know. Let's get out of here. That guy isn't going be any help to anyone, including himself.

I finished my drink and stood up.

When I turned there was a guy in a white dinner jacket, very suave looking guy. Young guy. Too young to be another one of The Patriarch's multiple personalities.

"What makes you think you're getting out of here?" he said, leaning toward me and running his face close to my navel.

I felt something sharp against my liver. Or the other side. Maybe my gall bladder. Could be a kidney in pain. Too low for my heart. Liver?

I looked down. It was a little gun.

"Walk straight ahead."

I started to walk as instructed and then I was walking alone.

When I looked back the guy was standing there frozen. Eve Solly was pasted behind him.

He looked pissed. And scared.

"Now you walk to that exit," Eve ordered. "Or I'll send a .38 slug right through your anus into your bollocks."

"I wasn't going to … "

"Shut up."

I followed the duo outside wondering what Eve was going to do with the guy.

She marched him across the boardwalk to a bench, pushed him down. She leaned against the rail, the .38 barely visible but it was pointing at him. I sat down next to the poor guy.

"Who are you and what did you want with this fool here?"

He gave me a sneer and then looked back at her.

"You're going to be sorry you messed with me," he told Eve, the sneer transported to his voice. "I'm Bogdan Pavlovich. They call me Junior. Nikolay Grigory was my cousin."

"So, you're … " I began.

"Don't fucking say 'so,'" Eve said, pointing the gun at me.

"I meant therefore you're the Patriarch's son?" I asked him.

He thought the question was funny because he laughed.

"I'm gonna kill ya whatever deal you made with the old man."

"Okay," Eve said, all sparky all of a sudden. "I'll have to kill you first. And I got the gun to do it."

"We didn't make any deal," I told him. "He heard Eve's confession is all."

"Did some begats," Eve added. "Didn't hear your name though. Bog Darn. What kind of deal were you thinking he made?"

Bog Darn shook his head.

"I don't know. Crazy shit."

"To be expected," Eve told him. "Your old man is more than unzipped. He's got a whole ensemble of players coming out of his head."

"You ain't gonna do nuttin to me," Junior told Eve, giving her the old sneer and menace look.

"Really?" Eve said, showing more of the .38. "I got a lot of reasons to cripple you with a well-placed bullet. First of all, I don't like your height. You're too tall. Second. Wait. One is enough for me. One in the foot. Knee?"

"Look, he thinks your friend here …

He turned to look at me in case there was some ambiguity.

"Is set up to take over big inheritance.

The fuck worth something."

"Fartsworth," I told him. "Really Farnsworth but Fartsworth is funnier. And I'm not set up to take over anything. I'm the fuck up in the family. Cast out. Abandoned. Fuck off they told me. I was sent to the Goolock."

Eve had just been staring at me but she was now shaking her head, the disbelief kind of headshake.

"That's all I know," Bock Dawn told us.

"Yeah, that's all a bag of nothing," Eve told him. "But I know you want to kill this waste of life here."

My eyes lit up.

"And you probably had his brother killed."

One of those accusations got Back Down riled.

"I don't know nuttin about his brother. I didn't kill him. Maybe one of my old man's whatevers had it done. But I ain't confused like that. I know your friend here killed Niky. And I'm going to pay him back for that."

"Well, it sounds like you're going to kill Dirk Bratter here," Eve said, nodding. "Bow Dine. Pavlovich."

"Bogdan. Junior is better."

"Got it," Eve said, smiling.

I didn't know what she got because what I got was he was going to kill me.

She pulled her phone out of her pocket and did some fingering, her eyes on Bad Dawn.

She held the phone up and we heard the last five minutes of our conversation.

"This goes to the cops," Eve told Junior. "My advice is to get far, far away. Maybe go back to Russia."

Junior made a lunging move off the bench, but I managed to grab his jacket and pull him back. He fell in my lap. I got up and he came along with me.

"Dump him over the rail," Eve said. "Aim his head into the sand. It'll soften it up."

He was making a lot of noises, but I got him to the rail, hoisted him just enough to leverage him over and down he went.

"Let's stop for a couple three Nathan's," I told Eve and she nodded.

"Yeah, you exerted yourself into hunger mode."

"Maybe we should stop at the Aquarium."

"It's closed. And anyway, those octopoi are tired of looking at a life form so far beneath their own. You depress them."

CHAPTER SEVENTEEN

THE CLARK GOBBLE EFFECT

"Let me sum this up," Eve Solly said couple of weeks later, as we sat in our usual corner spot at the *Pompey* bar.

"You say I've been invited to the memorial service for your brother, but I don't think I have been."

She looked over at Cag who was by the cash register, watching Sal count change.

"Yeah, but he's dead."

"You know the way I figure it, a lot of people are dead and they're not complaining. It's the Great Mishap is all it is as a great poet come in here once said."

Eve gave him one of her below freeze looks and Sal moved on down the bar.

"He's dead. Okay. You were told your brother died without a pot to piss in and he's got a shit load of debt. Then lastly, we don't know whether Dog Rag beat feet … "

"Junior Pavlovich?"

She nodded.

"Or he's outside right now waiting to put you out of your misery, all of which you are oblivious."

"Shoot him in the head!"

"You know, I could have just given Junior some of my inheritance," I told Eve.

She gave me a frozen eyed look, eyebrows arched up to her hairline.

"What the sweet Jesus makes you think you are going to inherit anything? If there is anything, it's already gone to pay this lawyer's inflated bill of services rendered."

"Look you, I told you to piss off!

"How does Gee let this loud mouth parrot in here?" Eve asked Sal.

"Gee says he's good for business. People like to come in now and talk to the parrot. Bar take has gone up 20%."

"You low, lousy, no good son of a bitch!"

"See?" Sal said. "How do you respond to that? But they do."

I remembered what an online reviewer stationed in his mother's basement had written on *Facebook* about our show: "Evangeline Solly is a high speed Seven Deadly Sins talking operating system. So twisted you'll want to run. Her stooge, Dirk Fatter makes a lot of sense if you're locked up in an institution. The parrot is a one bird Greek chorus with real balls. A fine example of AI, most likely made in China. The Dark Web at its darkest."

""You come to the memorial," I pleaded. " Just to see the look on the lawyer's face when you get up there and say a few words about how Theo was the good twin and how badly I sucked."

"Oh, yeah? First, I don't go up on anything. Second, neither of us should go."

"Why?"

"Why kill you? Let me count the ways. Your brudder? Either he got in the way of something going on or maybe he didn't want to go along with something going on. Commission or omission. Either way, he was murdered."

"I'm going to get them for that."

"Yeah, I'm sure they're shaking you'll come looking for them after you finish your sandwich. Tell me, your brother was in line to get it all? What's all?"

"The family holdings. Trust. The Estate. Like that. And the Foundation."

"Foundation?" You know, nothing is so full of snakes like a sacred, holy Foundation. It's the perfect front for dirty dancing."

"It is?"

"Your brudder was too clean to get wrapped up in that fucking shyster lawyer's backyard dealings running through the Foundation. He wouldn't go dirty, so he had to be killed. Get him out of the way."

"He had a laundry business in Paris."

"You mean like a Laundromat or a money laundering operation?"

"I think it was just clothes."

Her lips puckered and she let out a whistle.

"You still listening to that guy you see in your mirror in the morning? No. Don't Tell me again how you came into my life."

I started to say something, and she told me to shut up. I could see she was back to thinking.

"Maybe your taking over The Foundation doesn't work for whoever that lawyer is representing. "

"I told you. I'm banished. Cut off. I can't inherit my own socks."

"Look, your Mater is in a loony bin now. She was a loony when she disinherited you. Thus, that disinheritance won't hold in court."

I kind of felt good about that. The way Eve put things was always the way things were. Or would be. It didn't bother me a bit to think The Mater was always loony. There's less time for loving your kids if the loony is taking all your time.

"They could either stay with you and work you like a dough ball into any shape they want. Or they could send you to look for your brother underground. Didn't your mother marry a pool boy? He's next to inherit. Okay, here's what it is. Is the pool boy more of an idiot than you?"

"Fire when ready!" the parrot screamed.

Before I could respond Eve said she had to go.

"I'm slipping off this fucking stool some idiot named Sal waxed."

I remained at the bar. Nobody had to escort Eve out.

Sal came back to my end of the bar.

"Is it safe?"

I nodded. He poured me another vodka. I told him what Eve had said.

"Look, maybe you'll be killed and maybe you won't. But there's one thing you know for sure. Nobody gets out of here alive. Some get murdered, some fall down the stairs and break their necks, and some die in their sleep. Results? The same. It's worse if you get tortured first."

"Maybe I should just go along with whoever killed Theo. Do what they want so I don't get killed."

"Or you could do what they do in Texas. Stand your ground and kill them before they kill you."

"Yeah," I said then knocked back the vodka.

"Look, those Russkies might not kill you. They might just stuff you in a herring barrel and ship you to someplace along the Black Sea."

"The Russkies want to kill me too?"

"It's a war man. A red hot cold war. Don't let anybody tell you it's over with us and those guys. Putin is putting the band back together."

"He is? You know him?"

"Drop dead and don't come back!"

"Why would anybody want to come in here to talk to this twisted bird?"

I told him I didn't know and I really didn't know that. And anything else.

The next morning, I got a call from Wreckit, Sulmondson's robot mercenary.

The Memorial service was Tuesday, two days away. He'd come by my place at 8AM and pick me up and then we'd drive out to East Egg.

"You should be sober," he advised me. "And I'm packing so don't think you're gonna jump me like you did before."

He was the one with the machine operated voice. Scary.

"Mr. Sulmondson wants me to have a suit sent over to you. What's the size?"

I wanted to tell him to shove any size he wanted up his own butt, but I had already decided that I was going be the obedient prodigal son returning home. I wanted to get to the other side of ejected and rejected, just to see who was going to pop out of the woodwork and what requests they might have. I was going to find out what was going on, find out who killed Theo and then stand my ground.

I'd clean up all round for Theo.

The suit arrived two days later. I tried it on. It was snug. I shouldn't have given Wreckit the weight I had been thinking about trimming down to for the last five, ten years. It remained an ideal. The reality was different. So, I mean, thus, the jacket was snug. I put a lot of strain on the waist button, but it held. I just couldn't breathe deeply. I had a kind of flushed look in the mirror on top of my alcohol flushed look.

I'm standing there facing the bathroom mirror. Doughboy pale flesh flushed, blondish brownish sandyish thinning hair oiled straight back, pale, watery eyes, cataract looking but I didn't have any cataracts, 20/20 eyesight ... Eve told me my good eyesight was the gods' gift to illiterates ... a sharp, razor cut of a mouth, good teeth because I had never lived in England, which is what Sal had told me.

All of these features on one of those pumpkin sized heads that went long and not round, more of a blue Hubbard sized head. I had a pale pencil thin kind of mustache going but you'd have to get real close to feel its full effect, kind of Clark Gobble effect. Otherwise, it was kind of like a chalk mark on a snowman.

In short, I looked like a lump of grey modeling clay a kid had worked into a blob and shoved into a black suit. P.T.'s lump of primordial shard in a suit.

Eve and I had finally agreed that if she tagged along, there would be no chance that my mother would welcome me back into the fold. The money fold. The fortune fold everybody was anxious to get their hands on.

Cag goes around yelling "Greed is good! Greed works!" but that little bastard's kin are facing temperatures too hot for birds to survive. Or they could get flooded out of existence. Or wiped out in a continental slog of mud.

All of which meant to me that greed wasn't good. Theo said I had the kind of moral sense without a social or religious filter that only Venus fly traps, female praying mantises, and female mosquitoes had. It was instinctual.

Now, dressed sharp like this and with a repentant look in my eye, some tears too, my mother might open her arms and give me an all-is-forgiven crush.

I was prepared to tell her I should have believed her years ago when she said Gunner Farnsworth was partners in The Mob and Jabba the Hutt was The Mob's bee keeper and that her life was in danger because The Mob thought she was a moral hazard to their business. Etcetera. I'd tell her now that I believed in The Mob and I was there to protect her.

The actual truth was that Eve and I had listened to the parrot go on about The Mob in one of his dictionary sessions.

I got it all down in the Dictaphone:

"The Mob sent el Crapo to tunnel under your toilet."

"The Mob comes in caravans through tunnels under your toilet."

"The Mob is your 65 million friends on *Facebook* in a tunnel under your toilet."

"The Mob's body was found in a garbage bag in a tunnel under your toilet."

Stuff like that. The parrot made me think that The Mob's nothing but a toilet fantasy, like Dr. Fraud had told us. It's like everybody has a different hook up here. Eve thinks The Mob is tall. That's it. Sal thinks The Mob is all around us but we can't see them, like body snatcher invaders. Gee thinks The Mob is no more than gentrifying real estate developers. And so on. I think Gee would know because he got *The New Pompey* going with The Mob's protection. That's what Sal said anyway.

Like me, my mother didn't take the fitness path, Theo's choice, but went straight to the table and then signed up for as little movement as possible. She drank like me, too. She has two designer, handheld mutts she calls Oxy and Contin so beloved is she of both dogs and the drug. I guess they kept The Mob from breaking through the gates of her mind. More likely, considering how things wound up, they were a Trojan Horse. Mr. Spinalzo had us read Tales of the Illness by Hogan.

Wreckit picked me up at precisely 0800. I was already at the curb, the West End rumbling over my head as a Porsche pulled up.

I got in the front seat, which I noticed had been drawn back far enough so my knees weren't kissing my chin.

"Morning, Sir," Wreckit said, still with the smirk. "Seat belt. No pit stops. No smoking. No open bottles. No small talk."

"Drive the fucking car."

Like there was any way a seat belt would go around me. I heard the strategic button snap and I started to breathe more easily.

The driver gave me a cold assessment. He seemed to be sniffing the air. For the booze. I disappointed him. I had splashed myself, face and neck and hair with some Old Splice I hadn't used in years. It had probably gone bad or maybe it had *Twinkie* genes and stayed fresh forever.

"Nice ride," I said as we headed down New Utrecht toward the Belt.

"Porsche Cayenne Turbo S," he told me, patting the wheel fondly. "A hundred and sixty thousand."

"Impressive," I said. "Does it stop for a sandwich? I missed breakfast."

He pushed an elbow down and a lid popped open. He pulled out a thermos and a bag of Krispy Kreme's.

"Munch up," he told me, smiling.

"Ospina," he said, as I twisted off the lid and the rich aroma of coffee filled the car. I mean the Porsche Cayenne Turbo S.

"120 bucks a pound. How is it?"

"Incredible. Almost as good as Fogars."

"What's this suit cost?" I asked, pouring another cup.

"That's a Zegna. $2,795."

"Wow!" I said, pretending to be duly impressed. "Nice of Mr. Sulmondson to buy this for me."

The soldier would bring it all back to his commander. Sulmondson.

"Mitch Sulmondson must really be doing well."

"It's not his money," Wreckit corrected me. "The Farnsworth Foundation foots the bills."

I didn't say anything. He glanced over at me. Always the sly smile like I really amused him.

"Yeah, your mother used to foot your bills one time, right? Then she shoved a foot up your ass, and you went out the door."

I felt like punching his smirking face. Oh, yeah. I had done that. Hadn't changed his personality much.

"She fantasizes," I told him. "She's para something."

"Paranoiac. But you know sometimes somebody is really trying to kill you."

"The Mob?" I said, suddenly interested.

I thought about giving him Cag's take on The Mob.

After a while, he said:

"Maybe she'll think you've changed."

We were on the LIE, the sun was on its climb, not blocked by the El which shadowed my apartment. And I was still hungry. There had only been a baker's dozen donuts. High & Tight had gone all tight lipped, whether by military training or because he had nothing to say or because he had nothing to say to me.

"So, mercenaries fight for anybody who pays them?"

He let enough time go by to make me think he hadn't heard and then he said:

"Your family has got a lot of money, but you live in a shithole. Why's that? What did you do to get kicked out of the nest?"

"Eve said I made bad choices," I told him, closing my eyes.

He laughed.

"You don't think donuts were a choice, right?"

Yeah, I said to myself and closed my eyes.

I dreamed Eve was standing over me and there was a blackboard behind her. She had one of those old time teacher's pointers in her hand and she was pointing at stuff written on the board.

As she pointed down the list, I repeated what was written there:

"I'm assuming personal responsibility. Always go with that line of shite. Go with a public confession of totally screwing up your own life if you want to be welcomed back into the Heartland of Winners and Losers. You apologize to everyone. You weren't your best self. You don't know what got into you. You made some really bad choices. In fact, you never made a good choice. You wouldn't recognize one if you saw it. You always had a hard on for the bad choice. But now the group therapy worked, the lithium set you straight, you found God, you read Ayn Rand, you're ready to start a business you have friends on Fox. Stuff like that."

CHAPTER EIGHTEEN

THE CELIBATES OF MY BROTHER'S LIFE

The Captain … I decided on calling Wreckit that … was driving through the Farnsworth Royal Gates. I slept through our travel down the Sunrise Highway. Beautiful name.

Now I saw stone lions on both sides of the compound entrance. Theo and I used to climb them and shoot at each other with plastic ray guns.

First and only time I took Eve out here, she gave the place a thumb's down.

"Looks like one of those knock off Versailles designed by one of those Frank Lloyd Wrongs," she had told me. "I love it the way the mega-wealthy pay Howard Roaches to drop their genius and their pants, just bend over to a self-appointed architectural genius of big bucks. You have any idea, Babba, how much all round genius the wealthy soak into their genes by virtue of just having money? Your stock comes in big and next thing you got a great artistic sense and the mind of Immanuel Can't punched into you. It's a fucking miracle how money turns idiots into geniuses and canna sewers of everything."

I also remember asking her who Howard Roach was and why Manuel couldn't.

"Better get yourself together," the Captain told me, putting one hand on my shoulder and squeezing tight.

I shrugged the hand off and glared at him. Or tried to. I wasn't sure my eyes were opened. This wasn't biblical indolence.

Something was not of my personal choosing.

I reached for the coffee thermos. It felt empty. I looked at that prick, Wreckit. He had his sneering face inches from mine. I could see that clearly. I punched something soft, not his face. The car seat.

"You fucking drugged me," I croaked, swinging my right arm about an inch, which isn't a swing but more like a spasm or a failed orgasm.

"Hey, keep yourself calm. Remember, you want to make a good impression."

I kicked the door open lumbered out of the car. I mean the Porsche whatever the fuck. I swagged and swayed like a reed in the wind. Wreck had gone around to the back of the main house, the Versa chi mess, and I saw the tent, and a podium and about five thousand people seated on wooden chairs. Maybe 500. More like 50. A lot. More people than had shown up at Individual One's coronation.

Theo had a lot of passing acquaintanceships, lapsed friends lying about like lapsed Catholics, launderette corner boys, mysterious associates. But I was his only twin. Although, there must have been laundry loads of people in the laundry business that I wasn't seeing. The ones I saw all had suits like mine. Except the women. They were wearing hats Eve Solly would have coveted. All his friends from the laundering business in Paris is what I figured plus the East Egg locals who showed up at memorial services the way the villagers showed up in old black and white movies. Most of the people I thought I was looking at had more of the Paris look on their faces than East Egg.

I leaned against the Porsche.

My Presidential tie, black and long enough to reach my boys, was flapping in the Springtime frosty breeze. Beautiful day. Theo would have worked up a global warming message it was so beautiful. And endangered. I guess he thought we needed to launder the whole planet.

Theo loved the whole planet but especially I think the Airybvd's he rented in what he called topical paradises. And the moon and the stars and especially the sun. He wrote a gazillion poems about the sun when we were in Spinalzo's class. I wish I could remember one of them. He did a lot of big breasted women drawings too, mostly with a moon or a sun in the corner of the drawing casting shadows on undulant curves is how he put it.

"Steady as she goes," Wreckit said to me, taking a hold of my elbow.

"Your idea to drug me. Your boss wanted me presentable. Sober, steady. Able to leap tall ... able to fucking walk."

"No, sir. He wanted you just as you are now. Go ahead and show everyone what a worthy son and brother you are."

I thought of hammering that face, but I could see that half the mourners who had come to the service had been alerted to my arrival and they were all looking my way, hands at their brows, visoring the gleaming sunlight.

I couldn't step away from the support of the car. It felt like my legs weren't ready. Fact is, I couldn't feel where they were.

The lawyer, I forget his name, somebody's son, and the whole world came rushing up to me, his cocked up sweep of blonde hair combed in the hot new presidential style, blowing this way and that.

"Glad you could make it, Dickey," he said, thrusting out a hand.

I took it and squeezed it like it was a ripe fruit I needed to get all the juice out of.

Wreckit brought a shoe down the side of my foot and then poked me hard in the liver. I let the lawyer's hand go.

"Be a good boy," Wreckit whispered in my ear. "Go up there and make your Mother proud."

I regretted not having Eve along. You know, to get me out of there or some other plan. I had none. She had a gun.

I was struggling with the strategic button. I don't think my pants would fall down, at least not passed my ass, but my shirt was billowing out like a sail in the wind.

"How ... how do I look?" I asked, trying to focus on the podium ahead.

"I guess if you left a body in the water long enough, it'd look like you."

I didn't know lawyers were all shitty like that.

"Just so you know," the lawyer said, whispering in my ear. "As soon as this service is over, your mother's off to Ravine Farm Sanitarium. We got a judge to sign her in. She's not mentally able to handle her own affairs. Just wanted you to know. You're not able either."

I tried to digest all that. Thing that impeded that was the fact that I wasn't carrying my flask. I had been afraid that the fumes would have permeated my suit.

The three of us just stood there. They knew and I knew they couldn't manhandle me to the podium. One, I was far too big for that. And two, they didn't want anyone to see me as anything like

Theo. They wanted everyone to see me as the prodigal still prodigal. I was sure every Smartphone would be videoing my whole performance. Eve had told me that. Be prepared, she told me, You'd go viral on *YouTube* if you fuck up. Don't forget: sin dumps the wicked in a ditch."

"I for one think you can go up there," The Devil said, whispering in my ear. "Do your brother proud. He'd want you to show everybody here that you and he were brothers, identical, and not good and bad sides of the same coin."

"You think so?" I asked, rocking close to somebody's face. "Well, you don't know … anything. We had a private language."

I'm sure Eve or even the parrot would have something with more punch but that was all I had.

Somehow, I did the walk toward the seats on my own. There was a seat next to my mother in the front row, but she didn't lift her head when I sat down. I think she was dozing.

I hadn't seen her in about 140 years, but on reflection maybe I saw her couple of Christmases ago when I showed up with Eve and all we did was drink, fuck, eat, and sleep. Eve drank up the whole bar and then shot her .38 a number of times into the Christmas tree in the main foyer and then the private security army that patrolled the compound threw a net on her, hustled her into a van and drove her back to the city.

Oh, yeah, before that. Just out of the … cashed out of the Army. Moran and Williams. Moran wanted to burn the place down. Williams stole a painting of his sweetheart. My Mother told me in private about The Mob. So, there was that time too.

As I was recalling all these family visits, the lawyer was up at the microphone eulogizing Theo and then letting that go, told everyone that we were all fortunate that Theo's twin brother, Dick, was here to tell us all something about Theo that only his twin would know.

There was no applause.

This wasn't a variety show. I tried to button my jacket over my unbuttoned pants. Couldn't. So … don't say 'so.' So then, I used my shirt flaps to cover whatever was going on with my pants. In short, I did my best to look and walk in a respectable manner. I had the thought that Wreckit had misjudged my dosage. My body could sponge up solids and liquids like Panty's Gruel is what Eve told me. Didn't know what that meant. If you sin, they throw you in a ditch was running through my head.

Below the few steps I had to walk up was a giant photo of Theo. Smiling. He smiled a lot. He had good, white teeth, like laundered teeth. His eyes were clear and happy. His nose hadn't fallen into his chin, his jowls into his neck, his ball sacks to his knees, his eye pouches into sleeping bags, and his teeth into dark, volcanic magma. I mean he was my age. Somewhere between thirty and thirty something. When do twins stop looking like each other? Eve thought it depended on who they married. If both didn't marry, they'd always look the same. Not true for Theo and me.

It could have been any one of a gazillion photos. I can't go anyplace without seeing people aiming Smartphones at each other or at themselves. Selfies. Only the selfish take selfies Ms Solly told me but I figured her animalus stemmed from the fact that people took photos of her the way they were drawn to photograph General Tom Thumb or the lion faced lady. I said her beauty drew the cameras.

But I knew this photo. I remembered it. I took that photo when Theo graduated from Princeton, three years and six months after I had been kicked out. It had felt then like I was the one who had made it through, had spurned the drugs, the booze, the many late night escapades and had retreated to the Firestone Library and planned my climb on Wall Street and my journey to a Paris launderette.

I stretched the microphone upward to just about chest high. I looked down at the mourners. The celibates of Theo's life. What the hell did they know about Theo? I was his identical twin and I didn't even know he was in the laundry business. Or why he wanted to go to jail in my place. Or why somebody wanted to kill him. Or why I was alive and he was dead.

"I'm Dirk. Don't know Dick. I just saw this photo. I took it. Long time ago. I never forgot what Theo told me about time. He was quoting his favorite guy William Blax. There's a moment in time that Satan can't ... something or something or other."

I looked at my watch. It was a windup. The date was last week, the time was midnight.

"Long time ago, when we ... when you couldn't tell us apart. I took our shared chromatozoa, our father, P.T., was a genius-ist, and made what you see in front of you. Theo made it handsome. And good. You can see it in his eyes. You see broken, blood vessels in mine."

I did a wide eyed look and scanned. No laughs. No smiles. A lot of disgust and the kind of look kids get on their face when they say "icky." Truth is, I don't know what kids say to a guy older than nine. Probably just "fuck off and drop dead."

Suddenly, I saw a lot of condemning faces in front of me.

"Hey, I didn't force Theo to say he killed that kid, Nicky Gorey something witch. You know, truth be told, my brother Theo hit some bad luck with that judge. He was a real hanging judge. Gave Theo two to five when it was a stand on the ground homicide and he should have been let go. It was a self-offense. Man's daughter. He shouldn't have been in prison in the first place. Something very wrong there. His lawyer was blind and didn't see it coming. Somebody greased somebody to put my brother in Riker's. It's Sac of Confetti all over again."

I was getting louder and angrier as I thought about what Summer Arpeggio had said. "That judge was greased big time to put your brother away. I got blindsided. I didn't see it coming. I suck as a trial lawyer too. There's that also."

"And why the fuck Riker's?" I went on, hearing some giggles coming out of Billy Hashfries, the pool boy, sitting there next to my mother, who was still dozing, comatose or just opioid flying.

My own mother was the pool kid's December romance. If she wasn't a candidate for dementia old-timers' farm, I don't know who would be. Looking at her down there, head down, a tear came to my eye. She had asked me to protect her that time long ago and I hadn't. I didn't believe in The Mob then. Actually, I still don't.

Then I got angry again. They were getting her out of the way. Like now, getting me out of the way. Then I hear a big sound from the audience like you hear when you speed down a roller coaster. I was rocking so far forward and taking the podium with me. Somebody came up and righted the ship.

And I went on. I found it funny.

Then I saw pool boy Billy was standing up and waving at me or somebody.

He was wearing some kind of brown and white splotched suit a couple of sizes too small for him, cloth stretching across arm, shoulders and chest muscles. His pants were plastic wrap tight. The Fartsworth heir. Pissant.

"Sit down and shut up!" I screamed at him. "This is my brother I'm talking about here."

Anger like I get on the instant, impulse anger Eve calls it, sobers you up like ten cups of coffee and six slaps to the face and a bucket of ice water over your head and a dog bite to the boys.

I figured whatever stupifier had gone into the coffee or the donuts had reached about a fifth of my body mass, about twelve minutes of woozy and that was it.

"None of us here are worth one hair on Theo's head. My brother is still a better man dead than most of you droogs are alive. I'd slap some of you silly just for having the bollocks to come here."

That got the hive noise buzzing and I could see a few people get up and walk away. I could see Smartphones pointed at me. I'm going viral. Eve had said it would be inevitable like sleeping on your back and snoring.

"Somebody paid off that judge to put Theo away and I'm figuring that wanker is sitting here right now."

I looked down and stared at the lawyer. Winchell somebody's son, who responded by aiming his Smartphone at me and smiling.

"Get him off there," somebody shouted.

"You come up here," I shouted back. "Wait, I'm coming down there. I'll kick your gonads into your teeth, punch your glands into your nose, and push your sinuses into your ears!"

I was quoting something Cag had said to somebody at *The Pompey* who had passed out at the bar. Words like that stay with you.

I heard a scream and when I looked down I saw my mother standing, tottering, her face all blubbery red, her eyes like moon pies. It looked like someone had jolted her with a hypo of adrenalin. Which they probably had.

It was sad. We were both sad. Both of us were being coaxed down crazy's highway. Our destinies had been arranged for us. It suddenly came to me that the rich should have only fifteen seconds in the spotlight and then disintegrated. Funny, both Eve, Theo and Sal had told me that. And the parrot.

The Mater was screaming for what sounded like a donut as I got off that podium. Then somebody tripped me, and I tumbled forward onto the grass. Hands were on me, holding me down or trying to pick me up. I couldn't tell. I reared up like a bear and got free of the hands.

I was standing there by myself, the folding chairs empty, the podium empty. Everybody gone. No sounds.

I looked over at Theo's photo. I had taken that photo. Way back when. I think he was shaking his head but then he winked.

I'd punch him in the face, take him to the ground and wrestle with him like we always did. If he wasn't just a photograph.

I'll show you fear in a photo like that.

I had taken that photo.

CHAPTER NINETEEN

"TRIBES IN THE WOODS"

I called Eve and she said she was on her way, just meet her outside the gates. She'd be there in a few days.

I told her I think I got stoned.

"Biblical?" she asked.

"No, the usual. Maybe both."

There was some mud and grass stains on the new suit. Bad armor. The expense of the suit hadn't protected me. My pants had fallen just below my hips and no further.

I hid behind some bushes for a few hours, dozing off for some of the time. If anyone saw me, they didn't stop to say hello. I dozed in and out amid the peaceful beauties of this garden.

Every time I'm in a garden I think this is where I belong. This is where I come from. This is what I was kicked out of. Maybe I just don't have Adam's genes. Maybe I'm supposed to be Adam and I just haven't gotten there yet, a kind of pre-Adam. What if God picked up some clay, formed Adam but some of it fell and formed my ancestor?

Eve said someday I might evolve into a form capable of human understanding, even speech. I mean do we all have to come from Adam? Where's the diversity in that?

I stayed in that garden for two three days and then Eve showed up.

Somewhere in that time zone I had visitors.

I had picked a spot deep into foliage, bushes and such, the overgrown beyond the gates part of the domain. I must have been in a deep sleep. Day time. What time I didn't know. But when I opened my eyes, I saw two old guys in rags, each pulling at my trouser legs. My shoes were lying on the ground.

"What the fuck!" I yelled, just as they yanked the trousers off me.

I had been using my suit jacket as a pillow but now I saw one of the bums was wearing it. All I had on now was my BVD's, my socks and my shirt.

I was leveraging my mass so I could get on my feet and knock these guys around, but I got discouraged when one of the bums rushed up to my head and tapped my nose hard with a baseball bat. It brought tears to my eyes.

"Smash his brains out, Patawala!" his friend shouted.

I looked at the guy with the bat. Yeah. If you added twenty years or so to my tutor's face, rubbed in a lot of dirt, rotted out his front teeth and sweated him down to about a hundred pound, this old bum was Mr. Patawala.

And he looked like he was going to tee off on my head with that club. Today was the day I shouldn't have left under my bed all those hand guns Eve had given me over the years. I used the boxes for beds for my puppets, nestling them next to the revolvers and semi-automatic pistols.

"Hey! It's me Dirk!"

Swing stopped in midair and he looked at the other guy. I looked at him too. If you added twenty years, rubbed his face in dirt and so on, it was Mr. Spinalzo.

"Mr. Spinalzo!" I shouted. "Don't you guys remember me?"

"This stupid one got us fired," Patawala shouted to Spinalzo.

"No, it was the other one. My twin. Don't you remember?"

Then Patawala just circled his temple with his index finger.

"Border line personality disorder," Spinalzo said, nodding.

"What are you doing here?" Patawala asked me, angrily.

"What are you guys doing here? I was just having a little siesta. Why were you robbing my clothes? What the fuck?"

"Who told your mother I was wearing her clothes?"

"What? Were you? I didn't know that."

"You're a liar. You were a silent, stupid boy and now you are a liar. Who told your father I taught you alternate facts?"

"Not me. Water is H2O. No alternatives. You guys live around here?"

"We don't live. We're survivors. We poach. We steal. We hunt and gather. We graze."

"We grow poppies in the woods and sell the whole harvest to

Columbian buyers. It's a business plan."

"We don't deal."

"We live here in the woods close to the great wealth of your family. For us, it's a place filled with memories, sad memories of unjust affliction and daily oppression."

"Your mother and father are dead, hopefully?" Patawala asked me.

"No, they're not. My father is in his Lab and my mother is going to a nut house. Shortly. But Theo is dead. If that makes you feel any better. He was stabbed in Rikers penitentiary. I accidentally killed somebody, and Theo took the blame and went to prison."

"I know who stabbed him," Spinalzo told me.

"Who did?"

"A man with a knife."

I wondered how many crazies were in these woods. They must have heard me.

"We are with a tribe of tutors, nannies, butlers, gardeners, maids, cooks, chauffeurs, bodyguards, piano teachers, dance instructors, cotton pickers, delivery individuals, independent contractors, route individuals and servers. And others. Many others."

"Old and discarded. By your family. In the woods."

"Okay," I said, as if I understood. "Tell me. Is there a Mr. Rectum in your tribe? Theo told me that he was one of our tutors and I can't remember him because I forget."

"I wiped your memory pan clean," Mr. Patawala told me. "On the path to Enlightenment."

"You remember, Patawala, Mr. Rectum's three fold theory of friction?"

"Yes, I do, Mr. Spinalzo, come to think of it. He frictionalized the upstairs maid I believe."

"And was caught at it and fired. Unjustly. It was a consensual frictionalizing."

"Ooh! Anna!" I said, remembering. "Is she here? I mean in the tribe?"

"She is in a nunnery. You were a very horny boy as I remember."

"Mr. Rectum is not here. He had a bad end."

And they both laughed, or gurgled and choked their faces red, one or two teeth falling out. I felt sorry for them.

"I feel kind of bad for how I acted back then. You know I went to Princeton for a semester. Then they threw me out."

"And why not?"

"Into the woods then?"

"What woods?"

"You were an untutorable boy. Very bad Hindi. There are woods outside every Xanadu in America. Open your inner eye."

"And tribes in them, also."

"Wall street. And The White House."

This all seemed to me farfetched so I changed the subject.

"Theo owned a launderette in Paris."

"Of course, he did. There is no crime in launderettes. Only in the streets and the suites. Or the woods."

"Your brother could make money as clean as your shirt."

I felt then the need for them to be proud of me, that I had turned out better than they probably thought I would.

"I have a radio talk show. Or had."

"We listen."

"You do?"

"The wood is full of sounds."

"Mostly birds and angry squirrels."

"We get a lot of Likes on social media."

"We?"

"Me and Eve. Eve Solly."

"Ah! A friend. You were destined to have a friend, Dirk, and not only what was at the end of your fork."

"I gotta go. Eve. My friend is coming to pick me up."

"We'll wait with you."

"Not necessary. Really. Can I have my pants and shoes back?"

"You know, Dirk, the world took the friend out of us."

"By world, Mr. Patawala means your family."

"They disowned me. I haven't been part of that family for years."

"In that case you can join us in the woods."

"You mean join your tribe?"

"There is not really a tribe, Dirk. There is just Mr. Spinalzo and myself."

"No tribe?"

"And we are not really here either."

"You're not?"

"Drug and alcohol residue personae, Mr. Spinalzo and myself."

"We'll take the shirt though, " Spinalzo said. "It will go good with the jacket and pants."

"After they are laundered, I think."

They both laughed.

"What?"

CHAPTER TWENTY

"MONGOGIA"

"Okay, so it didn't go as planned?" Eve said, looking over at me collapsed like a deflated zeppelin in the passenger seat.

I gave her a thumbnail account. Bullet points too. I left out the part about being robbed.

"Well, you're out of the running for head of household," she said when I was done. "I should have figured Sulmondson would find the commitment route the easiest one to take. You were always too shaky a bet. You would have resisted making a whole lot of illegal money. There's no business plan in your life."

"You think so? What's the commitment route?"

"The usual," she replied, bored. "Strait jacket, padded cell, shit food, isolation, no off-light switch, Taylor Shift and Britannia Squeers duels 24/7, sessions with a pro bono shrink from a local commodity college. Textbook questions: Why do you think you're here and not there? How did you feel about your mother when she showed you the nipple? Do you have a penis to envy? Why do you cry when you look in the mirror."

I marveled at how much she knew about stuff like this.

"I went in one of those places for a time," she told me. "The idiots never had a strait jacket my size. I slipped out of it and ran away. Great mammaries. Memories."

She tapped the wheel. She was a great driver. She never observed a speed limit, a red light or a stop sign without cursing it.

"When's the last time you fell in line with anything anybody wanted?"

"Yeah, there's that," I admitted.

"Sounds like you threw enough fuck this and fuck that and fuck yous in there to warm your mother's heart."

"I don't remember. Anyway, they're putting her in the loony bin right after the whatever the fuck it was. The Memory Service."

"Don't get all choked up about it," she said, reaching a hand out and patting my knee. "By the way, what happened to your clothes?"

"I lost them. It got hot and I stripped down."

We didn't say anything for a longish time. Of course, there was no way those guys were real. I let it go. Eve wouldn't be interested.

"You know, I think I said back there what I would have said, drugged or not."

"You mean stupid stuff? Yeah, you're probably right. They went light on the drug. You need a rhino dose."

"You know, I was thinking … "

"How'd that feel?"

"I mean it was the stupidest thing I've ever done. I could have en something myself."

"Ingratiated yourself?"

"Well, maybe not that. That's a cheesy thing isn't it? Ingratiating yourself. But you know, I wouldn't mind living in that faux chateau and not under the El. I could be hearing the sound of chipmunks chirping in the morning, bats flying overhead, and not the rattle of the West End subway and garbage pickup. I'm really fond of Nature. I just took a different path as they say. I heard a different drum like Belinda Brownstat sang. Do you think it's a bad thing to want to live in the woods? I mean stupid?"

"Your stupid is usually different. It kind of takes people by surprise. Big guy in his underwear."

She laughed. I was a source of endless amusement for Eve.

"Maybe Sulmondson can get you committed and you and your mother can spend some loony time together."

"Where's the flask?" I said, totally disgusted. "Who's Sulmond's son?"

I made it on the social media the next day. I went viral. If all that shit is something like social, make me a hermit. Video of my whatever it was at the graduation service. Sal showed it to me as soon as I hefted my mass on a barstool.

"You know I'm beginning to think," Sal told me, "that the social part is less than the media part, if that makes sense."

"I don't care," I snarled.

"Calm down and go sit in the back!"

"I'm not in the mood for the parrot."

"I call her Sassy Feathers. You know you got a hashtag on Twitter," Sal went on, as he held out his Smartass phone and I looked at the video. #EvilTwin.

"You know, do I really want to know if my face friends run out of toilet paper or they're older than they were last year? My new approach is I just don't want the new approach. Know what I mean?"

"Hey, Don Cheech!" the parrot yelled as Gee came out of his office.

"Take a look at the big guy here on *YouTube,*" Sal said, holding his phone out to Gee.

"You don't look so good," Gee said after a long look. "Nice suit, though. I like the shirttail coming out of your fly."

"Hashtag is called Evil Twin in case you want to tweet along."

"If you hear me tweet, shoot me."

Gee handed Sal back his phone.

"You even made the prints," Sal told me. "You're in the spotlight, brother. You're a legacy."

"I need a drink, not a spotlight."

Whatever drug they gave me was still doing its thing right behind my eyeballs. If the old tutors I had met in the woods were drug dreams then who stripped me down to my shorts?

"A martini shaken, not stirred!" Cag shouted.

"Really?" Sal asked the bird. "He's drinking that?"

"Stop talking to the fucking bird, Sal and do your job," Gee told him.

"There's a piecc in *The Times* on pg. 22 about your mother zombying out at some sanitarium ... "

My flip flipped.

It was Eve.

"I got cash up front from *YouTube* for the podcast," she told me.

"What podcast?"

"The one that rides on the tail of your recent celebrity. You're a hashtag. Do you know how big that is? It's bigger than your ass and The Mob put together."

"I'm not doing that shit, whatever it is. I'm going to Mada Gas Car."

"Sounds good. You got the money for that trip?"

"I'm going to ... Montreal."

"Or you could stay here and become an Influencer. Listen to this:

"Most YouTube influencers past 100,000 subscribers land brand deals to endorse and authentically promote a product or service in their videos. YouTube influencers typically receive countless emails and daily inquiries from brands and agencies hoping to partner with them."

"Sounds like my worst fucking nightmare," I told her.

"Yeah, well how does this sound. I already got five brand sponsorships in hand. I got 5K upfront and we didn't even do a video."

I thought about that. I could go to Monte Carloff on that. Airline ticket.

"What do we have to do? Wait a second. What the hell is an Influencer?"

"It's a stool softener," Eve told me. "Listen up, Babba. An influencer is somebody who just naturally draws people to him. Or her. They get attached to you. They want to wear your underwear and use your toothbrush. They want to be like you. They buy your whole mess of a life. Can't get enough of you. You could shoot your father in the middle of the street and they'd love you."

I didn't know what to say. I suddenly felt wanted, as if I had never been ejected from the garden, family home, and livelihood. People I didn't know, call them strangers, wanted to be like me. There was something wonderful about that.

"Put your face on T-shirts and beer mugs. Merchandise. We could make millions real quick. It's all a thirty second kind of thing. You're a Haley's Comet flashing by once in a lifetime. You're a hashtag and then you're just hash. You've got to seize the day by the bollocks. Influencers go in dumpsters faster than chicken feet on hot coals in Savanah."

"Why the silence?" she snapped. "Too colorful way of putting life's realities for my Babba?"

I told her I'd think about it and pointed to my empty glass.

She hung up on me.

"Of all the gin joints in all the towns in the world, she walks in here."

We all looked at the parrot.

"That was a long sentence," Gee said, nodding in approval.

"That was Rick in *Casablanca*," somebody at the bar said. Professor Whatshisface.

"Tell me how much of a groin torque is Eve Solly?" I asked Sal, my voice full of misery.

"She's four feet ten of pure dynamite," Sal said to me, winking.

" Is that what she is? Four feet ten? She seems a lot taller."

"Yeah, she impresses a lot taller."

Couple drinks later, Eve called again and told me where to meet her the next day for a run through on our *YouTube* podcast, whatever that might be. And bring the parrot. She was going to push the sponsor's brands. All I had to do was buffet the carpet bombing coming in on *Twitter* faster than bed bugs run for cover.

I expressed my fear that maybe The Patriarch Junior hadn't left town and was still hiding in the bushes waiting to shoot me.

"Look, Brainiac, there are no bushes near your *pied a terre*. The Italians took'em out and poured concrete. And stop worrying about Junior. He's back in Moscow tweezing ice off his balls."

I showed up at the *YouTube* dress rehearsal only because I wanted my share of the 5K up front so I could lose myself in the Mongogian outback. I didn't know if Mongogia had an outback or maybe just jungle or desert, rocky peaks. Some geography where the West End subway didn't rumble passed while you were trying to sleep.

I might have been thinking of Majorca.

None of this mattered. All had been cancelled.

That's what the sign on the door said. What about the 5K? I asked the empty hallway. No answer.

I went home. I called Eve but got no answer. Probably in Montes Negro spending out the 5K.

Back at the *pied de terre,* noisier than ever but a sweet smell of something cooking from Mrs. A's apartment. I was about to do some exploring when the phone rang, the last of the old school home phones I was as attached to as my collection of hand puppets.

"Don't get in my way," a nasty voice instructed me.

"Okay," I said, hanging up.

I had heard Mrs. A's steps on the stairs and sure enough she knocked. I let her in. She was carrying what looked like a glorious Porchetta roast, crackling skin scored, the aroma of fennel, rosemary, garlic and lemon.

"I de-boned a suckling pig," Mrs. A told me, proudly. "Out back. You should have heard him squeal."

Why the fuck not was my thought but the parrot, sleeping it off like he had a hangover in his cage, woke up and screamed, "Push the old bag out the window!"

"One day I'll cook him," Mrs. A. said as she swept newspapers, pizza cartons and hand puppets off my all-purpose table.

"And I don't like these Bible thumpers he's letting in the apartment."

I didn't know what she was talking about. It seems two evangelists had knocked, and Cag had told them to come in which they did and according to Mrs. A when she burst in, they were sitting there listening to the parrot who was profane as hell and they told her he was possessed but they could pray him right.

"They started in on me. Two Jehovah's Seven Day Advantages. They gave me the Book of Mammon, like I needed another book. I got two."

"Did they leave?"

"They did after I showed them the Ruger-57. A bullet is the best defense against the Rapeture. You better eat this pig while it's hot."

For the next three hours I forgot about all the whatevers around me. I went viral on that Porchetta. Cag kept staring at me like I was just dirt beneath his fingernails.

"Our lives are miserable, laborious and short."

I wondered if she was talking about me, her or the Porchetta roast?

"Don't ask me," Eve Solly said right off as she walked into the *New Pompey* around 23 hrs.

"It all fell through. That's what happens when you take the word of someone taller than what's needed."

"That's harsh," I told her.

"Look at you. Could have made three, four decent humans out of you. But, no. We get you. You are the only reason I don't believe in God. What immortal hand or eye could frame your ass?"
I could tell she was a couple of tweaks away from pulling the .38.

"I thought I went viral?"

"You did. Like Ebola. Seems like six or seven countries already have clowns running the country going viral. They didn't need you."

"And the 5K?"

"Hyperreal. Simulacra. Nothing in hand. But I've got feelers out. You look unusually fucked up. You smell like you ate a hog from the inside out. You know a podcast is a visual kind of thing. And why does the parrot look hungover? Are you giving that bird alcohol, Sal? Because if you are, I will eviscerate you right here on the bar."

"No way," Sal said, raising both hands. "Not me. Never. He might stick his beak in a stray glass is all. True, he doesn't refuse if you're buying."

I was about to say I wasn't familiar with the clown who was going viral in the White House and why wasn't President Cartobamabushwa objecting when she waved me off and attended to her phone. When she put it down, she smiled at me.

"We just got a promise of a brand sponsorship from the NRA if we get the podcast up and running. All I have to do is turn whatever makes the headlines in *The Times* a move to take your gun out of your hands."

"Mine are in boxes under my bed."

"Yeah, I know. You're a collector."

"Mr. Refugio and Mr. Grogan are afraid of them."

"Who the fuck ... Wait. Don't tell me. Hand puppets?"

I nodded.

"What are they coughing up?" Sal sked. "Dese sponsors?"

"A couple of All-Wrong groups, League of Adolescent Influencers, Anti-Snowflake Coalition, Pedophile Lives Matter and some others. We need also to sponsor privately owned nuclear warhead drones, suitcase nuclear devices on rollers, and legalized 3D modeling of IED's."

"You could do that," Sal said. "Easy peas. You should call the podcast 'Fire Up!'"

"Go wash a glass," Eve told Sal and he moved off and did just that.

"So ... I mean thus then we're not cancelled?"

"We'll be sitting pretty, Pantagruel. We'll have more money and notoriety than Nicki Minaj."

"It's the world that'll probably be cancelled," Sal called out from the other end of the bar.

"Isn't that the guy," I said. "The Patriarch's nephew I threw into the wall? Niki Manajatoi?"

"Gee says I should cut you guys off. He says the place is getting too full of alcoholics and the gentrifiers come in get scared. You guys are like micronic aggressives to them."

"Alcoholics have a thirst they can't control, Sal. I always drink before I can get thirsty."

CHAPTER TWENTY-ONE

"BILLY HASHFRIES"

I half expected it was Eve knocking at my door later that night.

Actually, really late. Mister Tibia and Madame Uberalles were entertaining us with a silly kind of dance.

I hustled my balls as I headed to the door. When I opened it, I saw The Mater's boy toy, Billy Hashfries. He put a smile on my face right off because I remembered Theo giving him that name.

"I gotta talk," he said, trying to push past me but only nudging my belly and bouncing off.

I could have restrained him and flung him out with one hand, but I was curious.

He plopped into my one comfy overstuffed chair, gave a nose holding look around my room, the unmade bed, hand puppets, most of them pretending to be sleeping, hellfire tracts, toilet paper rolls I collected, chess board ,backgammon ... Eve had been mentoring me in both for about twelve years. I was still losing to everybody, including the parrot.

Billy stared at the huge parrot cage, now covered with an old quilt. It hung just below my hand puppet shelves.

"Is that the parrot?" Billy asked, nastily.

I put a finger to my lips.

"Don't wake her up. She's not going to like you."

"You ready for bed?" he said in that nasty, thin lipped way he had.

So, I wore PJ's with Pooh bear on them. He still had a hashfries on a plate face.

"Got anything to drink?" he said.

I shook my head as we both looked over at the half-filled bottle of Jim Beam rye on the night table.

He started to rub the side of his face nervously.

"Wait," I said, going over to him, lifting him up off my favorite chair and putting him down on one of my two lower back torture chairs Mrs. A had given me as a gift. For guests so they wouldn't stay too long.

I sat down on the overstuffed.

"Go ahead. If I doze off, don't wake me. Just get out."

"I've been thinking about what you said about Sulmondson. That he thinks he's running things and I'm not."

"Wait. When did I tell you that?"

"Well, maybe I just thought you said it. He says he's on some kind of forever retainer can't be terminated. I could get a lawyer to fight that but if I did that, I'd lose is what he said. I guess he knows. He's a lawyer."

I seem to recall Eve telling me something about me and Billy being in the run for something, my mother's money, and the lawyer betting on one of us to win and one to go in the loony bin.

"You're running the money, right? The Fartsworth business?"

That's what The Patriarch and his other selves wanted into. The business.

Billy shook his head, annoyed, nervous, looking at the Jim Beam.

"There's no fucking business. It's gone. Broke. It's the Foundation. That's where they're running the money through for The Mob."

Mention of The Mob sent me reaching for the Jim Beam. I took a hit and handed it to the pool boy. He looked kind of wasted, like he could float but not swim.

I had a sudden premonition of him dead. And me too.

"Alls I have to do is sign papers and let Sulmondson handle everything."

"You could still clean pools," I said, trying to perk him up. He took that the wrong way.

"Don't crack wise," he snapped. "I was good at it. What the freak are you good at besides scratching your ass in bed and talking to a freaking parrot?"

I pulled the bottle out of his hand.

"Thing is Sulmondson. He's a fucker. Real Wanker. He doesn't trust me. He thinks I'm going squeal on ... "

"The Mob?"

"He says I'm not steady. I'm liable to go off course and that would make them … "

"The Mob?"

He nodded.

"I need to shape up. Go into rehab. Fuck that. They're gonna send me where the old lady is."

"The Mob? I mean my mother? Where is she?"

"I don't look bad, do I?" he said, straightening up in his chair, ready for Miss Corliss in 2nd grade to commend him, give him a gold star and tell him to go water a plant. I spent a couple of months in a private grammar school watering plants, opening and closing windows, passing out milk and cookies, feeding the gold fish, cleaning erasers, sharpening pencils for everybody I had so many tasks is what they called them that I didn't have time to learn to read. Then when we had Mr. Spinalzo and Mr. Patawala for home schooling, they both thought I was heading at best for semi-literacy, which was dangerous to the country in their view, so best to leave me be in regard to reading and writing. They thought total illiteracy created character, common sense and enough suspicion to survive.

"You look good," I now answered Hashfries. "I personally got used to people saying I looked bad just leaving the house when I knew deep down that I was looking good. They just weren't looking at me the right way."

Billy searched my face, very puzzled.

"I'm fully three dimensions. They look at me two dimensionally. If you know what I mean."

"You on something or you're just naturally fucked up?"

Then he shook his head.

"Doesn't matter," he said. "You're right. People think you're a waste product of the Farnsworth's billions, but they think worse of me."

"Exactly. And do I give an ounce of waste product about what two-dimensional people say?"

It did, however hurt when Eve said it.

Kid was still nervous, now he was sweating. I saw it coming. That's why I got him out of my favorite chair.

"I think they're gonna kill me," he mumbled.

He was shaking all over.

"The Mob?"

He jumped up from the chair and grabbed the top of his head with both hands.

"I sign everything they tell me to sign.

What the fuck else do they want?"

That woke the parrot up. She started screaming bibulous blasphemies. I had to take the quilt off the cage to calm her down.

She looked at me and then at Billy Hashfries, standing there, shaking like he just came out of ice water.

"Ignore the Word and suffer!," Cag screeched.

Hashfries ignored him.

He gave me a squint eyed look.

"They want you," he said, pointing at me.

"Me?"

"Screw that!" he screamed and suddenly there was a gun in his hand.

At that moment, I was throwing one of my hand puppets, Mr. Armps, back and forth, something he got a real kick out of, and I just sort of side armed Mr. Armps at the gun and I actually hit it and it dropped out of Hashfries's hand but not before he got a shot off.

"Dump him in the ditch!," Cag screamed.

I hoisted up out of the overstuffed and made a grab for Hashfries All I got was a bit of his jacket. He pulled away and rushed out the door.

I didn't run after him. I went over to Mr. Armps. He had a bullet hold right in the middle of his checkered vest. The life stuffing had gone out of him. He needed more than a few stitches. He needed surgery. I bent down and picked up Billy's gun. It was an AMT Hardboiler. I put it in a gun box alongside Ooh! Anna! who had had the whole box to herself for quite a while.

Eve listened while I went over what had just happened with the kid. She didn't seem to care a fig about Billy pulling the gun on me or that Billy said The Mob would be wanting to kill me, or that Mister Armps had been fatally shot in the scuffle. I knew she thought only humans were destined for that bad end, death, but I thought there were other endings, maybe some not bad, like a snowflake to water or a caterpillar to a Monarch or skein of wool to a sweater vest or a log to smoke.

"He said The Mob is laundering money through the Farnsworth Foundation?" Eve asked me.

"He didn't use the word laundering," I replied, perplexed. "Said The Mob a lot and that they would kill him and me."

"Didn't you tell me that your mother told you that two of the clowns she married were in The Mob?"

"Yeah, Gunner and somebody and Jabba worked for them."

There was a long silence.

"They don't want to kill you but sounds like they'll kill the pool kid. They want you to take his place."

"Me?"

"Yeah, you're five IQ points away from being watered."

"Could you be more specific?"

"They'll teach you Mob reality and you'll soak it up. That's my distilled opinion."

That got me wondering.

"You mean like Nicky Williams and his sweetheart? She's not real but he thinks she is. I told you about him."

"That guy? No. You don't fantasize big. You only fantasize the next meal your fascist landlady is going to make you. Sounds like your friend Williams fantasizes on the cosmogony and theogony levels."

"He looked into the mirror and the mirror cracked and the world was made."

"That the parrot? Your brother taught her some crazy shit for sure."

CHAPTER TWENTY-TWO

#EVILTWIN PODCAST

The only time I saw Eve in the next few weeks was on the *YouTube* reruns of *Evil Twin* stuff we did when I was running viral.

She stopped coming to *The Pompey*. She told me there were lots of hills and valleys, switchbacks and over and unders, roundabouts, and procto stopic exams she was pursuing on my behalf, the half she said was worth keeping alive. I wondered what half that was.

The *Evil Twin YouTube* shows attracted the injured, angry and dangerous. They all have what Eve said somebody on *Counterpunch*, her favorite muckraking mag, called "shit-life syndrome." She said the best way to deal with mad dogs is to run after them.

Why we were successful for that brief run I don't know. When I asked Eve about that the parrot answered.

"First, I have couched a very profound mystery in the number of 0's multiplied by seven and divided by nine."

We did merchandize Cag big time after that. T-shirt with me seated, Eve standing and the parrot on her shoulder. Posters and screen savers too. People had Cag's voice as a personal greeting on their Smartphones: "Shut Up and Go Home!" "I Will Fuck You Up!" and "Parrots Rule!" were also hot merchandise. It all made me feel small but, as they say, it is what it is unless an Influencer tells you it's not.

As soon as we got a caller who wanted to make something

perfectly clear, Eve cut him off. Such trans parenting, as she called it, blocked the passions and constipated the show.

I have to tell you if you let that parrot and Eve loose in the life of any Everyday American, they'd suck the logisticytes out of every small brain pan in the place and shoot a jacked up dose of Fire Up! in their veins. Our sponsors loved it. They told us they were financializing the It. Eve said they meant The Id but it had to be The It because you say "It's in the closet" when you're scared at night.

I was a little concerned about the purpose of it all. I mean why would anybody call in to talk to me? Eve was worse. She was downright abusive. And the parrot? Lot of misdiagnosis, misapropism, Miss Cutes and miscellany came out of that bird's mouth. In Eve's view, we were doing something good by overloading the cyberspace circus tree, looping it around a gazillion times with Garble and Babble, send it up its own ass and the good of that was everybody would overdose, go into detox and straighten out. But we'd make our end before that recovery and wreck a cog nation ever happened. I didn't know Garble and Babble were on the show.

None of these dramas, which were really too much drama for me, got my attention the way the word The Mob did. The two words. I was always waiting for The Mob to call in.

We got into doing the show at *The Pompey* when Gee told me:

"You set up your podcast show here, I sell some whiskey. Help pay the bills."

"What's more you and Eve than this place?" Sal added. "Being by the cash register is the parrot's second favorite home."

I thought about it.

"They wouldn't gentrify your barstool right from under you," Gee told me, putting a heavy finger on me.

"You and Eve could just sit in your regular spots at the bar," Sal said. "And you'd have all the regulars come in and give you some grief. Like usual. Put a firecracker under your ass to keep you awake."

"Safest way to pay off your bar tab before I contract it out," Gee told us, with a wink.

"He's serious," Sal whispered to me. "Gee's put deadbeats in the dumpster out back."

Our director, Paolo Milio, or something like that, wasn't for the move at all but Eve had already seen the benefit and the genius of parking the show in such a convenient spot.

Eve, who had a personal vendetta against the invading gentrifying individuals living on their Dave Adens and Al Gorithms who were the ruination of the world, told Paulio Milo that if we didn't move the show to the bar, the show was over.

Hard to describe what that old neighborhood bar and its clubhouse members did to our young director's nerves. I think he came from a Mormon film and TV school in Idaho or Indiana. Cag said he was a Hard Shelled Anabaptist from West Virginia.

When this guy, Pedro Millennial, the director, got the hang of how Eve and myself hung with our friends, he began to direct, one or two of the regulars, and then most of them into the show. We didn't need any outside guests to interview. The bar was loaded with what our Director called good small screen faces projecting good chat.

"Yeah," Sal told him. "If you use the word chat, they'll kill you. We talk shit in here is all."

It went, like it came and it went.

I found out about Summer Arpeggio working for me one day when we were having lunch at *The Pompey* and Summer showed up. I still felt she should have done a better job of defending Theo, so I wasn't thrilled to see her. I guess she saw it on my face.

"I didn't kill him," she said, flatly, sitting down. "But he was in because I did a lousy job defending him. So, it's on me for the rest of my days."

I didn't look at her.

"Don't say 'so,' "Eve told her and that kind of broke the ice. "Babba here is getting excited about his return to the family compound. That's if Billy Hashfries is out of the picture."

"He's in the wind," Summer told her. "Nobody is saying anything. I even went up to that family compound. Quite a Downstone Abbey you were brought up in."

I nodded, saying nothing but Eve didn't let the opportunity go.

"Our man here had a silver spoon birth, Lord Brat private schools, family truss yachts, climbs in the Palps. Grannies and Tudors to ignoble his bearing. All that kind of good breading goes into making the Henry the Ate we got right here."

"Really?" the Director asked me. "Is that your background? A compound on East Egg?"

"He's not interested in going into any of that," Eve answered for me.

"I pissed it all away," I told the kid, sadly.

"I guess you can remember that day you pissed it all away,"

Summer said. "I know I can."

"How did you do that?" Paco Morales asked, still looking at me as if I was suddenly more interesting than the Three Effs.

"He did," Summer told him. "You can understand why our man here wants revenge."

"You want revenge?" Julio Castro said, wide eyed.

"The God of Jacob will not sleep," the parrot screeched. "His vengeance will not slumber long."

That screech, right in the kid's ear, stunned him as if he had heard a voice behind a burning bush.

"That's ... that's from this book," Chè Guevara stuttered, holding up a wormed copy of some book.

"She can read?"

"Her reading comprehension level is higher than this guy's," Eve told him, pointing to me.

"I just want to find out who killed Theo," I said, anger rising in me. As well as the wine.

"Theo is his twin brother," Summer explained to the kid, "he was stabbed to death in Rikers. Long story why he was in there. But he was innocent. I know everybody in there is innocent, but this guy was innocent. It lays heavy on his twin brother's, this guy here, his conscience."

I didn't feel it coming but I slammed the table hard and sent Summer's whiskey onto her lap. The parrot took to flight, and Juan Valdez jumped up. So did Summer who wiped at her dress with a napkin.

I got up with my napkin and tried to help her. She pushed me away and laughed.

"You owe me a drink. Plus, the two fifty a day which right now comes to more money than you have. So why the fuck am I working for you?"

That kind of stunned me.

"You're working for me? Doing what?"

"She is," Eve said, getting up. "She's trying to find Billy Hashfries."

"Why?"

"Because maybe he's dead. Which could be good for you or it could be bad. Go home, wash your face and your armpits and I'll pick you up in an hour."

"Where we going?"

"Visit your old lady at the Sanitarium."

"Your brother was stabbed ... in prison?" Our young Director, Claudio Cantalope, asked me.

"Didn't I tell you to shut up!"

CHAPTER TWENTY-THREE

THREE THINGS

That day we didn't get to the Sanitarium my mother was in because Eve said she had other more urgent business.

I went to the bar.

"Somebody left this here for you," Sal said, giving me a folded piece of paper.

"You need to do three things. Number one, get that two bit lawyer Arpeggio to withdraw her legal petition for your inheritance entitlement. Number two, tell your movie star friend, Eve Solly to stay away from the Russians. You should know that they're mobsters. Number three, don't go see your mother again."

"Drop this in the waste for me, will you?" I said, handing Sal the paper.

I shook my head. Lots of stuff didn't make any sense. I looked back at my drink. My drink.

First thing I did when I got back to the *pied a terre* was call Eve. Cag was sleeping in the bird cage which I had finally put by my sewing machine, in front of the shelf along the wall where all the hand puppets I had made sat quietly and studied the room. And me.

I left a message. "Call me. Urgent."

I decided to go back out for a smoke. It was still snowing. It was freezing. The whole neighborhood was getting ready for Christmas. All the shops. Christmas carols coming out of speakers perched over doorways. The rusted posts of the El had wreaths twined around them. Not all of them. In fact, there was only about one third the number of stores that used to be in business under the El. And there wasn't any music filling the air.

I huddled inside the sheepskin coat Ms Solly had made for me a couple three Christmases ago out of hides she bought on eBay. Fact was, I wasn't hearing or seeing what was really there. I was deep into pictures of stuff that were no longer there. I mean I never saw them when they were there. Eve Solly told me all about what now wasn't there. She grew up here, under the dark El, an orphan in the same orphanage – Darkness Visible Guardian Orphanage with a lot of somebody's little sisters without mercy.

Eve had drilled me on what was around when she grew up. I visualized it because I had a real incentive to see myself growing up there and not in East Egg with my mother, my absent genius father, his lab posse of screwballs, and our seriously bent tutors, Mr. Spinalzo and Mr. Patawala, who may or may not be living like animals in the woods. I should have told them I had made them into very companionable hand puppets though, always able to see the glass half full. I also didn't like seeing the disgusted look on my twin's face when he looked at the disgusted look on my face.

It was frigid. I needed to go back inside but I started to walk instead. Nobody knows what I'm going to do, especially me.

New Utrecht Avenue runs southeast from about the intersection of 9th Avenue and 39th Street a few miles to 86th Street just past its intersection with 18th Avenue. For most of its length, the West End elevated line shadows it. Compared to where I grew up, it is a shadow world, hard for me to believe anybody could love it.

I'm in front of Enrico's Calabrese Pizza, which is the old sign, but Enrico's dead a long time and it's now Sushi and Sashimi pizza. I go in and have a few slices with tamari sauce.

When I come out two guys walk up to me, then they go on each side of me and grab me by the elbows, kind of warm greeting elbow squeeze.

"FBI. Special Agents."

"Just keep walking."

"We just want to talk to you."

"Then you can go back to your place and have a beer."

"You can help us."

"You'd be helping your country."

"Your brother, Theo, wanted to help us."

"He'd want you to help us."

"He's not dead?"

"Don't talk. Just listen."

"Your brother was giving us evidence we could use against The Conglomerate."

"The Conglomerate?"

"No questions. He was a great help to us in making a case against The Affiliate."

"Your country was going to put your brother in WITSEC. He would have been safe the rest of his life."

"Unfortunately, he thought he was smarter than us and the Gathering."

"Your brother thought he would go to trial on a manslaughter charge and have us arrange a mistrial."

"He thought he could get free of the Amalgamation, stop giving us indictable info, and neither we nor the Combine would have reason to go after him."

"Your brother wanted to return to a free and innocent life without our help."

"Instead he got stabbed to death in prison."

"We warned him. The Matrix has a long reach."

"We couldn't protect him in there."

"He made a fatal mistake."

"We want you to be smarter."

"When you take over The Foundation, you give us what we need to put The Association out of business."

"We need you to testify."

"Lay out all the dirt in court."

"Then we put you in WITSEC."

"Think about it."

"You really have no choice."

"Specter is going to use you and spit you out."

"Or they'll decide you're too unstable to bring in."

"The way we see it Gruppo will need you. And we'll tell you why."

"Billy Hasborough is in the wind."

"Probably dead."

"Go home now and think this over."

"Here's where you can reach us anytime."

And then they were gone, faded into the shadows. I was calm. They weren't real. I mean they didn't even mention The Mob, the guy behind the guy behind that guy. No, these guys came from the same woods Patawala and Spinalzo came from. The woods in my own mind. I pulled the card they gave me out of my pocket. "Special

Agent Levandowski." The card was real enough but who was Wit Sack?

Cag was awake when I went back into my apartment. I sat down in the overstuffed, picked up the Eve Solly hand puppet I was doing some finishing hand stitching on, turned on the Dictaphone and listened to Cag work on the "D's.

"Druthers: what brothers are called after they're dead."

My mother had rooms at the Lodestone, which Google told me was a "chic, Scandinavian style boutique hotel" starting at $750 bucks a night.

Eve was working the clutch, brake and pedal like an Indy 500 driver. I was in the back with the parrot. We tried to leave her behind, but her screeching had brought Mrs. Angeloni to the door. A Hatfield/McCoy feud had opened up between Mrs. A and the parrot. She had opened her cage and a window and with a broom was trying to swat her out but Cag had pulled a matador routine by sitting on the window sill and then, just as Mrs. A swung at her, dropping to the floor. The force of Mrs. A's swing knocked her off balance and then out the window.

When I looked down, I saw that she had fallen into an open dumpster filled with stuff and was already scrambling out.

We took the parrot along.

"What's he been reading these days?" Eve asked.

"Truth is I don't know what book he's into now. Could be The Bag A Vita. Or maybe the Corun."

"You got those lying around?"

"It's the salesmen," I whined. "Door to door. You get free copies. Harry Kispy's followers."

"Good for you," Eve said. "Anyway, for your non-spiritual edification. Your mother doesn't own this place. The Foundation does. It's called how to avoid paying personal income tax. You never learned much about the finances of your own family, did you?"

"I got kicked out real quick," I told her. "Wouldn't have been interested anyway. Didn't do Theo much good. He knew all about financial shit and he still wound up running a Laundromat in Paris."

She laughed.

"What are you laughing at?"

"Give me some definitions of laundering, Cag," Eve asked the bird.

I flipped the Dictaphone on and held it out.

The bird did a lot of gurgling, burping, throat clearing and then told us in a Dublin accent:

"Laundering: an effort to get the yellow out of the whites."

"I see he's gotten a look at your BVD's," Eve said.

"What God has made clean, do not bother to launder."

"I liked him better when he had no religion," Eve snapped.

"Laundering: running illegal seeds through a good digestive tract."

"That's more like it," Eve said. "Do your religion quotes when I'm not around."

She was doing about fifty coming round the drive and then hit the brakes sharp, sending the parrot up to the ceiling of the car.

"Okay. Listen up, Dirk. I think you need to focus on how you're going to approach your mother. She might be so surprised she'll stroke."

"What exactly is it that we trying to get from her?"

"The Mob. We need to find out what she knows about The Mob. We need names."

"No way," I said, shaking my head. "Don't like that word."

"Don't be scared," Eve reassured me. "It's just a word."

"A word made the world. We're gonna die."

"See? Even the parrot is scared."

"You both have nothing to worry about."

"There's shit on somebody's shoe."

"Shut up," Eve told the parrot.

"It's still there."

"You're going in the trunk. The boot."

"Create in me a clean heart, O God, and renew a right spirit within me!" Cag shouted.

Eve pulled out her .38 and the parrot mumbled "What did I do?" and then shut up, putting his head under a wing.

"Your mother was afraid of her last two husbands, right?" Eve asked, directing her attention back to me. The gun still in her hand.

"Your mother knows they were using the Foundation to launder mob money. What I need is that kind of evidence and Sulmondson goes to jail. He's The Mob lawyer."

She parked in a space that had a "Dr. Grew" sign.

"They're not going want us to see her," she told me.

"What you do is go through the glass doors into the lobby, tell them who you are. They'll say no visitors. You make a fuss. Enough to get security out. I slip in behind the confusion and that's it."

I looked at the parrot.

"Grow a pair," he told me.

"How do I make a fuss? And why does that signage say Ravine Farm Sanitarium?"

"Tell them you're from the Central Office," Eve told me, patiently. "Show them your badge. Ask them by whose authority is your mother being kept in there. Demand to see the Director, the Head Honcho. Tell them you represent The People. Tell'em fat lives matter. Bang the counter. Occupy. Put up a tent. Start throwing things around. Open an umbrella. Here, wear this Guy Fawkes mask."

I told her I didn't have a badge and I certainly wouldn't wear that mask. She shook her head and gave me a pitying look.

She looked at Cag.

"Can you handle this? Try to keep his bulkiness here in their sight line to the door."

When I got out of the car, the parrot flew to my shoulder screaming,

"Come to my arms my beamish boy!"

Eve cowered right behind us.

"Flutter your coat out like a cape," she instructed me.

I did and at the same time the parrot stretched his wings out and we both entered the lobby like a feathered tornado and went straight up to the receptionist desk.

What happened, Eve hadn't counted on or she had and didn't tell me.

It wasn't just a Sanitarium assisting old ladies like my mother to take their dope pills.

It was a genuine lunatic asylum or whatever the PC name for the place was. Three hundred pound guy fluttering his overcoat like a cape with a screaming parrot the size of an albatross on his shoulder got the receptionist, a young woman in white, to immediately hit the "Escaped lunatic. Bring net and tranquilizer" button.

I don't know where the parrot went but four burly guys in white sprung out of an elevator, tazered me and I went down hard and fast. Out of the corner of my eye as I lay on the floor, I saw Eve shoot into the elevator, doors closed, and she was gone. And so was I.

I didn't see my mother but I did get a bed in the place.

I slept. Hours, days, weeks. The parrot woke me up, flew to an open window and out and I followed him. I didn't fly. I hung on the window edge, looked down and then closed my eyes.

I was about to jump when two lunatic handlers came running in and grabbed me by the waist, trying to lock arms around me. I think they were underfed because I lifted them both and went head first out of the window. I landed on top of both of them. I had a soft landing but they didn't move.

I stumbled in the dark, the parrot flying low and just ahead of me.

I followed her. Eve's car. I got in the back seat, Cag flying in with me, and she roared us from first to second to third to fourth.

"How many weeks have I been in there?" I asked her.

"Couple a three hours," she said. "Wrap that blanket back there around you. Your three piece set is touching my upholstery."

"This should wake you up," she said, handing me back her flask.

"Did you find my mother?"

"Yeah, doped to the gills. I zapped her with an adrenaline shot. She woke up. The Jabby husband, the bookkeeper?"

"Jabba the Hutt."

"Yeah, he kept two sets of books. One for the IRS and one for The Mob. I know where they are cause she told me. And if she didn't tell anybody else, they should be there."

I didn't know why these Jabba books meant anything, but I didn't let on.

"If they're gone, I still have our Patriarch."

I didn't know what having The Patriarch meant, especially since he had multi bill too many persons disorder.

I started to doze off, wondering if I had finished that veal piccata I had been dreaming about?

"Keep him wake," Eve told someone and the parrot began to sing. Not a bad voice. Rousing IRA tune.

As I was a goin' over the far famed Kerry mountains I met with captain Farrell and his money he was counting I first produced my pistol and I then produced my rapier Saying "Stand and deliver" for he were a bold deceiver.

Mush-a ring dumb-a do dumb-a daWack fall the daddy-o, wack fall the daddy-o There's whiskey in the jar.

I don't know how much of that the parrot sang or how much I sang, but I could hear it.

I suddenly felt ill, which I mentioned to Eve.

"Suck it up," she told me, eyes on the road.

"And stop stanking up my car."

I looked at the parrot for comfort.

He cocked one eye, orblike.

"It was the late summer, a humid breathless season that is inimical to comfort and personal freshness."

"*At Swim Two Birds,*" Eve said. "Flann O'Brien, his favorite. He likes the title he does."

I was stunned when I got updated on Billy Hashfries that same deliverance night.

Eve was lying on my bed lost in her cellular phone and I was recording the parrot who was in his cage and working on his dictionary.

"H. Hangover: a bat sanctuary in Germany; Hatchette. A young axe.

The phone rang. I picked it up, the last house land line phone in Brooklyn.

"Billy Hasborough is in a bad way. He's in a dumpster behind that dump of a bar you hang out in."

The voice sounded metallic and familiar.

I put the receiver down.

"Somebody just said Billy Hashfries is in a dumpster behind *The New Pompey.*"

It wasn't a long walk.

I didn't go in the bar but went straight around to the back. I had the forethought to bring a flash. I opened the lid. The usual stank. I don't know how dumpster diving became an in kind of thing, but it was sad.

What was sadder was Billy Hashfries, crumbled and swathed in what looked like some carbonara pasta. There was arugula bits stuck to his face. I don't know if this was irony or just the gods talking to me. I let the beam of light run down to his arm. Yeah. There was the needle still hanging there.

I let the lid drop down. Somebody had put him in there. He hadn't gone in there to shoot up, thinking it was a cozy place to get high. No. He had been pulled apart and then thrown among the garbage.

I was about six steps away from the dumpster when a cop car pounced at me, red light turning, flood lights in my eyes. Then another one wheeled in and came to a stop alongside the first car. There were four cops around me in no time. One frisked me.

Another went to the dumpster just like he knew there was something like a dead body in there. Sure enough, there was.

CHAPTER TWENTY-FOUR

LESSONS

It was morning before I was taken from my cell into what the cops call The Box. Interrogation.

I sort of recognized one of my interrogators. We had run into each other somewhere at some time.

He let me know right off when and where.

"Reynolds. I was on that case where you killed your girlfriend and her fuck buddy.

"I didn't kill them, Captain."

"It's Lieutenant. Oh, yeah. Your brother did. Then somebody killed him. Now somebody killed Billy Hasborough and you stand to inherit millions."

"Coffee. Black."

"So, you get a call. You show up. Dead body. We show up. You're in jail. Why's that?"

"Give me some coffee and I'll confess," I told him, rubbing my eyes. Out of an asylum, into a prison.

"We give you some java and you sign a confession?"

I didn't want to play hardboiled tough guy anymore. I felt like Sam Spladder being grilled in *The Maltese Fortune,* except he had scripted lines and all I had was drug withdrawal. I wondered if Reynolds was the good cop or the bad cop.

"The kid overdosed. I didn't put that needle in his arm."

"No, we know he did. Just before somebody sapped him hard and broke his neck."

"What?"

Billy's head had looked kind of off kilter body wise, but I wasn't CSI.

"Yeah, you sapped him just when he was at that all is beautiful moment. Then you picked him up like a sack of nothing and threw him in that dumpster."

"I want a lawyer," I said. "But not Summer Arpeggio."

"Do you want a coffee or a lawyer? We give you coffee, we talk more. Maybe you can convince me you didn't kill this kid. I mean you're a convincing guy. You convinced everybody that it was your brother that killed your girlfriend."

"Coffee and I want to call Eve Solly."

It was the Mob lawyer, aka the Fartsworth Foundations lawyer, Mitch Sulmondson who made a case for my bail. And I got it.

We drove to his office. Offices on Remsen Street. They hadn't had to gentrify this neighborhood. The only ethnic group they ever had were Peter Stuyvesant and his Dutch buddies.

"Somebody set me up," I told Mitch as soon as I fell into one of the leather chairs in his office. Bespoke furniture.

"I did," Mitch said flatly, smile on his face.

I gave it a few nanos. Actually, more than that. I get lethargic when things get overly complicated. I look to recline and lounge. Sloth, one of the worst of the Seven Dead Sins, I had heard Cag say one morning that I had slept through.

"I'm starving," I told him. "Powdered eggs is all I've had in there."

"We can send out," he said, smiling as if I had said something funny.

"You are about as much like your twin … "

"The *Pompey* delivers day and night," I said, interrupting him. I had heard before all the ways I wasn't like Theo. "Just a steak pizzaiola and a salad. Couple liters of vino Russo."

"Weren't you told to get that little bitch to stop trying to help you?"

He pulled out his smartass phone.

I believe he was referring to Evangeline Solly, but I didn't know what she was doing to help me or that I was supposed to stop her. I decided to change direction.

"Why did you kill Billy?"

"Billy? Why, he killed himself. Sapped himself hard enough to break his own neck right after he put the needle in his arm. Then after he was dead, he threw himself in a dumpster. Not hard to figure out."

I sat back as Mitch put my order in. Then he put the phone down.

"Okay. Truth is, I didn't kill him. Rechert was following Ivan."

"The Patriarch's muscle?" I said, very hard boiled.

"He lost him. When he picked him up again, he was dumping Billy near the Dyker golf course. He was already dead. Sapped. Needle in his arm. Rechert called me. I told him to put the body in the dumpster behind *The Pompey* and then call you."

I think he was waiting for me to figure it out.

"So, you'd get the blame," he finally said.

He waited again. I didn't say anything. I wondered where Wreck It was. Probably following Ivan.

"So, you'd realize that I could make everything dangerous for you and your nosey little friend if you didn't stay out of the Foundation's business."

I was cringing at the repeat use of the word 'so' when I heard the knock.

"Delivery," I said.

"Bring it in," Sulmondson yelled. "Door's open."

We said nothing as Gee's nephew came in, winked at me and laid out the dishes on Sulmondson's desk.

"Fifty-four is what it is," the kid told Sulmondson.

I leaned into the plate, the oregano sauce wafting into my nostrils.

When the kid had gone and I had dealt with almost half the steak, Sulmondson told me that once I signed a confession that I had killed Billy, he'd get me off. The confession would go in his safe.

"It's the leash I'm putting on you," he told me, smiling like one of those sadistinistas. "My advice is stop letting that dwarf lead you around like a dog."

He watched me eat and drink.

"Tell her to keep clear of the Russians. We're taking care of them."

"Got it?" he said, reaching over and pushing the dish away from me.

He was angry.

I nodded. I was thinking of The Patriarch, or one of them.

"If I sign that confession, do I get absolved?"

Sulmondson began to drum his desk with one hand.

"You know you don't compute at all smart. I think you're too dumb to learn the lesson Billy Hasborough's death has taught you. And that's bad, very bad. For you."

"You know," I said, reaching out to the dish and mopping some bread in the salad.

"You might be right cause that's exactly Eve Solly's opinion of me. And she just shy of five feet tall so don't call her dwarf."

"Whatever she is, she should know she'll get nothing out of getting interested in your problems."

"Evangeline and me have a kind of on and off again relationship. It's like a marriage and then a divorce that keeps repeating."

He gave me a pitying look.

"I don't give a fuck about your love life, Mr. Bratter. You can stay on her leash as long as you want. But she's got to back off on our business."

"The Mob?"

Looked like he wanted to hit me but he cooled down.

"Rechert will bring that confession to you over at your place. Sign it or I won't be there to defend you. And you'll go up for killing Billy. Won't be your twin brother this time. You'll go up for it. And maybe like him, you'll get stabbed."

I don't know what those words did to me or for me, but I think I had one of those Paul on the road to Las Vegas moments. I mean, I kind of woke up.

I went home and got into a hot tub and settled down in the warm suds to review everything I knew. I used one of the hand puppets as a soap sponge, Commodore Soapy.

I got to number one in my review and then woke up. I got back to one.

Eve had once told me that louche men turned her on. She liked a lot of louche. I think she meant sex and then I looked it up. Disreputable but appealing. Anyway, I was the exception. I was a louche who wasn't at all appealing.?

Two. What was two?

Three was easier. What the hell was Eve Solly up to"

Oh, yeah. Two was I had to sign a confession that I killed Billy Hashfries otherwise I'd go to jail. For having killed Billy Hashfries. Sulmondson would keep the confession in his safe as long as I stopped Eve from doing what she was doing. Then I got to three.

The tub water had gotten cold. I lumbered my way out.

Four. The towel was four.

I looked at water draining in the tub and Commodore Soapy hanging soapy and wet on the edge. I had some rubber ducks too. They weren't mine. I got them second hand. I liked to watch the way they shuffled in the bath water a bit when the West End thundered by.

I took myself and the towel, never big enough, into the parlor.

I sat down and looked around.

The parrot woke me up some time later. I reached under his cage where the dicataphone was and turned it on.

"You will be shown hell and you will see it with your own eyes."

I know Eve preferred what the parrot picked up on *Twitter* at his hashtag site #TheRealCag to his holy books quotes but I was undecided. I didn't want a parrot to remind me that I would be shown hell, but I also didn't like to come home and first thing I hear is "Hey, you. Go fuck yourself."

I turned off the Dictaphone. I was close to throwing the quilt over his cage but it was too early.

Two days later, I was dressed and at the door.

"And we created you in pairs," the parrot mumbled, one eye fixed on me.

I slammed the door.

I was about two blocks from the Sea Beach line, snow flurries forcing me to keep my head down when just as I was crossing 63rd Street a car stopped in front of me, window rolled own and there was Wreck It leaning over, looking up at me.

"Get in," he said.

Repeat performance.

I hesitated and he pointed a Walther P99 at me. I was about to get in when Eve's car made a truly wicked two tire turn on the corner, a hand stuck out the window on the driver's side, .38 Special in the hand and bullets banged into Wreck It's car. He took off, tires squealing.

Eve shouted at me to get in. I did.

"What the hell, Eve?" I said, my knees up to my chin and my nose inches from the windshield. No chance of getting the seatbelt on.

"Why didn't you tell me that lawyer, Sulmondson was making threats?"

"Threats? I didn't get the feel of that. You shouldn't do this or he'll do that. I have to get you to back off from what I don't know. Somebody killed Billy Hashfries and that should be a lesson to me. Where we going?"

"To your *pied a terre*," she snapped. "I got to get your brain into gear before they kill you. And far more importantly, kill me."

"The Consortium?"

She glanced at me and just sighed like I was a burden she

couldn't go on with any longer.

"I'm not scared of The Affiliation anymore," I told her, trying to cheer her up. "It's like a monster. And they're not ever there. If they were, they'd be at *The New Pompey*."

We found the parrot poring over a pamphlet some Letter Days or First Day Witness or Seven Day Advertists, who had come to the door, had left.

"You will perish during the great tribulation."

"Throw something over that cage."

"I will shoot you dead, mudderfucker," Cag screamed as I dropped the shawl on his cage.

"Want me to call out for pizza?" I whispered to Eve.

She shook her head. She plopped into the overstuffed, her flask nestled in her shoulder.

"Don't talk," she ordered. "I need to prep for the lesson I'm going to give you."

"A lesson? For what?"

"Shut up."

I lay back on my bed and closed my eyes.

Cag wasn't asleep. I heard him mumbling.

"They say that life is an accident, driven by sexual desire, that the universe has no moral order, no truth, no God."

"I can still hear him," Eve sighed.

I opened my eyes and looked guiltily over at Eve.

"He's just annoying. Half the time."

"Then half a bullet will do it."

Jeez, he could be annoying. I was about to repeat when Eve pointed a finger at the hand puppets I had on the shelf over the parrot cage.

"Get those things down and put'em on your bed," she ordered.

I got up and reaching over the cage pulled down the hand puppets and laid them in a sitting position against my pillows.

"Okay," Eve said, standing up. "You got names for these guys, right? I've heard you call them by their names. Who's who?"

"This guy here is Dr. Serdab Patawala. He doesn't speak English. This is Mr. Spinalzo."

"Mister? In a dress?"

"He was our tutor. Used to dress in our mother's clothes."

"This is Madame Uberalles. She always wore a hat with a feather on top. Prof. Cranialhemorrhage with the red face. Dr. Crumblerumple and Dr. Gruppenfuhrer. They came from The Lab.

Gunner Fartsworth and Jabba. My mother's husbands."

"Which one is your father?"

"He's not here. He's in The Lab. You don't see him much."

"This guy with one red eye and one blue eye?"

" Moran. He and Williams, over here, were in the Army with me. Boot camp and then the Stockade. I told you about them."

"And the tall blonde hooker here with a tramp stamp?"

"Williams's Sweetheart. Nobody knows how she looks so I made her up."

I had no idea how Eve knew she was tall. The puppet was the same size as the others. Nobody knew how tall Williams' sweetheart was. She probably didn't exist except in Nick Williams' mind. I had made her to look like Ooh! Anna!, the upstairs maid of my youth.

"Okay, put the ones that belong together in your head on one side here and then the others across from them."

I started to move them around, one side and then the other, then made some changes, thought more about who fit where and made some more changes. I was switching Mr. Spinalzo for Dr. Gruppenfuhrer when Eve stopped me by trouncing down hard on my foot. She either wore high heels or harness boots. She had the harness boots on now.

"No more changes," she said.

"We urge you, brethren, admonish the unruly, encourage the fainthearted, help the weak, be patient with everyone."

"Really?" Eve said, shaking her head and looking at me.

"He likes Tess Alonian," I said in the parrot's defense.

"Okay, this is you," Eve said, putting her flask in between the two rows of hand puppets.

"Where's you?"

"Right in front of your sorry ass trying to explain the situation you're in."

"A crushed spirit dries up the bones."

"What we've got here are two mobs," Eve told me. "These guys here represent the Russians. The ones over here represent the Farnsworth Foundation. This guy here ... "

"Mr. Spinalzo."

"He's Victor Pavlovich. The Patriarch."

"Which one? There's three."

"Which ever one you want, sweetie."

"The monk. Though He's not really a monk, is he? He told me he was multiple persons all disordered."

"Don't talk. Just listen. Two mobs, right? Here and here. You in the middle. Follow?"

I realized I had placed Dr. Patawala with the wrong mob and I moved him. Eve slapped my hand.

"Leave him be. Do you follow what I've said so far?"

I nodded.

"Yes, I do," I said.

"Thanks to your feet."

"Where's the dumpster with Billy Hashfries in it?"

"He doesn't matter."

Her eyes narrowed. I could tell she was getting really pissed.

"Except as a lesson. They killed him. They could kill you."

I plopped down on my overstuffed. I felt myself sweating. No one could exhaust you like Eve Solly, in so many ways.

"You better run," the parrot whispered.

"I'll have my throat cut in a dumpster," I told the parrot.

"The old Russian is multiple things. All of them dangerous. He wants in on the laundering operation being run through the Foundation. That puts him at odds with The Mob. Sulmondson is the point man for The Mob. The other two who got their hands on that money ... This guy Jabba ... "

She pulled the Jabba puppet out of the line.

"And this guy, Gunner. They're dead but Sulmondson is the liaison now. Illegal money gets sorted with Foundation money and Sulmondson does the sorting."

She paused and looked at me.

"You follow?"

I nodded. I didn't mention the fact that Theo had a launderette in Paris but I was wondering which hand puppet represented that. My money was on Mrs. Angeloni hand puppet.

"The Foundation mob over here is not interested in you because they got Billy Hashfries to inherit and they run him like a Swiss clock."

"Somebody killed him and dumped his body in a dumpster."

"He brought me up out of the pit of destruction!" Cag screamed

"The Russians killed Hashfries as a message sent to the Foundation."

"Which is The Mob. And also, The Conglomerate."

"Whatever. It's big. Your family foundation is a front. The Russkies also figure if you inherit they can handle you. Sulmondson thinks the same thing. You're clay in everybody's hands. Of course, it might be easier in the long run just to kill you and let Sulmondson fight for control of The Foundation in the courts."

"Kill him and stuff him in that suitcase."

Eve went a little ballistic after that. She swept key players in both mobs off the bed.

"We're done," she said, pulling her phone out of the side pouch she was wearing.

"Who you calling?"

"Shut up. This is Eve Solly calling. I'm a friend of The Patriarch. Is he around? He is? Right now? Okay, can you tell me when Mr. Victor is around, but The Patriarch isn't? No. What I want is for you to call me when he's not The Patriarch. Got it? I need to talk to the secular Victor Pavlovich. That's right. When he's not dressed like a Russian monk. You've got my cell. Call me. Yeah, I already confessed, and The Patriarch gave me absolution, so I don't need to talk to him. There's a Franklin in it if you call me. Do svidaniya."

She looked at me.

"Class is over," she told us. "You're a fucking mountainous moron and the parrot is a ball buster."

"Talking about The Mob. I mean whatever the FBI called them."

"Yeah, I'll try to slow it down next time. Ease back on the details. What FBI?"

"I think they came out of the woods my old tutors are living in."

She said nothing but just went for her flask.

"I saw this film the other night," Cag told us in a very meek voice. "She died. He lived."

CHAPTER TWENTY-FIVE

WORDS

"What's that piece of paper you keep taking in and out of your pocket?" Eve said to me in a surly tone as we sat at a booth in the back of *The New Pompey*.

Cag was perched at his usual spot at the bar. It sounded like he was keeping the daytime regulars amused.

Eve was telling me that it wasn't safe for me or the parrot to stay in my *pied a terre*. She held out a hand.

"Let go," she said.

"Something that lawyer, Sulmondson wanted me to sign. But I'm not."

I gave her the confession to Billy Hashfries murder that I was supposed to sign.

"More coffee?" Sal said, coming over to the booth with a coffee pot in his hand.

He leaned over Eve to see what she was reading. She slapped him away and at the same time threw the paper on the table.

"You didn't think to tell me about this?"

"Why? I'm not going to sign it. I didn't kill that kid."

She pushed her coffee cup toward Sal who was still standing there with the pot of coffee. He poured. I pointed to mine. For some reason, we were drinking a non-alcoholic.

"Watch my fingers," Eve said, then held up one finger. "One, the dummy front for the Foundation that the Mob is using to launder money is dead."

"Billy Hashfries," Sal, said, squeezing in next to me.

"Two," she said holding up two fingers. "You are now the dummy front."

"Why keep saying dummy?" I protested

"Three. The way they can keep you in line is by holding that signed confession."

"Yeah, I didn't sign it."

Eve did one of her yoga deep breathe through the nostril routines and then slowly exhaled. I was getting into this, but I seemed to be a natural mouth breather like a fish thrown into the bottom of a boat.

"And that means they've got no leash on you."

"Is that four?"

"Five," Eve said, holding up five fingers. "Now, you're a danger to them. A danger to their operation."

"I'll sign the confession."

"Don't bother," Eve said. "I'm their problem. As long as I'm with you, you can't be trusted. They know I want to take them down. I'm getting the back story on their operation. Send it to the *Times*."

I shook my head in disbelief.

"I wouldn't do that for me if I was me. I mean if I was you and I was the me that's taken up a lot of your life."

She gave me a very sweet smile like you give a puppy that does something bad, but you can't be angry.

"You wouldn't last long fronting for those gangsters, Dirk," Sal told me. "Somebody has to save you."

I was thinking about what the job of fronting would be like when Eve's phone did its ring, "Bad to the Bone."

"Eve Solly. What? He's the jazz musician now? Victoire? No, that doesn't work. The last personality I want to deal with is a fucking musician. No, it doesn't help that he's not a bass player. When is he the guy who gives orders that keeps everything running in the black at that joint? Once a month? End of the month? Okay, tomorrow? Around noon? We'll be there."

She put the phone down.

"Mr. Victor will be at the club tomorrow at noon. This Patriarch guy has got his schizoid on a time table."

"Good to know," I said, hearing someone singing "Wild Rover" over at the bar.

I didn't want to think it was the parrot because truth is it was getting to be like what the terminator said in that movie about something becoming conscious at exactly 11:45 or around there.

At noon next day at *The Sea Bird*, I was wearing the clothes Eve had set out for me. I looked like I was ready to golf. Eve was skirted and high heeled, what she called her Mary Magdalena look.

Eve guessed that The Patriarch went in phases like the phases of the moon and what you had to do was get him in a sane phase, or at least in a normal state of mind, or something approaching that.

I didn't really know why we had to see him at any time but as I didn't want to get another five finger lesson, I asked no questions.

Mr. Victor had ordered us a nice lunch of caviar he said was from the Caspian Sea, followed by Borscht, followed by Golubtsy, followed by Chak-Chak and Bison Grass vodka. I got busy on the culinary side of things and left Eve to have her talk.

I caught pieces of it here and there.

"I need what you have," Eve says. "Muscle."

"They have a very sweet operation indeed," Mr. Victor says.

"They'd be out and you'd be in," Eve says.

"He has control?" Mr. Victor says, looking at me.

"Of The Foundation, yes. And I have control of him."

"You have to expose it to expose them," Mr. Victor says.

"I can flay them without flaying that Foundation. Not to worry."

I noticed that I was the only one drinking the vodka. They were both as sober as sleeping people.

"We need leverage to move them your way," Eve tells him.

Mr. Victor laughs.

"I'm afraid, Ms. Solly, that your way will blow their house down and I'm left in a Siberian winter."

I could see that scowl moving across Eve's face.

"They're big. They'll crush you. You know why? Because you're only a good fighter once a month. You've got a mental problem. You are so vulnerable."

Mr. Victor didn't like that.

"So, what's you point."

"Don't say `so'."

His face went dark but then it lightened up quickly. I guess the way multi-people personality inside one guy can do.

"You've met The Patriarch?"

"And the musician and I've been told there are other Victors. You're the only one who might successfully muscle in on that laundering operation, but you're only around one day a month. Mr. Victor, your secret selves are not sane the rest of the time. And everybody knows it."

Now the scowl was on Mr. Victor's face to stay.

"I've got that under control," he told us angrily. "So ... "

He paused. Eve said nothing.

"We're done here."

We watched him head for the bar. Eve got up quickly. I said I had to hit the men's room. She told me to hurry up.

Minutes later, I was jacking up my fly, heading to the bathroom door when the walls exploded, the floor sank, and a door slammed into my face. Then tiles from the walls began to shoot out from every direction and I was on a sinking bathroom floor, my ears ringing, the ceiling went all Chicken Little sky and fell on me.

I didn't think bomb until much later, a long time later. And even then, I couldn't say the word.

Part Two

CHAPTER TWENTY-SIX

"GOOD MORNING NURSE"

"It's all going to fall into place, Bratter. Don't pretend you can't hear me. Those bodies will be identified. It'll all come out so do yourself a favor and give us your side. You'll be doing yourself a favor. There's no sense in keeping mum. Do yourself a favor."

"I've told you Lieutenant Reynolds, Mr. Bratter's vocal cords were damaged by the bomb explosion. He cannot speak. He has some small movement in his left hand. Otherwise, he is paralyzed. And he doesn't hear better when you keep repeating words loudly. Loud English doesn't come out French."

"Okay, just let him know, Doc that clamming up won't help him in the long run. He needs to do himself a favor and talk to us."

"When you're ready to talk, Bratter, we'll be ready. Once we know for sure that nothing like an innocent accident happened in that club, you can say goodbye to your bail. You're going to lock up."

"Well, Lieutenant, his whole body is in a terrible lock up right now. It can't be pleasant for him, you know."

"No, I don't know, Dr. Grew. This guy should have been sent up for killing his girlfriend. And the guy we found crumpled in a dumpster. Look at me, Bratter. You're going to fuck up and I'm going be there to put you away. Remember that.

Go ahead and do yourself a favor and confess."

∎∎∎

"Holla, amigo. One credit card. Get you everything you need. Your nose is working? Go like this. Bueno. Get card. I get you the coke. You snort, you get better? Esta todo bien!"

"What are you doing in here, Alphonso?"

"Este pobre hombre que da un poco de compañía, Nurse Foot."

"Get out. And speak English. And my name is Nurse Fourth."

∎∎∎

"Good morning, Fort. How's our patient this morning?"

"I did what you ordered, Doctor Grew. I kept repeating loudly that he wasn't able to speak or move and that his girlfriend was dead."

"Excellent. Repetition and volume do it every time."

"Don't you find it strange that he's able to eat?"

"He can? Excellent. Nothing like our S on S here at The Sanitarium to get the body going again."

"He didn't have that, Doctor. It was delivered from outside. It had a fantastic aroma. He ate quantities of garlic along with a whole bottle of red wine. Is that unusual, Doctor?"

"For breakfast, yes."

"I meant it's atypical for total body paralysis."

"That will be all, Fort. See that I'm not disturbed. I need to examine the patient's corpus callosum, specifically the Broca and Wernicke areas."

∎∎∎

"Good morning, Nurse Frack. How is our patient this morning?"

"I believe he's a bit tipsy. A friend joined him for breakfast. A Mr. Moran. They drank three bottles of wine. Should I have stopped them, Doctor?"

"Not at all. There is truth in wine, Nurse. Perchance, you see Mr. Morgan again, tell him I'd like to talk to him. Now, some privacy. I have some news to give our patient."

"Good, I hope?"

"My objectivity in these matters, Nurse, forbids to presume the morality of my conclusions. There is neither good nor evil in diagnosis. Truth is in a diagnostic sentence."

"Of course, Doctor."

"In fact, I think I'll hold off until I have Mr. Moroney here. Has any other friend come by?"

"His landlady, Mrs. Hemangioma brings his breakfast and

dinner. He has his lunch here at the hospital. Oh, yes, a young man who said he was Mr. Bratter's mixologist has also visited. With a parrot who asked me if I knew why Jesus died."

"That will be all, Nurse. Wait, did you? Know? Why?"

"Sepsis, I would think, Doctor."

"Of course. See that I'm not disturbed."

...

"Thank you for coming, Mr. Moranus. I wanted you to hear my diagnosis of your friend."

"Moran, Doc. Moranus was what my teachers called me. Happy to hear it, Doc. Your patient and I were in the Stockade together. Before it burned down. We became good friends. I've plundered, so to speak, the family mansion and imbibed in the family wine cellars. I'm what you call a friend of the family. A couple of times removed for health reasons."

"I'll try not to be technical, Mr. Moran. Unless of course you have some background in brain injury?"

"I do in fact. I was born with it, but I meditate. Let me ask you, Doc, could our friend here possibly convince a judge he was fiscally competent?"

"What's that? He doesn't speak or move, Mr. Moran. He eats competently I've been told but that is the limit. May I proceed?"

"Shoot."

"The Broca area of the brain lying in the left frontal lobe was damaged by the explosion, the result being what we call Broca's aphasia. He cannot speak or write. The motor strip of the frontal lobe has also been injured, to what degree we do not yet know. But right now, no body movement is being activated. He can do yes and no eye movement."

"So, he understands what we're saying?"

"Double wink. That means yes he does."

"Okay. Dirk boy, I'm holding down your Peed Atari in Brooklyn. Williams is spending a little time in lockup for unwarranted removal of accessories and impedimenta from your family's mansion. Want I should bring anything by, make this joint more homey? How about some hand puppets? Yeah? Good. I'll bring them over."

"Hand puppets?"

"I could bring his parrot over too. Was his brother's. Keep him company."

"I believe Nurse Fooks found the parrot a disturbance to the patients when the bird last visited. Nurse Fooks said he was too evangelical."

"That's okay. He doesn't mind."

...

"Good morning, Doctor. Mr. Maroon would like to speak to you?"

"I've been thinking if we could get my friend operational, Doc, you could get some nice funding for your own operation here. By the way, how did my friend wind up here? In your sanitarium."

"His mother is here. Funding in both cases from an outside source I am not at liberty to reveal."

"Fair enough. But like I say, put my friend here on his feet, he could expand your funding big time. He could swell your bottom line faster than milk swells an udder in Oshkosh."

"I'm afraid what you're asking for is something medical science at this time cannot give you. His brain damage is neither operable nor self-recuperating."

"More things in heaven and earth, Doc. By the way, it could be somebody shows up wants to turn the lights out totally on my friend here. Anybody with a Russian accent, give me a call pronto."

"Seriously? Someone wants to kill him?"

"We all owe life a death, Doc. Somebody might think my friend here blew up his old man. Blew him to hell, as they say."

"I don't understand. Mr. Bratter blew himself up so as to blow up someone else?"

"And, of course, my friend is innocent but try to tell that to a son choked up with grief and was a little aft of the beam before that. You know what they say about the Russian mob."

"I do? I mean I don't know anything about the Russian mob. You mean Mr. Putin?"

"Fair enough I guess when you think about it."

"Think about what?"

"Just saying if you hear a Russian talking around here, call me."

"Not the police?"

"Well, you could, Doc, but you know what they say about the Russian Mob and the chumps who squeal on them."

"I do? You mean they'll turn the lights out on me?"

"Fair enough. Do me a favor and decorate my friend's room with some of these hand puppets. Having friends around may lighten his load. He made them. He knows their names so don't worry.

They're all friends. You know what the bond of friendship is, Doc. Conversation."

···

"Nurse, if anyone with a Russian accent comes here wishing to see Mr. Bratter, call the police. Don't mention my name. Give them your own."

"I don't believe I've ever heard a Russian accent, Doctor. I think I would confuse it with a coastal accent."

"Really? Incredible. Get a copy of the movie *Dr. Zhivago*. Do that immediately. We have no idea when such a person may show up."

···

"Good morning, Doctor."

"Any accents? Did you see the movie?"

"I did. Which one had the Russian accent?"

"That will be all, Nurse. Do you have any sort of weapon, Nurse. A pistol or revolver? An automatic or semi-automatic, for instance."

"I have a new Russian Udav in my car. Oh, Doctor, before I forget. Miss Alice wants to talk to you."

"Alice? She's talking? I told you to keep her sedated."

"She comes out of it now and then, Doctor."

"Fugue, are you a nurse or are you an idiot?"

"Before you go any further, Doctor. I should tell you I carry a Makarov on my person, as you advised. And my name is Fourth. I was the fourth child."

"Really? I don't know how I lived so long without knowing that. Well, if you hear a Russian accent, I'm ordering you to shoot first and question afterward."

"So, you don't want to talk to Alice? I'll tell her."

"Just put her under, Nurse. Can you do that? And watch that goddamn Russian film again. Who was Russian? Incredible."

···

"Fair enough, Nicky."

"I knew you'd understand, Moran. You know, some people don't talk because they have nothing to say. They use their words sparingly. Or, perhaps they are tired of hearing themselves talk and would rather listen. I think our friend, Dirk is a good listener and that's what he's doing."

"Shut up and go back to bed!"

"I wish this parrot would listen more and talk less. We gotta send him over to our friend as a permanent resident. Let Dirk practice his listening."

"More as to what I think could be the case here is that some people are so far beyond human communication ...

"That they talk to birds and hand puppets?"

"Yes, that, certainly. But they are so removed in another realm that talk to them would be like you or I regressing and walking on all fours or taking to the trees. Or wondering what a wheel could be used for. My sweetheart is not fond of talk."

"Tell me, honestly Nicky, has she ever spoken to you?"

"Oh, yes. Many, many times. But she wasn't talking."

"These bitches lookin bitter because I be lookin better !"

"Twitter has infected that parrot's brains. I wish he'd go back to the Koran."

"We're a little cramped in this *pied a terre*. I'm going over to the Sanitarium and push the Doc our way some more."

"Back for dinner? Mrs. Angeloni is wafting glorious aromas our way."

"Fair enough. You know, Nicky, I'm thinking Doctor Grew is about as up and up as me and you. That whole Sanitarium thing looks like a scam enterprise to me. I keep hearing Alice screaming."

"Who's Alice?"

"Fair enough but that's what she screams. Alice! Alice! That Sanitarium ain't sanitary is what I'm thinking.""Possibly. It's certainly an enterprise wafting in the Mysterium."

"You. Shut up and get out of here!"

...

"Good morning, Doctor. Mr. Mortuary would like to speak to you."

"Who? Moran? Again? What was that banging noise this morning?"

"I unloaded a few rounds at someone suspiciously Russian."

"Good God, Nurse. Was he? Russian? Did you kill him?"

"I missed three times but got him through the heart on the fourth."

"What? Who in God's name was it? Where's the body?"

"He is ... he was a drifter who just wanders in at all hours. We call him John Doe."

"He just wanders in? How is that possible? What is he looking for?"

"He says he's looking for some Sanitarium or Salvational relief.

One of those, which of course, without insurance, we cannot give him. I'm sure I heard him distinctly speaking with a Russian accent. He had a towel wrapped around his head."

"Sikh."

"Yes, I think he was. Very. But he has no insurance,"

"Not in this place certainly. And where is his body now?"

"Fortunately, Alphonso was on duty. He's the Puerto Rican who removes the toxic waste and not a Russian."

"Alphonso?"

"He picks up the toxic container once a week. He always sings in Spanish as he works. Arrivederci Roma. He's quite the Godsend around here. He came on a ship, not a caravan. A rubber raft I think he said. He has a large handkerchief he kneels on in the mornings and at twilight."

"Well, tell him to get that body back here. We'll have to notify the police."

"That's not possible, Doctor. Alphonso has already incinerated the body. I am also thinking that I would be arrested for murder, accidental as it was."

"My God! Alright. We have no choice but to remain mute about this. After all there is no body. *Habeus corpus*, you know."

"That sounds Russian."

"This is terrible, Nurse. We need to be able to identify a Russian accent. You obviously cannot."

"I could ask Nurse Stalin. She speaks Russian at home. She …."

"You aren't serious, Nurse? You mean we have here on staff … Are you a total idiot, Nurse Foot?"

"I have three bullets still in my gun, Doctor. It's Forth."

"Alright. Alright. Tell Nurse Trotsky whatever to be on the lookout for any visitor with a Russian accent. Tell her to call the police at once and give her own name. Now, where's that pain in the ass Moran?"

"In Mr. Bratter's room, Doctor. And may I say that from now on I will be carrying a loaded gun. Understood?"

"Well, just don't be firing off indiscriminately."

...

"Buongiorno, Commendatore. Qui la cocaine. Dove La Visa"

"What are you doing in Mr. Bratter's room, Alphonso?"

"Dannazione! È io amico, Nurse."

"Get out. And speak English, Alphonso. You're not Russian are you?"

"Mi dispiace."

"Stop speaking gibberish and get the toxic waste out."

...

"Good afternoon, Mr. Moran. What can I do for you? Your friend remains the same. No change. In fact, I predict there won't be any change for the entire length of your own life. The Earth will burn up before there will be any change in your friend."

"Fair enough. Doc. None of it to be denied. Did I tell you that my friend here could come into a fortune with your help? You know forces, Doc? One force pulling one way, another pulling another way? One with the most cash on hand wins?"

"That's either a market efficiency theory, Mr. Moran, or pataphysics. Not medical science."

"Actually, it's business. It's always business, Doc. Like your Sanitarium here is a business and that means it can go out of business. Your staff, for instance, isn't what it should be. Certified wise. Or, you yourself ain't exactly who you say you are."

"Do have a point, beyond insulting me, Moran?"

"What I'm saying is that if you don't think you can handle that kind of spot check, let me help you. Which I can do if you help me. Alls that's needed is to juice my friend up so he's moveable. Bluetooth his vocal chords like that guy Stuart Hawkman. Use some of your science to get him up and out of that bed. You won't be forgotten when he's got his hands on his inheritance. Be a lot more than whoever is paying you to keep him in here."

TWENTY-SEVEN

"THE PATENT"

"I gotta tell you, Nicky, I think the parrot is driving our friend deeper into the pit of darkness he's already in. Parrot kept yelling 'Patent number 2939990!"

"Well, he could be holding a patent for something he invented," Mrs. Angeloni said, clearing up the dishes and noticing that as usual Williams and Moran had consumed everything down to the last morsel.

"I'll need the rent money," she said, on her way out, tray of dirty dishes in her hand.

"We need to fence some treasures that Nicky picked up. Give us a week or so. Or, we could give you, say, some priceless items."

"Hot items, you mean. No thank you."

After she left, Williams went back to the parrot's patent.

"He repeats what he's heard."

"When's the last time you quoted *The Koran*?"

"Heard or read. But he does have audio books. But I think he heard someone say that patent number. Somebody who was visiting Dirk."

...

"Doctor Grew cannot see either of you gentlemen today."

"Fair enough. Our friend have any visitors since last time we were here, Nurse?"

"No, why should he? I don't mean that. I mean who would visit him?"

"So, that's a no?"

"Yes. No. No one. Did someone say he had a visitor?"

"Thanks. Can we have some privacy?"

"I'll need to tell Dr. Grew that you gentlemen are here."

"Fair enough. Good bye."

"Did she seem rattled to you, Nick?"

"Hey, parrot … "

"Cag. That's her name. Did Dirk have any visitors recently?"

"Hugh Dubartas is at the door!"

"Besides him."

"Madame Uberalles is on the phone!"

"We're not going to get anything out of him, Moran."

"What's that patent number, Cag?"

"Patent number 2939990!"

"Where did you hear that?"

"Why don't you just drop dead and leave us alone!"

...

"Mr Moran and Mr Williams would like to speak to you, Doctor. I don't think you should."

"What? Tell them I'm busy."

"The Doctor is busy right now. Do you wish to make an appointment?"

"No, we'll go right in. Thanks."

"Gentlemen, really?"

"No, we're not. Somebody visited Mr. Bratter?"

"The parrot's repeating some of what some visitor told Dirk."

"I was not present."

"Somebody let this visitor in."

"Nurse!"

"Yes, Doctor?"

"Did Mr. Bratter have any visitors recently besides these gentlemen?"

"I couldn't say. Nurse Stalin is in charge of that section."

"Call her."

"I don't think we'll be able to reach her under the circumstances, Doctor."

"What circumstances?"

"She killed someone late last night. She said she recognized him from Auschwitz. She said it all came back to her, although she was only a child then. She put several bullets in his head. A Herr Gasmeister. She heard him speaking German."

"Incredible! You can't be serious? She had a gun?"

"She packs a Mauser Hsc."

"Good weapon. Nicky,
 and I have used them. So, where did she go?"

"I don't know. She didn't say. She's quite old, late nineties I believe, and I think the excitement may prove too much for her."

"You are telling me Nurse that this truly ancient woman carrying a loaded gun heard German spoken …

"That and she recognized him. She said he was called The Gasmeister. He was married to the Hyena of Auschwitz."

"Are you delirious Nurse? What the hell are you talking about? Hyena married to a gas miser?"

"She shot him. We heard the shots. Alphonso and I."

"Where's the body?"

"Yeah, me and Nicky would like to search his pockets. See what we can find out about him."

"The body?"

"Did she take it with her, Nurse? You can tell me anything incredible. I'm ready for it."

"Alphonso took it. We put it in the toxic bin."

"You didn't go through the pockets?"

"No. We … Alphonso and I. Nurse Stalin had already gone. We dumped it in as was. Alphonso takes it to the incinerator. Probably done already. He gets off from work at noon. It's past two now."

"Gentlemen, I'm sorry."

"Get our friend on his feet, Doctor. You know, shooting visitors and then throwing them in an incinerator is not legal. We could call the cops."

...

"Very quickly. Where is your plastic card? I need to go back home. You know Tabriz? My home. It's beautiful. You will come to see me and my family This is not a holy place."

"What are you doing in here, Alphonso?"

"Arrivederci Roma."

"Get out. Wait. Did you dump that body?"

...

"Are you sure you're not Russian, Professor Betz? You sound foreign."

"Please excuse my English, Nurse Foots. I am Brazilian. On both my mother and father's side. I was born after the war. I injured my ankle this morning and so I must use this walker. It is extremely important that I speak to Herr Dirk Bratter at once."

"I'm afraid he doesn't speak, Professor."

"It does not matter. He was not a very verbal child. He will understand."

"Are you sure you're not Russian? You sound like someone I heard in *Dr. Zhivago*."

"Absolutely. I am too old now to become a Russian, Nurse."

"I see he has a Papagei for a companion. What are all these Handpuppen over there? And here? Ah, I remember this one? It's what he made of me."

"It is?"

"Gruppenfuhrer is what he called it. And me. I see by his eyes that he remembers me."

"You can? Well, don't tire him. I'll leave you two alone. Nurse Stalin should be by momentarily."

"I'm going to move this chair here. Like this. And sit here like this. Wunderbar. First, dear boy, I need to see what is what here. Mein Gott, you are as large as this large bed. You and your twin were riesig at birth. Like giants to come. I hit you here. And here. Now slap you here. Again. I grab your head. I'm out of breath. And, pull it forward. Schnell. Then back. Two more slaps to the cheeks. Punches to the Abdomen. Ah, you can make a sound! The vocal chords are exzellent. Snap my fingers in this ear. Here. Now here. Loud clap again. Close your nostrils. Your eyes tear. Sehr gut. Now, if I can, roll you off the bed. Not too easy. Kick you hard in the Niere und Liber. Sehr gut. Now you stay there and listen. Achtung."

"Madame Uberalles is on the phone!"

"Ah, Wunderbar! The papagei remembers ... no, you remember Madame Bovardelier! You and your twin called her Madame Uberalles. But she cannot be on the phone. She died many, many years ago. In the Lab is where she died. They all died over their Bunsen burners. A reason why I never enter a Lab. Our work was cursed and so were we. She was in fact working on just what I came to tell you about. Falling asleep? One, two, three kicks. Achtung. Your father, my good friend in and out of the Lab, P.T., put his discovery in your name. Why? He thought and we all thought that you would have great financial need in your life. Your twin was destined to succeed. By transparent genetics. You were unfortunately already transparently genetically inferior to your brother. So, you now hold the patent for what will compensate for this. Patent number 293990. Remember that. 2939990. Patent number 2939990."

"Patent number 2939990! Patent number 2939990!"

"Wunderbar! Wunderbar! Der Papagei erinnert sich!"

"Excuse me. What is going on here? Why is Mr. Bratter on the floor? Who are you?

"Bitte legen Sie die Pistole weg, Madame."

"Wait. I know you. You're the Gasmeister! You were married to the Hyena of Auschwitz!"

"She wasn't that bad, Frau. My lovely Bovardelier!"

"You son of a bitch!"

■■■

"So, I believe, Mr. Thwaite, that we should be concerned about the ownership of this patent."

"Do you have your head up your ass, Sandwich? We didn't get off the ground with a patent we didn't even know about. None of the Conglomerate's shell have anything to do with such a patent."

"So, research says that most of what we've done comes out of the start that patent made. So, it's sort of the Prime Mover. We didn't know there was one. I'm an atheist myself so the whole concept of a creator? I personally assumed …

"Do I give a flying fuck what you personally assumed? Let me know when you impersonally assume anything. "

"So, what I don't assume, Mr. Thwaite is that every planet in the solar system has a New Testament starring Jesus Christ."

"Are you out of your mind, Savage? There are no humans on any of those planets. Where there are no humans, there are no gods. Jesus is personal to this planet."

"So gratifying to hear, Mr. Thwaite."

"We don't fry frogs on hotplates, Salvage. And we don't need patents."

"So, if that is all, Mr. Thwaite?"

■■■

"Eloise. See that kid coming out of my office? Yeah, Sandwich or whatever. Get rid of him. Fire him. See that's it done. Tell me, do you say so? No, I know you didn't say anything. The word. So. You use it? So, you don't know? So, you don't know you just used it? Why are you giggling? No, I'm not in such a good mood. No, I don't give a fuck, Eloise, that you really appreciate it and the whole staff does when I'm in a good mood. What's that?

So, you didn't mean anything. So, again. Stop crying. Okay. Okay. No, I'm not going to fire you. No, I'm not going to fire my own daughter so calm down. No, I won't be home for dinner. When have I ever been home for dinner? I'm taking Sandwich's wife to dinner. So, just fuck off and do what I told you."

CHAPTER TWENTY-EIGHT

"JUNIOR PAVLOVICHSAINTPETERGRAD"

I was relaxing in this Sanitary world of flat on my back perspective when Junior Pavlovich walks in like he owned the place.

"Hey, it's Junior Pavlovichleningrad!"

Junior shows the parrot his gun and the parrot ducked her head under her wing. If I could have moved, I would have done the same thing.

Junior comes up to the bed, leans over and slaps me hard, multiple times, back and forth across the face. The last time someone slapped me around, he got shot. Prof. Gruppenfuhrer The old nurse called him a gas bag and emptied her gun in his gut. I had no idea what that was all about.

Now Junior puts one hand under my head and lifts it, shakes it and then drops it. He surveys the tubes running into my arms and head. He steps back and scowls and then laughs.

"I thought you went back to Russia?" I asked him without sound. "How'd you get in here? What do you want? Get lost. Go fuck yourself. Drop dead."

He pulled the visitor's chair close to the bed and sat down. He smelled like he was wearing Bison Grass vodka cologne.

"Well, big, fat boy, it looks like you're losing some poundage. Skinny boy now."

He leans forward and pinches a cheek, hard. His eyes light up. Nothing like an immobilized body to get a sadist's juices flowing.

"I'd kill ya but I think I like you better like this," the sadist told me. "You start walking and talking again, I'll come back and kill ya."

I tried to make my eyeballs express my view of that.

He took out a cigarette case, pulled a cigarette out and lit up. He blew the smoke in my face.

He sat there smoking and smirking.

"Who blew up my father, Mr. Victor Pavlovich, Senior's place?" he asked me.

"The Mob," I said to which I asked myself wasn't Junior The Mob, or one of them? I was totally confused on The Mob's identity but then again wasn't that its thing? Plus, I had heard it said that I had irreparable brain damage.

"My thinking is that," Junior said, leaning over and sweeping some of the bedcover off my left leg. He held his burning cigarette over my leg. "Correct me if I'm wrong."

He touched the cigarette to my leg. Didn't feel it but I tried to show pain in my eyeballs.

"My thinking is that my Dad wanted to stick his beak into whatever business you're involved in."

"The Foundation," I told him. "It gives money to laundries overseas."

"I checked it out. You stepped up as the guy who runs the Farnsworth Foundation. The guy who ran it before had his throat cut."

"And dumped in a dumpster," I added.

"Left him in a dumpster," Junior said, seeming to get some amusement out of Billy Hashfries passing.

"That," he said, applying the cigarette to my leg again, "leads me to think that the same killer cut a throat also blew up my father, who was a Patriarch as you know."

"And Eve Solly," I added, feeling that I was tearing up again.

"Alls I have to do is follow the blood trail," Junior told me. "I'm the head of The Patriarch crew now."

I congratulated him.

"Yeah, I run my crew. But you don't run yours. There's a whole law firm Asshole, Asshole, Jerkoff and Cockblock representing what they call a blind power of attorney so you can't see who's pulling the strings."

I told him I had never heard of that law firm.

"We could speak privately to the partners," Junior said, suddenly punching me in the balls. I wish I could say it hurt that's how much I was yearning to feel anything.

"Like I'm speaking to you now."

He laughed.

"But I think the quicker way is for you to drift off so the blind POA dissolves and I wait for the next douche bag to take over The Foundation."

"There's nobody left in the family," I told him. "What do you mean drift off?"

He made a quick grab for the oxygen tube going into my nose and yanked it out.

"I was lying," he told me, as I wondered if my lungs were going to kick in. "More fun holding out to you a little hope. Soon as I stepped into this room, you were a dead man."

He sat down, dropping his cigarette butt to the floor and stamping on it.

"I'll just sit here and watch you croak."

In a few minutes, he told me I'd be turning blue.

"You should be dead by now," he said after about ten minutes. "You got the lungs of a whale."

■■■

I must have drifted off to sleep but when I opened my eyes Junior was still there. But he was slumped over and blood was trickling down from a hole in his forehead. I called his name but even the dead don't respond to silence.

Then I heard a voice from behind me.

"These punwits are studying your head like a nuclear suitcase. That's as funny as it gets."

It didn't sound like the parrot. It sounded like Eve. Auditory hallucinations. Dr. Fraud had once told me that they were definite preludes to lunacy. I could never get him to understand that the voices I heard were coming from the TV Theo put on in my room when I was asleep.

■■■

"Incredible, Nurse. This man is dead. Shot through the head. You really must relinquish all firearms."

"I didn't shoot him, Doctor. I didn't even know he was here until now. Does he have a Russian accent?"

"Well, we won't know that now, will we, Nurse? Unless of course the dead go on speaking."

"Maybe the patient heard him, Doctor? Maybe they were talking?"

"Mr. Bratter has lost the use of his vocal cords. Correct, Nurse? But let's consider that they were conversing and then this man was shot."

He looked at me.

"Did you see who shot this man, Mr. Bratter? Nod or shake the head of … of this puppet."

She shook her head vigorously.

"He must have been asleep. Call the police. Of course, if we do that, they'll close this place down after three shootings. Wait, are you sure Nurse Stalin wasn't on duty. She could have easily shot him. Such a quick draw mentality."

"No, Doctor. She's unavailable."

"Oh, that's right. She was arrested. In jail, no doubt."

"She was but she died in solitary. She was 96, Doctor, and I'm sure the stress of the shooting incident was too much for her."

"Too much for her, Nurse? I'm overwhelmed. Tell me, do we have other nonagenarians packing revolvers on the staff?"

"We have two others assisting in electric shock therapy, but both are gun control advocates."

"Incredible. I'll be in my office. Could you make me some tea, Nurse. I'm beginning to feel the impact here."

"Shall I ask Alphonso to get rid of the body?"

"What? Why would we do that? You call the police, tell them this man's been shot to death and when they arrive, there's no body? Does that make any sense, Nurse?"

"Might I point out, Doctor, that this is only the second accidental murder. The first body was not reported. However, even a second incident might threaten the Sanitarium's licensing. Perhaps it might be best to have Alphonso do what he usually does. Without calling the police."

"Incredible. But then again, perhaps you're right. Tell me, Nurse, when you say what he usually does, you refer imprecisely to the one murder you committed?"

"An accidental shooting that proved fatal, Doctor."

"I believe you said you fired four rounds on that occasion, Nurse. Time to see who you were shooting at, I would think."

"Better safe than sorry. As to the number of Alphonso body removals, are you distinguishing parts from whole bodies?"

"Whole bodies shot to death on these premises, Nurse."

"I'll have to get back to you on that, Doctor."

"Incredible!"

...

Memo to Henry Thwaite"

"The patent ownership by a living member of a family owned enterprise pre-dating all prior arrangements of inheritance establishes legal precedent of ownership. That's the legal reality. The Board doesn't care if your tenure here is vacated. What we care about is whether the Farnsworth Foundation continues to be a reliable asset to the conglomerate."

"I flew from Doha. And thirteen is an unlucky number. And tomorrow is the 13th. See you then.'

Jeez

"Where did this letter come from, Eloise?"

...

"Jeez, a gun?"

"Kimber K6S. No ordinary gun, Mr. Thwaite."

"Jeez, what are you going to do shoot me with that extraordinary gun right here in this restaurant? Take a look around. Every table full. And they all have phones they like to take pictures with. You shoot me here and your face will be all over the Internet."

"Okay. Tell me where I can find Moran. I'll shoot him instead."

"He's on a boat. Jamaica Bay. *The Sweet Cheeks.*"

...

"Are you telling me, Nurse, that a man totally immobilized is now gone as well as all his assorted companions, feathered and woolen?"

"Took all of them with him, Doctor. Which I am glad of. I was very close to shooting the parrot. He was obscene, disrespectful, and ill mannered. Told me to do unspeakable things to myself. I didn't like one or two of the hand puppets either. They had a foreign look."

"I suppose you would have shot all of them had you your pistol with you. But, of course, you left it home, as I instructed."

"Of course, Doctor."

"And when you say he took all of them with him, you realized that a man who cannot move any limb cannot take anyone anywhere. Which means someone came into the Sanitarium, unobserved by Staff, as usual, gathered up all the hand puppets, got the patient into some large conveyance, as our patient was cargo van size, arranged for the parrot's transportation and as silently as all that left us."

"I think Alphonso might have helped whoever it was."

"What? Incredible. Alphonso was of assistance in this escape? The man is truly ubiquitous, and I've never met him. I've never seen him. I pay his salary?"

"He and the parrot became close friends, I believe, Doctor. He called him Ellie Papa something. I believe the parrot is a she."

"Never mind that. Where is Alphonso now?"

"That is such a terrible thing that happened, Doctor. ICE took him. He was an illegal you know. Mexican. Not Puerto Rican as he claimed. I believe he's back with some friend he called Isis, I believe."

"You know where I'm going, Nurse?"

"Shall I make you some tea?"

"No. No. I'm going far, far away. Tell anyone who's looking for me that I've gone far, far away. Can you do that, Nurse?"

"Yes, Doctor. But if you're following Alphonso … Omar is his real name … to Mexico, you might want this."

"What is this? Your gun?"

"It's a .380 Bodyguard. I've got another. I'd feel better if you took it, Doctor. You never know when it will come in handy."

"Incredible."

■■■

"What the hell are you doing in my car, Jeez? Where the hell is my bodyguard, Rechert?"

"Rechert resigned, Mr. Thwaite. Now, here we are. Just the two of us. No witnesses with phones. Silencer on my …"

"Yeah, I know. Kimber K6S."

"Ah! A fellow handgun enthusiast."

"Sure. How about this Bond Arms Snake Slayer derringer? Try this bullet out in your belly … "

Thwaite shoots.

"Sorry," Jeez told him. "Tactical Multi-Threat Vest on. Here's a .357 Magnum bullet in your head."

"Wait, Jeez! I told you where Moran was."

"I thank you for that. I will be paying Mr. Moran a similar visit. In time. We are all shells with floating nomenclature played on a chess board without a bottom, Mr. Thwaite. A whale was once a land resident. You were once useful. Now you're going to be dead."

He shoots.

Part Three

CHAPTER TWENTY-NINE

"SHARDS"

You could say that my own mind was a combination of many variables. I could mention the besieged and crippled minds of Mr. Patawala and Mr. Spinalzo, both suffering from what Theo called Dizzy Floria, but Eve translated as dysphoria, a deep dissatisfaction with life which Eve said I was immune to, along with any ailment defined by the word "deep."

Both Theo and I had gone to St. Xenophobia by the Bank Academy at one point where Theo learned Chinese and Arabic and I learned cursive. I did have scattered childhood Q&A's with PT. on the few occasions he came out of The Lab -- "The male inserts the penis" and "Give him enough gas until he's on his back with four legs in the air rigid" talks -- a brief run at Princeton, collapse into shit-life syndrome, sometime in The Stockade with Nick Sweetheart and Moran, and the life instructions of Ms. Evangeline Solly.

One of her reflections was I seemed prime order something resistant to instruction, nor could I be diverted from my own mind nest.

As the many hand puppets resting on shelves in my *pied a terre* indicate, I can sew and stitch fabric into arms, legs, bellies and faces that have names. In short, I can create.

That's when I wasn't frozen except for my eyeballs and my inner monologue.

My daily sessions with Dr. Glue did not help.

He plastered a lot of tabs connected to wires connected to computer consoles he positioned alongside of and at the foot of the bed and every once and awhile would say "Incredibly gaseous" or "Anal recursiveness."

After about a gazillion of these sessions he sat by my bed and told me what he had discovered.

"Thus, what we see is that your mind is fragmented. Fragments are what we see. Shards. Which create a fragmented mind. One of the fragments is this, which I quote from memory: *Now I do not know whether I was then a man dreaming I was a butterfly, or whether I am now a butterfly, dreaming I am a man.* We believe that was said by somebody who would fit that category of genius DNA we wish to harvest for insertion in embryos and thus create a human race smart enough to not soil its own nest to the point of probable extinction of itself."

I gave him a WTF look but as my face did not change and only my eyes moved, that message was left to my eyeballs.

"Well, be that as it may."

He stood up.

"We're making progress."

And he walked out.

I gave him the finger. If I had Eve's .38, I would have shot him in the ass.

"He doesn't like you, Mr. Bratter," the Nurse told me one morning, right after the Doctor had left and she was fussing with my sheets.

"But no need to worry about that. He's not a real doctor. He's a Google doctor. And I think he is a gangster, but you know what, I get paid maybe ten times what a real nurse gets paid. So, what do I care? And I fool him. He thinks I'm a nurse. And, look here. This Mauser 7.65. My gangster protection. I shot a Russian the other night, but I haven't told him yet. I mean the doctor. The Russian has been incinerated."

If I could have gotten a shocked WTF look on my face, I would have but I think I kept the expression of Mister Spinalzo, one of my hand puppets. The real Spinalzo always looked like his face had just come out of the freezer.

"You know what I think, Mr. Bratter? I think if you got a real medical team to look at you, they'd say you were either concussed or constipated or maybe both. Just don't sleep too much and drink gallons of water is my advice. But really, what do I know? That is funny because you sleep all the time. Sad too I suppose."

Those words really, really depressed me and I would have stayed depressed forever, but I fell asleep.

Lieutenant Reynolds came by every couple of days to see if I could be moved to a prison hospital but Dr. Flew told him that moving me would cause irreparable damage to my Werenicki. That mystery led the frustrated Lieutenant to shout in my ear that he was going to get me, and I should do myself a favor, which was another mystery as to what that was.

Mrs. Angeloni came by the first week to tell me that the parrot had to go. Also, as it looked like I wasn't ever getting out of the hospital or a prison, she needed to rent my *pied a terre*. I should note she said that I hadn't made my rent in months. She wanted my permission to drop the parrot off at Animal Control and to call the cops on Moran and Williams who she was tired of feeding.

I tried to shake my head and I did the two eye blinks in a row which meant "NO" but that always produced tears and she just said that of course it was sad and though she didn't think a parrot belonged in her soon to be renovated, gentrified apartment building as was fitting in the New Paris of Brooklyn and she certainly didn't think Eve Solly, rest her soul, was the girl for me, she wasn't going to leave me with any bad feelings between us. I might get better and become the heir she always thought I would be.

I haven't moved anything but my bowels in five weeks. I can't speak and I can't move. I hear gunshots in the night. I'm being fed and watered intravenously. Day and nighttime shifts of nurses slip bed pans under me, wipe my ass and then turn me. The biggest fear of ICU's nurses is semi-corpses with active diarrhea. Luckily, I didn't have any of those kinds of nurses. I had a Nurse who told me she wasn't really a nurse. Also, a doctor who was a gangster and not a doctor.

I don't know who was paying the bills, probably The State who wanted to keep me alive so they could put me in jail for life or execute me.

So, yeah. I'm the alive guy dreaming he's dead but I'm really the dead guy dreaming I'm alive. Dr. Flea, my gangster doctor, had it right. Alive in just a few ways you can be alive. Why's that? Because I'm so freaking dead that I can't imagine myself more alive than this: a big slab of unmoving, mute flesh, slowly de-slabbing. I should have had more purpose and ambition.

That didn't stop people from visiting me.

The lawyer Sulmondson himself came around.

He told me that I should concentrate on getting better. The opioids would help with that. Meanwhile, he had power of attorney and was running the Foundation the way he believed I would have run it.

He said something about a patent and about Moran owning the patent or something that didn't make sense. I was to remember that the Foundation was wrapped up in about 209 subsidiary financial services corporations secretly serving 666 shell companies spread over 26 jurisdictions all over the world and run by a quantum arrangement of guys behind guys behind other guys who communicated by encryption of G5 cell phones.

A lot of money settled into The Foundation like it was a settlement account for doing good. There was no way I could inherit control of it through inherited control of the Farnsworth Enterprises. Even if I weren't in a less than vegetative state right now.

Nevertheless, he wanted me to get better.

He wanted me better the way evangelicals want Jews to be in the Holy Land so at the End of Days, Jews can either convert to Christianity or be thrown into burning lakes of fire.

Really. When you can't move and can't speak you see the worst in everybody and everything. What I did figure out was that with my mother in a Sanitarium, the same one apparently I was in, I was the living heir but Sollenoid had proven to the Courts that a guy going to jail for murder if he came out of a body and brain freeze had no legal competency, as he put it.

I told him to fuck off but I didn't even hear me.

On the way out, he told me that if a scary guy named Jeez came by I should say goodbye to the world.

***

CHAPTER THIRTY

WICKEDPEDIA

Eve, who wasn't convincingly dead, didn't haunt me like she was dead. I dreamed her. But The Patriarch haunted me like the Dead are supposed to do. All three of his personalities had blown up in the *Sea Bird* bombing. I was throwing cold water on my face in the john at the moment that bomb went off.

Even though The Patriarch was probably in many pieces, he came by in one solid piece to hear my confession and grant me absolution of my sins

I gave him a wide eyed WTF look via my eyeballs that he picked up on.

"Yes, I know you can't speak. It's not a problem. I can't absolve you either. I'm dead and not in a place set up for absolution. Besides, being a Russian monk is part of my personality disorder. I mean was part. I wasn't a monk either. Now that I am unified in death, I've found that out. You find out about things like that when you're dead. I don't see how it's useful but it's a plan. Whose plan I don't yet know, and I've got a feeling when I find out, I'm not going to come back and tell anyone. Still for all that and all that, I can't help thinking that the only thing real about any part of me was the psychosis. Do you know the Order of Angels, Dirk?"

I signaled another WTF look, but he ignored it.

"Cherubs, guardian and Christmas time angels are actually the lowest order in the hierarchy of Angeology," he told me, crossing his legs and looking up at the ceiling. Angels. He wasn't fragmented but he did look bad, as if he needed a drink, a bath, soap, a dentist, a manicure, a barber, new shoes, a change of clothes and a nose hair clipping. Oh, yeah. A shrink. But he wasn't going to get any of this. Death isn't a spa. He didn't have to worry about death having sewed his personalities back together to fit the Norm. He was Dead and nuts. I think the plan he was talking about had him nuts alive and dead. A really awful consistency I thought.

He droned on about the angels.

There was it seems three levels, low, middle and high. They were all a better brand of creation than humans who, however, were higher than certain animals but not parrots, octopoi, dolphins or crows, and lower than devils, of which there were, according to him, about sixty orders of.

"Now this is not approved theology but I think there's crossover."

He paused. I waited. Actually, it's all I can do.

"Do you know, Mr. Bratter, that genetic studies point to a hybridization between archaic humans and modern humans. There's about 4% of human DNA that is prehistoric. When the permafrost melts, we'll see another 10 to 20%. There's talk of ancient Neanderthal DNA, DNA that goes back as far as Adam. Non-modern or biblical. Primitive. Naïve. Rustic mentality. You may be a perfect example."

I was trying to close my eyes and ears. How did his hallucination of The Patriarch turn into P.T. Bratter, my father, on one of his infrequent visitations out of The Lab and into the bedroom Theo and I shared? I'm not questioning visitors who are dead or dreamscapes so I just let The Patriarch disappear and P.T. Bratter sit there and mini-lecture me.

"I came by to tell you, son, that no one is looking for you. Not even science. And that's good. No one will ever look for you or remember you. I mean once I'm gone."

I told him he was already gone and to get out before I threw him out but none of that was said or done.

"Okay," he finally said, with a deep sigh. "That's all I've got. Turn off all the lights before you go to bed. Oh, I'm passing on the primeval lump to you. It's your origin, after all. Only fitting. I took a patent on it in your name. Should turn your life around. Inside out. Upside down."

After all my hallucinatory visitations, I was always kind of glad to see Dr. Growth come in the door even though he was most of the time an hallucination but at least I knew he wasn't dead. That somehow made whatever went down more real to me.

The hallucinated Dr. Growth had a hypertensive red face, a throbbing carotid neck artery and sported what looked like a Harpo Marx wig on his head. He looked like a capo de capo of an amusement park disguised as a doctor.

Today, he began by telling me that sometimes the human mind goes off on its own. As I knew it was all just my lucid dreaming, I let the cameras roll and just lay there and listened.

"In other words, Herr Doktor," Eve, the star in all my dreams, told Dr. Glutton, "it's like he's going or has gone up his own ass, assuming that there's little anatomical difference here between his ass and his brain. He's circling someplace in there."

"Not precisely," he told her. "But apt. He's in what we call a recursive absurdity of thought having nothing to do with his ass and all to do with his injured brain."

"That happened at birth," Eve snapped. "What's new here? When is he going wake up and talk? Forget what I just said. Leave him alone. He's okay."

She was in a chair about the same height as the wheelchair I was in. I mean it was a dream so why wouldn't I get myself out of the fucking bed? Her legs were crossed, and I wondered if she was wearing underwear. I wondered if this dream was lucid enough to take me all the way to sex.

"Reason is not what we're looking for," Dr. Gowan said. "Reason won't take us to where Dirk is."

"What does, Doc?" Eve asked. "Lithium? LSD? Mycology?"

Gaylord's smile was just his mouth opening wide and a bulgy eyed stare.

"Story," he told her. "I like to hear stories. As Don can neither write nor speak, I will be relying on others. Do you know Don well, Miss Solly?"

"Long enough to know his name is Dirk and not Don. I also know that he's been fucked up a long time. The only story he can tell you is a sob story, how somebody pulled the silver spoon out of his mouth and how he's been filling it with groceries ever since."

Dr. Gruel's lips seemed to get extra blubbery. I wondered if the Eve I was dreaming knew Dr. Groth was a gangster with a degree from Wickedpedia?

"Long time damaged psyche," Eve went on. "Took this long for it to manifest into what's sitting right here?"

She nodded in my direction.

I noticed that my hand puppets Madame Uberalles and

Mr. Spinalzo, were unusually silent but they had sneaky looks on their faces. They often lectured in my lucid dreams. Madame Uberalles would demand that the prisoners line up and leave their eyeglasses and teeth on a table and Mr. Spinalzo would explain why he was wearing my mother's underwear, as if my mother cared. Why would she care about that when she didn't care about me was my thought.

That absence of blather from both puppets now aroused my suspicions. I wondered what they had told the doctor?

"Could be a slow incubation," he told all of us and Mr. Spinalzo said he agreed.

"Naw," Eve said, waving that off. "You incubate into something. No metamorphosis here."

"Perhaps you can tell me, to your knowledge if anything recent occurred in Mr. Brady's life that was upsetting, perhaps traumatic?"

I was going down a huge list when Eve, who had a voice, piped up.

"Well, I don't know about Mr. Brady's life, but Dirk here killed one of his tramp girlfriends and let his twin brother take the rap."

"Ah!" Dr. Grape exclaimed, eyes wide. "What kind of gun did he use?"

Grape? I had been told by my Google shrink that the first thing that goes are proper nouns. Followed by the knees.

"A twin you say?"

"The better half of the egg," Eve told him.

Dr. Grind levered himself up from his desk.

"Is that opinion shared by the patient?" he asked.

She gave me a quick once over.

"Yeah, he thinks he's a shit sandwich but he's too much of a narcissist to care."

"That's a contradictory diagnosis, Ms. Solly, if I may say so."

"Well, I'm just storytelling, Doctor. And I'm not real. Then again, you're a phony doctor so who gives a fart what either one of us says in a dream someone in a vegetative state is having? He dreams like a narcissist. We really want to be here?"

We made our exit then. I mean the word exit flashed in my dream. I stayed in the bed and Eve vaporized.

But I think Eve and me had one time been real. And now maybe neither of us was. Then again, I knew she was alive. It was a matter of getting to her. I need to rush to her house and warn her. About everything.

CHAPTER THIRTY-ONE

"LORD BYRON AND THE DOG"

I hadn't heard any shots and there weren't any cop cars in front of Eve's house.

Somehow, I realized I was trying to get to Eve's house. I had stopped at a bar. *Lord Byron's Gin Pub.* They served everything but gin and the barmaid thought Lord Byron was the owner of the place, but she had never met him.

Now I was at Eve's front door.

It was our secret knock. Morse code. My name: -... .-. .- -.-. Dash three dots dot dash two dots dash dash. Dash.

It was kind of silly as Eve already had a video camera and could watch any one at her front door on her monitor in the kitchen.

I stood there long enough for me to do some imagining.

It had taken me longer to get to her place than I figured.

So, The Mob could have already shown up, did some black ops entry bullshit and wrapped a wire around Eve's neck and dropped her like a small sack of potatoes. The Russians could have disconnected her video surveillance, gone in a window, climbed up the chimney and entered from the roof or from a second story window. Rechert could have shot a high wire from the next building and then skimmed across like he did in the jungles of Iraq. Wherever they broke in, she would be waiting, looking, ready. Of course, he would be someplace else, and she'd be a goner.

As it was, I had lost so much time on the way to her place arguing with the barmaid about Lord Byron that whoever blew up *The Sea Bird* could have already gotten to Eve's house. For all I knew, The

Launderers from The Foundation might be inside right now, Eve tied to a chair and gagged with a newly laundered shirt. They would be waiting for me to show up so they could force me to sign a confession that I had killed Billy Hashfries. Then I would inherit gazillions in the laundry business.

I stood there at the door long enough to realize that either Eve wasn't home or her video feed wasn't working or some part of what I was imagining was true.

I slowly lowered myself to the top step and sat down.

The Glock 19 couched in my back like I had seen a private eye on TV wear it, dug fiercely into me and I reached back and jostled it into a better place.

It was twilight now. Quiet. Very little traffic. If there had been shots fired or would be shots fired, there was a chance they would go unnoticed. That made me think that maybe everything had already happened. I mean let's say whoever killed Theo in Rikers had shown up first, not found me there. He'd try to slap Eve around and she'd pull out that .38 Special faster than Hickok could pull out his Navy Colts and she'd drill him. Then she'd drag his body into the bathtub, cursing me all the way, and wait for me to show up.

No, I showed up. I was here. That couldn't be it. What she would have done was shoot the guy and then get the hell out of there, go back to *The New Pompey*, tell Gee and he'd arrange for some of The Perpetual Help seated at the bar to go back to Eve's house and dispose of the body. I was sure they knew exactly how to do that. You can't tell me that the body disposal business was new to that place. I had heard that anyone who disappeared had probably been incinerated at Dino Kim's funeral home.

I had been in *The Pompey* once when a couple of real shadies had come in, made some fuss and then Sal had told them they shouldn't expect to get out of there alive but they could if they just shut up, paid up, apologized for being dicks and walked out. I had seen that happen. It was a rough place. They served gin and they knew who Lord Byron was. You couldn't gentrify a place like that. You'd have to bring in the Great Exterminator and the Great Communicator, strong, presidential agents of change.

Okay, so, I been sitting here now a long time. No one has shown up to get rid of the body. Sal had told me that the Underclass is good at getting rid of bodies. To which Eve said, that the thing about a permanent Underclass was this: the only thing permanent with them was never knowing they were already dead. Hence, she said, their bodies were disposed of at birth.

Of course, it could be that The Mob showed up, one of the two that Eve had pointed out, showed up, got angry, disappointed and then, being a seasoned Mob, had probably won that gunfight with Eve Solly. Could be there hadn't even been a gunfight. She might not have seen it coming, just like I hadn't seen the bomb as I was jacking up my fly in the men's room at *The Seabird.*

Rechert would have said something like "You little bitch, where's that jerk? Where are the papers he was supposed to sign?" I began to sweat thinking of Eve lying inside that house, maybe bleeding out. That wonderful, beautiful goddess of a woman, Eve Solly, could now be lying in there bleeding out or already dead. If I wasn't sure that a Special Forces Seal was in there waiting in the walls to ring a wire around my neck and squeeze the life out of me, I would have stood up and rescued Eve.

You know the idea that she needed to be rescued made me laugh. Not Eve. That was impossible. What happened most probably was that she was in there, drink in one hand, smoke in the other waiting for me to show up. And on the floor in front of her, probably the parlor, there would be Theo's killers, the Bombers, all the Patriarch's multiple personalities, Junior, all of them, lying dead. All of them dead.

Everybody dead and Eve alive.

You see, just at that moment where Rechert, who shows up first, has realized that he's been played and is about to get rough with Eve, Russians come in and he's surprised. Getting into places where she's not supposed to be, where she doesn't belong, that she has no legitimate claim to is Eve's thing. You can't stop her. Her M.O. Method of operation.

So, she totally surprises all of them. She's got two guns in her hand, .25 caliber silver handle and her .38 Special. She points both guns at him. He laughs. She looks deadly, beautiful but deadly. She's the real fatal part of femme fatale. Everybody's got some bullet proof underwear on and all like that so they all know slugs won't slow them down. Somebody could flip a knife into her, pull his own 9mm Browning Hi-Power and shoot her, do a double flip Bruce Lee kind of deal and crisscross her head with his legs. He could do a lot.

But before he does anything, The Lawyer, Sulmondson, that sneaky, slippery son of a bitch, comes up from behind ... comes out of a wall Ninja like and digs an evil looking knife into somebody's back. But that guy is armored, all muscle in places where I've got love handles so he manages to turn and give one brutal, fatal hand chop to his attacker's neck, turn again, with the 9 milli in hand and trade shots with him. They both drop. Right in front of Rechert, who's crumbled on the carpet with a broken neck.

And Eve Solly has been the spectator of it all. Front row seats.

That required … I mean that scene required a lot of gunshots.

I looked up and down the street. I saw a guy in the distance walking a tiny dog. Dog stopped and relieved himself. Guy leans over with some kind of poop shovel in one hand and his cell phone and a baggie in the other. He's talking on his cell and at the same time wrestling the poop into the baggie. He drops the phone. And the leash. The designer dog runs into the street. He yells. Into his phone.

That's a kind of slice of the everyday that makes you want to go back to dreaming. So, when I look down the street now, I see it's Lord Byron with a bottle of gin and he's just watching the dog running around a corner and it's okay.

It's getting hard to make out anything now, just the time of day in early Fall where twilight seems to come on quick and go just as quick, where you can't tell night from day, life from death, a dog from a wolf.

At some point, I stopped thinking about what was going on wherever I was and fell asleep. I was in a repeat cycle and then I fell asleep, a sleep like death where if you dream, you don't know it.

I knew Eve was safe. I would get a call. She would wake me. She would make me move.

***

CHAPTER THIRTY-TWO

"ENLIGHTENED"

To: Sulmondson

"The patent ownership by a living member of a family owned enterprise pre-dating all prior arrangements of inheritance establishes legal precedent of ownership. That's the legal reality. The Board doesn't care if your tenure here is vacated. What we care about is whether the Farnsworth Foundation continues to be a reliable asset to the Conglomerate."

"I flew from Doha. And thirteen is an unlucky number. And tomorrow is the 13th. See you then.'

Jeez

"What does this sound like to you, Rechert?"

"Sounds like Jeez is going to kill you tomorrow."

"Who the hell does Jeez think he is? I'm tired of hearing about him."

"Don't worry. He's just somebody who dies tomorrow."

...

"I think I've found my sweetheart, Moran."

"A real one, Nicholas?"

"Beyond real. Her name is Eloise. She works at The Foundation. Or she did. She thinks I am perfect Foundational material."

"That's perfection for you."

"I'll bring her around to *The New Pompey* so you can meet her."

"Fair enough but I'm avoiding that place. Sore losers, a bar tab, and it turns out that woman I married? Susie Q? She's got a husband and he's looking for me. There's also another guy looking for me trying to stop me from helping our friend Bratter out."

"I heard our friend Dirk got out of the Sanitarium. I heard the police raided the place and when they got there our friend was gone. He just walked out."

"I was all set up to get him out but the night I showed up shots were fired, and I thought it best to retreat."

"I'm going to take Eloise with me."

"Fair enough. Where are you going? Isn't there a warrant out for your arrest for emptying out the Farnsworth place?"

"Eloise knows all about that. She doesn't see it as a problem. She calls herself an enlightened materialist."

"Fair enough. What kinds of materialism did you take from that place?"

"Well, it was several loads, mind you. They included oak flooring, fireplace stones and marble, crown molding, banisters, paintings, sculptures, drapes, copper pipes, sideboards, chiffoniers, commodes, escritoires, lockers, davenports, safes, tombs, bunkers, seed vaults, vases, all hardware, chandeliers, tapestries, bed frames, cupboards, shelves, kitchen and dining room tables, automatons, spinning wheels, antiques, books, utensils, crockpots, tajines, toasters, microwaves, flat screens, laptops, bar and bar stools, jams, whiskies, sourdough starter and bidets."

"Fair enough. I see enlightened self-interest in that load. I gotta tell you that some people think I'm trying to muscle in on their money laundering operation which is not my intent. We just want a foot in at any level. We want to dip a beak into the waters."

"We do?"

"The patent stirred the pot. Of course, we could stay outside and just get paid for doing that."

"Patent for what?"

"Mystery patent."

"I wouldn't want to get Eloise mixed up in something like a mystery patent."

"Fair enough. But the thing is they might find you before they find me and want you to flip on me. If you don't, they'll probably shoot you after they Patriot Act you."

"Maybe you should disassociate yourself from that patent."

"I could of course but I'm in there for our friend, you know. I couldn't leave him hanging out there by himself."

"I went to see him once at Sanitarium. I don't think there's any life left out to hang. Perhaps, they've already found him. And he's permanently gone. He can't own the patent if he's dead."

"I think he's around and they're looking for him. For us and him."

"And Eloise."

"You know, Nicky, I kind of wish you hadn't met your sweetheart at this very moment. I mean you've been looking for her as long as I know you. Any time in the last twenty years would have been problem free. I mean especially since you didn't have definite specs on her."

"What are saying, Dennis?"

"I'm saying now is a fucked time for hooking up with your sweetheart. Right now, I got more sweethearts than I can handle and none of them is around in the morning. Makes life simpler. Yours is a good approach too. As long as you don't actually find her."

"My sweetheart is not like that and you know it. Where are you getting all your good time money, Dennis?"

"I told you. The Foundation's attorney. Sulmondson. I showed him the patent papers and he got jumpy like an electrified frog."

"How much?"

"As you know, it's my practice to start out expansively and then by force baby step backward, like I was going under ether. But here he okays the first number. I'm all Eureka! But I'm not showing it."

"How much?"

"If I give you half, can we get together on this in the old manner and see where the hurt might be coming from?"

"Of course, I'll have to do it for my sweetheart. I need to protect her. Where do we start?"

"Usual. You inside. I'll take the front and the back. Carrying?"

"I've got my old Makarov PM, the Ceska brojovka CZ 75 you gave me last year, the M9 Beretta that's always with me, of course the Glock 19, and the Sig Sauer P226 also the Rattler for long range."

"Compelling enlightenment, Nicholas."

"Yes."

"And my friend? I'm really happy you finally found her."

"Thank you, Dennis."

...

"Keep both hands on the bar, Jeez, and I'll do the same."

"Agreed."

"I don't see how this is neutral ground, Rechert. Doesn't Mr. Gee own this museum?"

"So, why did you come, Jeez, if you knew all that?"

"I figure I can convince you to walk off before you do whatever you plan on doing to me if I showed up here."

"Sal, set us up here. What are you drinking?"

"Anchor beer."

"We ain't got it."

"Fuck, I hate Brooklyn. Give me a shot of any rye and a beer don't taste like grapefruit juice."

"Same for me Sal. Shoot. By which I mean talk."

"Your lawyer is out of the game, Mr. Rechert, so you'll be out of a job."

"Jeez…I hope you don't mind me using your name as an expletive?"

"Go right ahead. I stole the name."

"Here's the view from my side of things, Jeez. Sulmondson is right now not out of the game, if you mean the game of life? And if I let you take him out of that game, then I suck as a bodyguard and it'll be hard for me to get another job as a bodyguard."

"Roger that. Hey, bartender, I said any rye. I didn't say dishwater in a rye bottle.",

"Oh, sorry. I thought I could get that passed you.

"Give me a shot of Wild Turkey and shut up, thanks."

"I'm Delta. Was and forever. You know what that means, Jeez?"

"Jeez! No kidding. I thought you guys were a myth told by hashbins who kiss the asses of crooked shysters."

"You offering me some disappear money, because it don't sound like it. It sounds like you plan on shooting me right here."

"Right in front of Sal? Sal would you allow that?"

"I'll allow that seeing it's this particular guy."

"We'll give you 25K for disposal of Moran."

"I can't let anything happen to Sulmondson. It's a reputation thing with me. The guy's a dick but I'm under contract. I break a contract, nobody will touch me."

"Then we're at a stalemate, Rechert, because Sulmondson is buried meat. I just hate Brooklyn. Nothing is easy here. Speaking of easy, why did you kill that kid?"

"I didn't. The Russians did."

"Listen. What if we make it look like the Russkies killed Sulmondson and you were shot trying to save him, but you lived?"

"Naw. That sounds like a lot of trouble for you and a lot of pain for me."

"Don't concern yourself with that. I'm paid to handle trouble. And consider this: a through and through bullet to a nice locale is better than a bullet to the head."

"We get down to it."

"I guess so."

"Hey, Gee! These guys are about to shoot it out."

"Oh, no they're not. Take it the fuck out of here, boys. Shoot yourselves a couple three blocks away from here."

"Not so good, Gee. Jeez here has some people waiting for me right outside the door."

"Like you don't have your people waiting for me right outside the door?"

"Tell you what, boys. I'd better settle this. Sal? See the sawed off in Sal's hands? Now both of you go out the door together like good little boys. Share the bullets."

"There will a lot of fireworks, old man. Cops will close this mausoleum down."

"I'll take 50K but I'm not going for Moran. I heard about that guy."

"Deal. I was hoping you would leave him to me. I heard about him too."

"Okay, kiss and make up and get the fuck out."

"I hate Brooklyn and I hate this place. The drinks suck."

"Tell him to go fuck himself, Sal."

"Gee says … "

CHAPTER THIRTY-THREE

"THE SWEETHEART"

"I'm glad you called, Nicky. So, you remembered me? We did the third grade together. It was so strange running into you at The Foundation after all these years. You haven't changed a bit. You knew I worked there? At the Foundation?"

"You appeared like a vision to me back then. I thank you for meeting me here in this lowly place. But, you see, I have friends here and I feel safe."

"Not at all. I've always wanted to see this part of Brooklyn. I read a novel about New Utrecht Avenue once. *If You're Ready, Then Run.* Or maybe it was *If You're Here, Then Run.* Such interesting characters. But you don't feel safe elsewhere?"

"Your usual, Nick? And for the lovely lady?"

"She walks in beauty, Sal, and like the night of cloudless climes and starry skies and all that's best of dark and bright meet in her aspect and her eyes."

"You've got words from the honeypot, Nick. I think you and Moran could talk your way into Heaven. Or out of Hell, as needed."

"A bottle of white wine, Sal. If it's not the best, it won't be the worst."

"Coming up. There were some guys looking for you and Moran the other day. Okay. It's like magic. They just walked in. Mister Jeez. I remembered that. Anyway, they parked outside. They're still there, I think."

"Right off, I'd say this doesn't look good, Sal.

I think it's dangerous for us to be here right now, Eloise. Is there a back exit, Sal?"

"Through the restaurant then through the kitchen."

"Go along with Sal, will you, Eloise?"

"No. We'll both be safe together."

"This may get ugly, my sweetheart."

"I don't think there's any ugliness in the world now."

...

"Mind if I'm join you two? We've got mutual friends."

"Don't sit down, Jeez. The young lady and I are having a private conversation."

"I'm going to sit down. If you want to fire off that gun you're holding under the table, go right ahead. Eloise here might get caught in a crossfire though."

"Nicholas does not have a gun pointing at you, Mr. Jeez. He's a strong supporter of gun control."

"I am?"

"Pardon me, people, but Susie Q's husband, Big Willie, and a posse just came in looking for Moran."

"Bring me a Jamison, waiter. Neat. Is that bunch of recruits coming over to us the posse? Know them, Williams? No? Then where's Moran? I'm not going to all the trouble of getting over to that boat he's on."

"He's always on *The Sweet Cheeks*."

"That is such a sexist name for a boat, Nicholas."

"I did prefer the original name. *My Hottie Sweetheart*."

"Is that the way you think of your sweetheart? As a hottie? Is that the way you think of me?"

"Pardon the eruption, but where's Moran, Williams?"

"He says he's on his boat. *The Sweet Cheeks*, formerly *My Hottie Sweetheart*, which this young lady correctly objects to. Now get lost, Wee Willie."

"Who the fuck are you, Mister Suit?"

"Mind your language in front of my sweetheart, Wee Willie."

"Big Willie, not Wee Willie."

"Get away from this table, Big Wee, or he'll shoot you in the foot but I'll shoot you in the head. You've heard the name Jeez? That's me."

"Shut up, Suit. This is none of your business."

"My boyfriend, whom I just discovered believes approaching

women by grabbing them in the pussy is a wonderful thing to do ..."

"I don't. Moran does. Gentleman, Mr. Suit, Mr. Willie and friends, I must tell you that I draw near to the end of all my desire in this woman."

"Shut up and take us out to that boat Moran is on."

"Pray do, Nick. Take us all. Me and these jerks."

"I told you to shut up and get out of here, Suit."

"But Wee Willie, a couple of associates of mine with their hands in their pockets don't want me to shut up or get out. They want you idiots to do that. And they're right behind you. In their pockets are guns."

"Don't you want to get the guns out of the hands of people like this, Nicholas, or, do you think if we all had guns and we all shot each other all the time, the world would be a better place."

"Oh, Eloise, guns don't matter. Any moment might be our last. Everything is more beautiful because we're doomed. You will never be lovelier than you are now. We will never be here again."

"If you mean you and me, you're right."

"It's horseshit is what he's saying. When I find Moran, I'm gonna make him eat this marked deck. And cripple him for messing with my wife."

"This is getting boring. Get up, Eloise. You're coming with us. If you want her back, Williams, you and Moran come to this address. We shall conduct our business on land. My associates will escort you to our car, Eloise."

"Get your hands off me! Shoot me! Go ahead and shoot everybody here! It's what he wants."

"You know, Jesus in a Suit, we don't think this lady wants to go with you and these other suits."

"Unlike your wife, who went along easily enough with Moran."

"She did, didn't she? The bitch. I'm gonna kill her if I find her."

"Gentlemen, this has been entertaining but we have to depart. I promise you that we'll take Mr. Moran out of your hair. I can't promise to return your wife, though."

"Naw, this young lady stays here. It don't seem like you guys have the proper respect for where you are right now."

"You mean this place? Jeez, it's long past burial, isn't it?"

"I like it, Mr. Jeez."

"Ah, my associate, Mr. Lupinek, likes it. What is there to like, Mr. Lupinek?"

"You don't have to ask for the toilet as because the whole place is a toilet."

"You'll have to forgive Mr. Lupinek his use of the American language. He's a traveler from Romania. As is his associate, Mr. Bogus."

"Not really. I was born a couple of blocks from here."

"It doesn't matter, Bogus. Escort the lady to the car."

"Hey, Evelyn, you wanna go with these guys?"

"No, I most certainly don't. And my name is Eloise."

"Okay, you clowns step back. Eloise, you come along nicely or … see this gun? I'm going to do what you say and fire some bullets. Right into your Nicky boy. Want me to do that?"

"Say something, Nicholas!"

"Moran is outside."

"What?"

"You won't need my sweetheart. She and I have much to talk about."

"Susie Q's husband. Why don't you and your buddies go see if Moran is outside."

"Fuck yeah we will."

...

"Nothing. I don't hear nothing."

"Anything, Mr. Lupinek. You don't hear anything."

"That's what I said. I think they went home."

"Another round?"

"Excuse me, Eloise. I need to sit and ponder. No gun shots. No sounds at all."

"He wasn't outside."

"Maybe he was and the posse is chasing him. Maybe they did away with him silently. Maybe he did the same. You know what the universe was before The Big Bang, Mr. Lupinek?"

"Alive?"

"Silent. It was silent. That's the original condition of the planet. We shall all return to it."

"There was five of them, Mr. Jeez. All big guys. They would have made big like noise."

"My observation also, Mr. Bogus. Except in proper English. If he wasn't out there, that posse would be back in here once again protecting Eloise from abduction. Wee Willie had the air of a female rescuer."

"You know what I think, Mr. Jeez. They go to work. Lunch hour over."

"Don't force me to say jeez in response to your stupidity, Mr. Lupinek. I don't think they looked like they were conscientious employees. Let's go out the back. Eloise, you are with us."

"Are you going to sit there and let them take me, Nicholas?"

"Moran is out back."

"What the fuck?"

"You are beginning to frazzle my patience, Williams. He is out front and out back? Does he defy laws of physics?"

"No, he's an atheist. Nihilist atheist. Moran walks passed prohibitive signage. The Bible and so forth."

"You can't be serious, Nicholas? What bond of friendship could you have with such a man? I mean these suits are threatening my life, your sweetheart's life, and you could stop all that by just taking them to that awful boat."

"I told them. He's out back."

"And out front?"

"That too."

"How can I be your sweetheart as you say I am if you don't believe in God."

"Actually, I don't believe in anything. The world is everything that is the case. And celestial entities are not the case. Any case."

"Jeez..."

"Yes?"

"Nicholas, tell me truthfully. You don't believe in God, but you believe in guns. You have a gun pointed at Mr. Jeez at this very moment."

"Actually, I have two guns pointed. And another two on my person."

"Mr. Lupinski. Go check the rear exit."

"Should I go out and be shooting?"

"Your choice entirely. But don't do it in the subjunctive."

■■■

"Nothing. Not a sound. I guess Mr. Lupinski didn't go out shooting, or be shooting as he expressed it."

"Or get shot."

"Yeah, but if he went out, he would go shooting. That's what the Lupinski does. But could be maybe I think, Boss, he's eating a sandwich back there. We missed to eat the lunch."

"They finished lunch. You missed lunch. Mr. Bogus. Get over it. Lunch is to you what a nail is to a hammer."

"Veal Cacciatore. Gino makes it every Wednesday."

"Thank you, waiter. We'll pass. Is Moran really on that boat, Williams? So much depends on your answer."

"Moran is in the dining room. Eating."

"I suppose he's not a vegan, your friend the nihilist, is he, Nicholas? And how could I be your sweetheart? Nihilists don't have sweethearts."

"Moran is an opportunivore, my dear. Vegan and meat. I believe in nothing but you, my sweetheart."

"You think Lupinski is back there eating the sandwich, Mr. Jeez?"

"No, I don't, Mr. Bogus, because that is too absurd for anyone of any intelligence to conjecture. Nevertheless, Mr. Bogus, go back there and see what's what. Report to me without delay."

"Should I go out the back door if nobody is in the restaurant?"

"Yes, but go out shooting a lot of bullets as loudly as you can."

"That's what I'm usually do. I use my Mach-10 machine pistol."

"Whatever. As long as you make a lot of noise. What I don't want to hear in the next five minutes is silence. Understand?"

"The original fate of the universe. I understand, Mr. Jeez."

∎∎∎

"I thought I heard something."

"Sal broke a glass, I think. Would you mind if my sweetheart and I discussed some matters?"

"I don't think there's anything to discuss, Nicholas. You're not the man I thought you were."

"We met only once before, dear, and that was in the third grade. I was a different man then. I once dabbled as a vegan. And I also could never quite believe in nothing though I can't say what I found to believe in besides you."

"Well, I don't think I could possibly be the sweetheart you're looking for. You obviously require an atheistic, nihilistic lifetime member of the National Rifle Association who answers to the name *Sweet Cheeks* and can't stop killing animals and eating them."

"Nihilists don't join. Not even nihilism. I hope that makes sense."

"Nothing about you makes sense, Nicholas.. Mr. Jeez, can I leave? I don't think using me as leverage with Mr. Williams is a workable plan any longer."

"You're right. But before you go, I'm curious. Nicky, tell me, how do you stand on legalizing pot for plain old enjoyment?"

"Be happy for this moment. For this moment is your life. Omar Khayyam. Righteous weed is a path."

"So, that's a yes. Eloise?"

"You are also a drug addict hedonist, Nicholas?"

"That's Moran. It takes more to make me happy. And less. I am slave to a Springtime passion for the earth. To everything, there is a season of parrots. Instead of feathers, we searched the sky for meteors on our last night. I quote Mr. Frost and Aimee's `Summer Haibun.'"

"Goodbye, Nicholas Williams. Somehow I know that you know that you need help."

"Goodbye, my Sweetheart."

■■■

"I've lost Mr. Lupinek and Mr. Bogus and you've lost your sweetheart. Not our day, I think, Williams."

"You haven't lost Moran. He's about to come through a door."

Part Four

CHAPTER THIRTY-FOUR

"NON SERVIAM"

"I don't like hospitals," I said in a low voice. "The smell of Tea Tree oil, whiskey, burnt toast and fumigant, the disinfectant flowing, the moans and joans, the screams the nurses make, the bodies being shoved in bags, the loose joints, knuckles and nodes, the gun shots at all hours of the day and night.

And the numerical examination. Where are you from one to ten? I have never known that. I know I'm not a ten. Zero is when you're dead. Right? How are you? Should I say "Fine" or "5'?

"Yeah, but at the same time, a lot of people were looking for you," Sal said. "We heard you were fighting for your life. We didn't know where they had you."

"He's a veteran of foreign wars," Moran said, dreaming over his Negroni. "The three of us served brilliantly in the Stockade for many months. Falsely accused of *non serviam*.""

"They had Nicky here under observation. Treated him like a weaponized device. His brain I mean. You know, those ass gowns would harsh the mellow off anybody's brain."

"I am celestially and eternally devoted to my sweetheart, Dennis. But she left me. I didn't pass the questionnaire. I am no more than meat with a gun and no god."

"Fair enough but she looked hot," Moran said. "I saw her exiting as I came in. She was like an unfolded rhomboid."

"She's celestial, not infernal," Williams replied, calmly, dryly. "I remain devoted to my sweetheart. Supernal beauty and innocence."

"I think I'm passed my dancing days," Moran said, sadly. "My sweethearts wore me out. I wish I could find one cheap sweetheart like you, Nicky."

...

On this occasion, I had walked into the Pompey to a lot of cheers.

"He was down, friends," Moran shouted, "but he's inherited the entire Fatsworth gazillions so up time is coming!"

"That's what is going to get me killed," I moaned to myself.

"We will not let that happen," Williams said, greeting me and putting a hand on my shoulder.

It was then that I saw myself in the bar mirror. It wasn't me. It was Theo. Tall, slim waisted, muscular, cleanly groomed Theo. More flaccid than muscular probably. I had meta something into the better half of the egg.

About one hundred and sixteen hours later, Sal was announcing last call.

I opened my eyes. I saw Williams sitting across from me. He was staring at me. Sal came over to the booth.

"You passed out," he told me. "You were hitting the vodka hard." He looked at Williams.

"Still, about half of what this gentleman drank. And I think he's cold sober. He was drinking to the memory of his sweetheart. He found her and lost her that quick. Eloise. A kind of square name. I guess it had its moment in Oshkosh. Utrecht is hot now. A name, a place, a fantasy, a drink. Kill me if I don't name my daughter Utrecht."

"I thought you had been spayed, Sal?"

"We should depart," Williams said, standing up.

I looked up at him. Sober as a judge and looking as calm and unruffled as ever. Damn, Nicholas Sweetheart was elegant. I kind of concluded that a mind focused on an impossible dream, like Don Quickette, did good things to you. Eve thought Williams had the elegance of Dracula and that he had probably been sucking the blood out of sweethearts since Jesus.

"I should be back at the boat. Eve told me to wait there. I didn't. Sailor and I came ashore as the sea wonderers say."

"Eve. Damn. I didn't think you could kill that lady with a bomb," Sal said, shaking in his head.

"What boat are you talking about, Dirk? And who's Sailor?"

"I don't know. He came with the boat. Who is he, Sal?"

"He's Tommy Lemon's first cousin. He was in the Sands. He's watching that boat for Angelo Bari till Angelo comes back from where I don't know. They say he's on the continuum but where nobody knows. Sailor, that is. Not Angelo, though he's a strange dude too."

"We're on that boat until Eve finds out who's trying to kill us."

"That's very good. Moran is working on a détente package in lieu of you and me and Moran being killed."

"Where is Moran? I got to get back to the boat. Safe there. Do you think Moran would be at home on a boat?"

"Moran is at home anyplace. He'll be at home on your boat."

I gave Sal a quizzical look.

"The Moran left with one of his sweethearts," Sal said.

"Sex is often an emergency situation for him," Williams told us. "He doesn't spend a long time searching for true love."

Sal scratched his head. He looked tired. He had had a busy, unexpected kind of day from what I had heard.

"Sailor rows me out to the boat. I gotta go. Eve is waiting for me."

"Of course, she is, Dirk. Never alone. Never forgotten. Moran and I will catch up. We'll swim out to the boat."

"A man in a fine suit who called himself Mr. Jeez said he was going to swim out to the boat to see Moran."

"He's a very persistent man, is Mr. Jeez," Williams said.

CHAPTER THIRTY-FIVE

"SAILOR"

Sailor liked to row so I let him do it.

Besides, I rowed right side dominant so we would just circle endlessly out in Jamaica Bay.

Sailor, fought in what he called The Sands, which I figured was Afghanistan or Iraq or Syria or Somalia, but was, he told me, born on salt water. He learned to swim in Coney Island when he was two. Both his mother and his father had tried to drown him, but I doubted that. Theo had been a good friend of Sailor's. He said he enjoyed the company of the autistic who could do phenomenal things like lift cars and count sand grains.

It was a pitch-black night, lots of stars but no LED power down here on the water where Sailor was rowing. I couldn't see *The Sweet Cheeks.* I couldn't see my hand in front of my face. I saw Sailor as a shadowy hulk sitting in front of me, working those oars. And talking. He liked to talk about this voyage he was going to take after he found a treasure of gold dust at the bottom of Peconic Bay or something like that.

He had a gravelly voice, like that of Senator Sherwood Bronze. Listening to him was relaxing me.

"I plan to sail through the water gap into Chesapeake Bay and then into the Atlantic, up to the *la Voie Maritime du Saint-Laurent* access, into the Great Lakes waterway on to the Illinois waterway and then the Mississippi River system straight down to the Gulf. Navigable channels with some off locks bypassing rapids and dams. From the gulf through the Panama Canal and then sail straight across the Equator."

I nodded. I didn't follow the trip but it relaxed me.

...

There was a stern ladder to climb up into the boat and Sailor went up first and then leaned over and helped me up. He humped me up on deck like a heavy bag of cargo.

When I stood up, I saw a shadowed figure behind Sailor. I saw a gun in his hand. I just pointed and Sailor turned.

"K6S. No ordinary gun," Sailor said.

"You know your guns, my friend. Where's Moran?"

"He doesn't own this boat, is what it is," Sailor replied. "You shouldn't be on this boat."

"Remember the gun. You Bratter? Or maybe this guy is Bratter. You both fit the description. Big and stupid looking."

"The thing is you should not be on this boat without I say you have permission to board."

"Jeez, I didn't know that was the thing. I thought the thing was I shoot you both in the head and throw you overboard."

"Moran is out front," I said.

"What? Not that again."

"What it is he means the bow," Sailor explained.

I don't know why I said what I said but one-time Williams told me that if I ever get in a tight spot just say `Moran is out front.' I don't know how that was supposed to help but I said it anyway.

It kind of worked because the guy with the gun twisted around halfway and looked behind him, keeping the gun pointed at me and Sailor. I noticed that Sailor had taken some steps toward the guy. There's all kinds of craziness in this world is what I've come to believe.

"Step back, Captain," the guy ordered, and Sailor just froze.

"Moran is in the back," I said, again not knowing what the hell I was saying.

"He means the stern is what it is," Sailor explained and at the same time he lunged at the guy, the gun went off, but Sailor didn't seem affected.

I watched as he picked the guy up, held him over his head, the guy screaming "Jeez!" and then Sailor threw him over the side.

I looked over into the water, but I couldn't see anything. I did hear some thrashing and screaming. He kept yelling "Jeeze!" and then it was just silence.

"You think sharks got him?" I asked Sailor who was standing by me.

"No sharks in Jamaica Bay," Sailor told me. "I think he shot me. .45 slug. The thing is they're big slugs."

Then he dropped to his knees. I pulled my flip phone out of my pocket and dialed 9.1.1."

"999. Coast Guard," Sailor mumbled. "Let me talk to them."

...

Moran and Williams rowed to the ship before the Coast Guard. I told them what had happened. Sailor had a tree age kit and I had done what he told me with the wound.

"Whoever it was, is out there drowning," I told them.

"Yeah, we ran into him," Moran said. "Nicky hit him with an oar. He went down for good."

"You mean you killed him?"

"Fair enough," Moran said.

"He came here to kill all of us," Williams told me.

"Yeah, he's the guy the mob sent. Mr. Jeez."

"He did keep yelling that," I said.

"Same with us. That's how we identified him."

"He killed Rechert. Sulmondson's guy," Moran said.

"How do you know that?"

"He wouldn't be here if Rechert was alive. I would have like to have seen how that all played out."

CHAPTER THIRTY-SIX

"BETTER THE LONE WOLF"

"All you need to do is show up at this hearing, answer some of the judge's questions, then we petition for a vacating of the POA Sulmondson is holding, and then it's all yours. We move into the chateau. It's getting a little cramped on this boat. You give up the patent and they'll get out of the way of you inheriting. That's the deal. You don't get everything. You get something. The You Get It All app hasn't come out yet."

Moran smiled and spread both hands out. He was happy with his own words.

"That include him going up for killing Billy Hashfries?" Eve asked, stretched out on the deck sunning herself.

I attributed the fact that no one seemed to see or hear Eve to a repercussion of my own recent brain injury.

I restrained from referring to her because I didn't want to wind up back at The Sanitarium cared for by a faux doctor and a faux nurse. I could have thought she wasn't there, but she was too there to believe that. I believe what I see. And I saw Eve. P.T. once told us that you can never know what others see. That's why he used a microscope.

Anyway, Eve didn't like the deal Moran had made. She didn't think we could stop worrying about guys like Mr. Jeez coming after us. I don't know why Eve said that because she knew Mr. Jeez was dead. Drowned. Then again, she knew a lot more about how dead people behaved than I did.

I didn't care about getting control of The Foundation, the

Fartsworth Estate, the patent P.T. Bratter had left me, a swimming pool and a tennis court. Never my interest. I'm like one of those rare things: an interest free entity.

I did care about going on trial for a murder I didn't commit. But then again, maybe it was my destiny to go to jail, Rikers, get stabbed and die. Kind of make up for Theo's death. I also thought Eve was right in believing Moran had gotten more out of the deal with gangsters in the streets and in the corporate suites than he was letting on. He was an eat the whole birthday cake guy and it wasn't his birthday. Eve was smart and more, two tears in a bucket and fuck it enough to put up with the messes made by intelligently designed puppets and parrots and the people they associated with. Me.

I was, as always, with her. Besides, if I didn't side with her, she'd probably post herself in a gonad torque spot and run a new kind of hell up and down my spine.

Still, it was Moran that took to prepping me for my competency hearing.

"Now I'm going to tell you that what appears to you as true," Moran said, putting on some foreign accent I don't know why.

I was lying on my berth sewing a hole in Madame Uberalles' outfit and he was swinging from his hammock. Williams had been right. Moran would make anyplace home.

"What appears to you as true is not true at all. Your twin, What's was his name. Rio?"

"Theo."

"Fair enough. He was always half dead. Not good genes or bad genes but only strong and weak genes. Your brother was a trusting, obedient, passionless dog. Who else would go all the way to Paris to work in a laundromat?"

"A life of total prudence is no life," Williams interjected from his hammock where he was tossing Mr. Spinalzo from hand to hand. Mr. Spinalzo seemed to be enjoying it.

"You, on the other hand," Moran went on, "eat up the whole world. Like a wolf. Wolves don't punish themselves because they don't heel and sit and obey like dogs. The dog can't vanquish the wolf. Only the wolf can do that to himself."

I remembered Williams telling me that Moran was more a wolf among men than a man. So, he's talking about himself, not me. I kept on listening because I didn't want to antagonize a wolf. I also got the impression that the parrot and most likely one or two of the hand puppets had told Moran a great deal about Theo.

"If your twin was the good half and you're the bad half and the good half is killed because of something bad you did, then guilt builds up in you until you can't move. The guilt subsides. You know why you suddenly jumped up and scrammed out of that Sanitarium? You know why you can move and speak now? Because you reconnected with the wolf."

"Better the lone wolf than the cringing dog, in the words of Orwell," Williams added."

Then Moran jumped up and screamed,

"You're the wolf! So, howl like a wolf."

He started to howl and kept it up until Eve shot down into the cabin.

"What the hell is going on?"

"Moran says I'm a wolf."

"Oh, jeez," Eve said, totally disgusted, and went back up to the deck.

...

"Eve, you think Moran is right and I won't go to jail and that I'll inherit?"

It was after midnight and we were topside looking at the stars. She was smoking a sweetened cheroot.

"Moran's a guy in front of another guy who's behind another guy ad infinitum. The Buddhist wheel of life it ain't. The Noble eightfold path. It ain't that either. What it is is The Great Chain of Fuck All. A lot of holes in the fabric of anything bringing it all together. You're not listening, are you? You're pulling on your lower lip and your eyes are closing."

"You know when I was in the Sanitarium, I dreamed about you. I thought you were dead, but I still dreamed about you. Why didn't I ever dream of Theo? How come I can't talk to Theo in my dream like I could talk to you? He's my identical twin. I should be able to. We had a private language."

"How many times am I going to tell you that you didn't have a private language? You grunted and farted, and he spoke six languages. Here's the thing. You don't want to ask him why he was laundering money for The Mob. So, you don't dream him, and you don't have to ask him. You don't want to know the answer."

I didn't follow that.

"What was Williams talking about at meal?"

"Transparency," Eve told me. "Who could commune with his sweetheart and who couldn't. Crock of feces, of course.

But he sounds like he's talking from behind a burning bush. You listen closely though, and you know it's words coming from a Black Hole with a mouth."

"Kind of, I guess."

"Do you ever wonder why that shit rock was patented and then passed on to you?"

"You mean the prime ordeal shit stone my father said I came out of or something like that?"

"You might have been pulled out of that shit stone for a reason. Everything began with a lot of such shit stones flying around. A lot of different, very different things got made. Follow?"

"Kind of, I guess."

"Good. That solves your identity problem. What I did find out is that a lot of money has been made over the years on the back of that patent."

"I didn't come out of a shit stone, Eve. I was born like normal like everybody else. Except bigger."

"Look, Mr. Normal, you need a piece. Beretta M9 should do the trick. Big guy like you could conceal two three pieces. I recommend a Smith & Wesson Shield. Two of them. Along with the Berretta M9. Anybody approaches you who you don't know, show the piece. It gets results. Like showing a lady your hardware."

"That's what Sal always says is how he approaches women."

"Don't pay attention to Sal. He treats women like objects. And that's only the ones who will talk to him."

"I think Sal thinks you're like the Queen of the pack."

"Why not? What I am is even obvious to him."

■■■

"What's the good word, parrot?" Moran asked Cag.

"God is under repair. Check back."

"Spot on!" Moran laughed.

Moran grabbed his Bomber jacket and put it on. He reached one hand inside an inner pocket and pulled out a gun like my own."

"I also usually got a Raven Arms P25 MP25, .25 caliber holstered just above my ass crack. I got a Colt Mustang XSP in an ankle carry. I know more about weapons than the SEALs."

"Anybody tries to board this vessel, Bang!"

The parrot put his head under his wing. I think Moran puzzled him, probably not more than Williams did.

"Nicky and meself were equally drawn to the sea. Lie down on land was forced on us. Now it's not as easy to get a ship as it was when my Dag was sailing. It's the long furloughs on land that bring the troubles to me."

Moran could put on a Dublin street accent and throw if off like a sweater.

Even though we were anchored and had no worries regarding a lee shore as Sailor told me, I still felt like I was moving back and forth with waves and tides and whatever. I had been anchored like a rock in my *pied a terre,* even when the West End rattled by.

"Ships made me think," Moran said, dreamily.

"You think people are still looking for me?"

As I said this, I looked around the cabin. Eve had gone ashore again. Ever since she was dead but wasn't and I was brain damaged immobile but wasn't, I didn't like being away from her.

I could hear Williams and Sailor talking on deck. Sailor had been trying to convince us that he knew where gold dust lay at the bottom of the ocean. That vision appealed to Williams, who had been somber since he lost Eloise, his sweetheart. A false one as he admitted to us, tearfully.

"People looking for you?" Moran asked. "You're packing triple heat and you're ready to howl like a wolf. What's the worry? No worries."

I remembered my renewed vigor and plopped down on my berth, pushing a couple of pillows under my head.

"Why did The Mob blow up Pavlovich's club?" I asked Moran.

"Probably a deep fry in the kitchen touched off the gas. The country has been left without enough kitchen inspectors. Half the air in the U.S. is toxic grease and that's a factoid."

"The police found traces of a bomb."

"Fair enough," Moran said, closing his eyes. "A terrorist snuck into the place with a bomb, drawn by the aroma of a deep fry. They say there are six terrorists in Brooklyn every square mile. Living in retro-fitted lofts near the old Bush Terminal."

"You know I thought Eve had been killed in that explosion."

"You know, Dirk, I've been watching you for a long time. Ever since we were in the stockade together with Nicky and I've come to some conclusions."

"Anything I should know about?"

"Well, I think you are a very ignorant man."

"I am what is and what is not!" Cag screamed.

"Thanks for that, Moran. I just know what I know is what I know. You know, that suits me. I don't go looking for more than I know."

"Fair enough. The known unknowns and the known but

forgotten knowns and the unknown unknowns and the knowns falsely known as well as the unknowns known but not included in what you know. But you get my point. What you just said is a very ignorant thing to say."

"So that's it? You watch me and you decide I'm ignorant?"

"You don't know a thing about the art of the deal. You've not read the book. You don't understand financial structuring, the art of bankruptcy and such. You don't know the codes to protect property and assets, which lead of course to private wealth and income. You're not proprietary. Sad."

"I thought you made the deal? I sign over the patent and they get me reinstated as sane enough to run The Foundation."

"That's just our opener. We're going for it all. And I'll tell you why. I've got the App. Just kidding. Your patent gives you prior claim to remove the whole structure and privatize it in your name."

"The shit-rock does all that?"

"What it does is put fear in them. Which is good. And bad. Enough fear gives us leverage in a new deal."

"I'm waiting."

"What's the bad? Well, Boyo, people like these, split between legalities and illegalities as they are, between dog and wolf such as yourself, kill what puts too much fear in them. That's why we're enjoying life in exile on this vessel at this moment. That's why we pack guns. A lot of them. We're in the competitive arena, Boyo. Guns and bullets is what it is. That's where we are, true enough."

"We are?"

"Your mind is your greatest enemy."

We both looked at the parrot.

"He's been quoting from the Bag of Ether," I told Moran.

"Fair enough."

■■■

A couple of days before my competency hearing, Eve and I went ashore, right to the *New Pompey.*

It was safe for us she said. And I needed to be aired out in public before the hearing because days on the boat had given me a last dried biscuit in a barrel appearance, which wouldn't appeal to the judge. Besides, she thought listening to Sailor, who was caretaker of the boat and somebody's cousin, too long would leave me more stunned than was usual.

"Limited liabilities?" I said, repeating what I had just heard Gee who had joined us at the bar had said.

"Owners without faces," Eve said.

"Owners without faces?" I asked Gee.

"Several. One face behind another until you go up your own ass. They want to renovate the building so I should be apprized … apprized … that there might be some noise, dust, and rats making a getaway. So, I told the flunky they sent none of that is going to get me to break my lease. Which is until I croak. So, the asswipe tells me that all the renovation might scare off my customers, especially because there won't be any way to get in the place except through the alley. I told him that was okay because most of them go in and out via the alley but stay out of the basement cause there were bodies in the basement I didn't want found. Gnats that came around and annoyed me."

"What's in this building they have to renovate?" I asked, wondering what all this had to do with me.

"Nothing. And nobody. They just want their hands on the bar. It's a threat. To bust my balls and get me out of here. I'm paying right now about one quarter the market rate. Place has untouched value.

I felt sorry for Gee; he was like a Dodo bird facing his own extinction from feral cats.

"They're buying apartments six figures your mother and my mother couldn't afford if they worked two hundred years."

"Not my mother."

"I forgot," Gee said. "Hamptons. Oyster Bay. Wherever. Well, places rented for five hundred bucks a month. Maybe less, rent controlled. They're worth in the mils now."

"Pray tell, how did you end up with the limited liabilities flunky?" Eve asked him. "I would have put a bullet in his ass at the second full sentence."

I repeated what she said to Gee.

"I told the limited liabilities flunky he could renovate his ass off but if it reached a point that I took it personal, I would come looking for him. I told him to do his homework and find out who I was around here and if I was a man of my word. I told him I started out with Quadroon. Then I told him to fuck off."

Eve laughed. She threw an arm around my shoulders.

"You to have to tell some people just to fuck off. Or just shut up. Everybody I knew was at their best when their mouths weren't working."

"Enough of my troubles," Gee told me, refilling my glass. "I know you got your own worries."

"Him?" Eve said, "Idiots don't worry. They got to think too much to find what they're worried about."

"I've got no worries," I told Gee, angrily.

"Yeah, you do," Gee said. "You need to give some time to your grief We all know what Eve meant to you. And, now, don't get angry. But you need to be told that that guy out there? Moran? He's on a lot of people's list. You don't want to be around when they come to settle up."

"He's going with me to court. Petition of airship."

"Inheritance," Eve said.

"Inheritance," I told Gee. "That's going to vacuum this lawyer … Soldmyson's power of attorney."

"What I am saying is that you don't want to be there when certain parties talk to that fellow Moran."

"He thinks he's a wolf now."

"Stay hard, kid. And listen to what I'm telling you. You might think you're a wolf but these guys hunt wolves for sport."

CHAPTER THIRTY-SEVEN

"THEY HOLLOWED OUT THE WHOLE PLANET"

The court we showed up at was the King's Country Surrogate Court on Johnson Street. We took the Flatbush Avenue bus because Moran said his car had been stolen.

"Taken back by the rightful owner is what he means," Eve said, as the three of us sat at the front of the bus.

"Williams will meet us there?" I asked, noticing that Moran was eyeing an attractive lady who was sitting across from us.

"I forget to tell you," Moran said. "Nicholas is already at your place. The Fartsworth compound. He's doing some remodeling before we move in. After his sorrows, he needs a bit of respite."

"Respite my ass," Eve snapped. "He's probably stealing everything that's not nailed down."

I knew Williams had already looted the estate and been caught at it and was out on bail, but I didn't say anything. It was difficult for me to know what Eve knew at this point. The dead might see all and then again, they might not see anything. If I were Cad lick, I would have had the answer to that.

"Not the guy you want as a character witness," Eve said.

"I think Nick is reliable," I said.

"Right. Nicky will not let us down. It's not in his nature. We're both as reliable as duct tape on a banana peel."

"Well, what about now? Who's representing me here?"

Moran slapped my knee.

"You got me," he told me, as an elderly man got on the bus and didn't move far from the driver. He was looking for a seat.

I started to get up, but Moran jumped up and pointed to his seat. The old man fumbled toward it. Moran went and hung right over the attractive blonde across from me. I could hear him say something, but I couldn't make it out.

I was totally surprised when three stops short of our destination, the blonde got out and Moran did too. I pressed my face to the glass, but he wasn't looking back. She crossed the street and so did he. The bus pulled out.

"Well, there goes another character witness. His face is on a wanted poster right outside the courtroom. It was a bad day when you crossed paths with those guys. Where was that again?"

"Army Stockade."

"My point. They're not your friends. They're nightmares."

...

"Looks like they sent the Dream Team from the Mother Ship," Eve said as she and I sat at a table in front of the judge's bench.

She was looking at the suits, three of them, sitting at the table across from us. I didn't recognize anyone. I had expected to see Sulmondson.

There was a myopic clerk standing behind the judge's desk. I read the nameplate on the desk: Judge Marshall Solomon, named after the silent screen movie star, I guessed.

The clerk motioned me to sit in the witness chair. I did. I had on my shipboard attire.

"You, Mr. Dirk Bratter, wish to revoke the Alpha Zed Holdings power of attorney and executorship of the Farnsworth holdings including the Farnsworth Foundation, Farnsworth Global Enterprises and all properties including the East Hampton Farnsworth Estate. You do so based on the fact that you are the last living relative of Mrs. Sarah Sorrow Bratter Farnsworth, who according to the Mental Incapacity Act has been judged to be incapable of making any decisions regarding her own care and treatment as well as any decisions regarding the aforementioned Farnsworth Holdings."

Judge Sourmash raised his eyes from the paper he was reading and looked at me.

"Do you disagree with any part of what I have just read, Mr. Bratter, and if so for what reasons?"

I was about to say it sounded okay with me when Eve, who was now standing alongside the myopic clerk, said:

"His mother can't decide if a tree is talking because this illegal conglomerate is keeping her doped up in an asylum so their shysters here can prove this preternaturally impaired last, living heir, who doesn't need to be doped up, can be vacated as legally unsound. I submit to Your honor that the mentally unsound run the country without objection and so Mr. Bratter is good enough to run a goddamn Foundation whose mission is to launder the money of The Mob, which Alpha Zed Holdings is merely a front. A shell extended into hundreds of other shells all over the world. They hollowed out the whole planet. His mother's head is just a sample."

"Now, Mr. Bratter. Your response, Mr. Bratter. We're waiting."

"His … I mean my mother is incapable of talking to a tree because she's doped up by order of my mother's lawyer Pitchell Pecansomething, in a Sanitarium, which is kind of bogus place, as I know from firsthand experience as I was there with brain damage which I didn't have at all. And, I submit to your Honor that there were gunshots every night. Also, the mentally unsound deserve a shot and I'll do everything I can to see that they get it. Meaning me. My Mater is just a shell of what she once was, also a shell as far back as I can remember. Thank you, My Honor."

"Did you get all that?" the Judge asked someone.

"Who is Pitchell Pecan, Your Honor?" the stenographer asked.

"Record the name as heard, Ms. Flowers. "The Court adjudicates words. You simply record them."

I turned and saw that there was one of those court stenographers' types in a far corner typing away.

"Mr. Bratter," Judge Socksalmon said turning back to me. "While the Court recognizes your liberality regarding the mentally challenged, we are not here to rule on such or to review any decision regarding your mother. That has been adjudicated and she is where the law says she should be. So, I ask you once again, are you here to revoke Alpha-Zed Holdings power of attorney of the Farnsworth holdings?"

"I am."

"On the grounds that you are legally entitled and mentally sound?"

I nodded.

"The Court will hear Alpha-Zed Holdings."

"We do not question Mr. Bratter's legal entitlements nor do we question his mental soundness, although we believe we could make a strong case that he lacks judgment, agency, durability, facility, and overall soundness of mind while suffering memory loss and abysmal attention span."

Eve whispered in my ear.

"Repeat what I say."

I did.

"Your honor, adiposity, a naive I.Q. catachresis, flatulence and torpescence do not mean he's nuts. He's just an autochthon."

"I didn't get everything he said, Your Honor."

The stenographer began to read what she had typed.

Judge Lockrock stopped her.

"Please, don't, Ms. Flowers."

"A case of no mental competency then is not being made by Alpha-Zed?"

"No, your honor. We object to Mr. Bratter's petition for the simple reason that he is presently on bail for Murder One and the chances of him being found innocent are, upon review of the case, negligible. His imprisonment would vacate any opportunities to oversee the Farnsworth Holdings."

The judge now looked at me with new eyes.

"We have the indictment charges here for your review, your Honor."

Papers came out of an attaché case and were handed to the judge who began to read them.

He looked up.

"I will review these and make my decision by noon tomorrow."

"I didn't kill Billy Hashfries."

Judge Simon Parker, the Hanging Judge, looked at me and then at the Dream Team table.

"Clearly," he said.

"All rise."

...

"The trick is to convince our enemies that you're not their enemy. Convince them that you can do a better job as a laundry service than your brother Tim did."

"Theo."

It annoyed me the way Moran could never remember my brother's name. I think if you can't remember a person's name it's a sign of narcissism. Theo always said that identity was just a proper noun. Not remembering someone's name was like nullifying their existence.

"Sounds good," Eve said, angrily, "until you go on trial for murder and they will find you guilty and then you're in Rikers and they stab you like they stabbed your brother."

"The Mob?" I asked Eve and she nodded.

Moran was what Eve called a demonic force but for me it was all Eve, my suppository of wisdom.

"We make the deal with the patent," Moran said, ignoring Eve, as if she wasn't there but I didn't see that as proof that she wasn't there. I saw that as opinion.

"Once we do that, those contracted to kill us, will be contracted to protect us. This is what it is, Dirk. They can't take your fate from you. It's a gift."

"His Fate is to get tied up with you and your partner until he strangles himself," Eve shot back. "That's not a gift. And guess what? We don't like you using the 'we.' You're pitching for something we don't want."

I repeated that to Moran.

"Fair enough. Okay, just stay put," Moran told me. "Don't go up. Don't go down. The easiest target. Advance and attack. Patent in hand. Proprietary rights with priority in our hand."

"You don't have any idea what that patent means," Eve shot back.

"You know what, Dirk?" Moran asked me, smiling. "They don't know what it means but I know they see fear in that patent in our hand."

...

"Bring the parrot up on deck. He needs an airing. And so, do you. He needs help with his dictionary."

I shook my head. I wasn't getting the support I needed.

"I can't help him with that dictionary," I moaned. "He's scrambling my head. For, you know, words. He's going through the Good Books like a red ant at a picnic. He's says the truth is a sentence. What the hell does that mean?"

"Let the parrot know that The Patriarch absolved you of all your sins," Eve said. "Oh, yeah. He wasn't a priest. He was just crazy, so I guess you're not absolved. You still got a rank smell of sin, like you've slept in the same sheets for a year and pissed them more than once."

At that point, totally under fire, I started to cry, or at least I felt a tear forming.

"Stop crying!" Eve shouted. "All you got from that bombing was an annoying case of Catachresis. Don't repeat this word. I don't want to hear what you'll do to that word."

"I worry about you, Angelo," Cag said in what I guess was a whisper for a parrot. I had no idea who Angelo was. The parrot was full of himself as a result of countless idiots retweeting his nasty, punitive tweets. I couldn't get his phone away from him. He was tweeting at all hours of the day and night.

"No, don't worry about a Murder One charge," Eve told me, sarcastically. " Listen to the parrot. He's another fucking genius like Moran."

"She's talking but she's dead," Cag whispered.

And I cried.

CHAPTER THIRTY-EIGHT

"THE TRIAL"

Eve advised me not to show up for the trial.

According to her, the prosecution had more than one smoking gun.

I had motive. I did a Richard the Turd and bumped off the guy ahead of me in the line of suppression. And I had been arrested at the scene of the crime, standing right by the dumpster. And I was big and strong enough to mangle Billy Hashfries' body, rip his head from his neck, and fling him into that dumpster.

Oh, yeah. They found traces of his blood on my hands.

The trial was Thursday. Today was Wednesday. I looked over at the parrot who was back to working on his dictionary. I was relieved. I had become a fearful, nervous wreck listening to squawks like "A little, wretched, despicable creature; a worm, a mere nothing, and less than nothing; a vile insect that has risen up in contempt against the majesty of Heaven and Earth." "Light yourself on fire with passion and people will come from miles to watch you burn." "Blood alone moves the wheels of history."

That kind of talk, a litany of fucking tweets, even from a parrot who doesn't know what the hell he's saying, makes it hard for you to sleep. Me, also. He had 72 million followers.

So, it was okay when he stopped tweeting for a while and resumed working on the "B's."

"Bolivion," Cag squawked. "A state of stupor, landlocked, south of Argentina and Paraguay; also, a vile insect that revolts against the majesty of Heaven and Earth.

"Boredom," he continued, "the sleepy kingdom of prophylactics, nonetheless fertile; also, a state of burning while others watch."

"Blood, a lubricant on the wheels of history."

"Bovine, a vine much favored by parrots for its appearance."

I didn't wait to hear anymore. Somehow this bird had gotten twisted, most likely from listening to Eve, Moran, Williams, Sailor and my brother, who I've come to see as a launderer of The Mob's money.

All of us still trapped in what Sailor called a Kvetch, a kind of Hebrew sailing vessel.

The night before I couldn't sleep. Moran found me on deck, measuring my worth against the brilliance of the stars.

"If you got to go and we all got to go then you got to go. Some time. Of course, death ain't like a trip to the bathroom. I'm more an advocate of the intensity of life rather than the duration, if you know what I mean. Of course, duration has its attraction. Especially in the ICU."

I could smell the whiskey on Moran's breath.

"You'll always have Eve. Of course, you're wrong for her."

That woke me up.

"I'm not wrong for her. I'm just not as … as right as she deserves."

"Put your big boy pants on," Moran said "Tomorrow's the trial. And you're a wolf."

■■■

Lawyer Summer Arpeggio was already in the courtroom when I arrived. She told me immediately to sit down and look as small and harmless as I could.

Her voice was thin, cracked, shaky, barely audible. I had never seen this lady nervous. Eve had once told me that Summer had been brutalized by her gangster father when she was young, but Jim Beam had erased all that, if you took your daily allotment.

I sat down. I smelled whiskey on her breath.

I told her she looked nervous.

"I got the court version of white coat syndrome," she whispered. "Listen, I'm gonna argue that you got back problems. Too weak to dump the victim into a dumpster. So, look small and frail."

"I thought you said he was tall and slim? This guy looks like a big, murdering slob that would off his mother."

I looked at the speaker.

"My co-counsel," Summer whispered. "And my AA sponsor. Individual Aspen. "

"Individual?" I repeated.

"I'm agender," Aspen told me. "Non-binary. You can refer to me as ze. Are you aware that there are 76 different genders at present? Are you aware which one you are?"

I shook my head. I could smell whiskey on her breath.

"See? We are each in a prison house we think we can't choose to get out of."

"We are? I don't want to go to prison."

"Another of my strategies," Summer whispered to me. "We're going to destroy the substances and materiality's of the charges by barraging the court with formalities. I didn't go to matchbook cover law school for nothing."

I noticed she was reading that from a scrap of paper in front of her.

"Look at me," Individual Aspen commanded. "The first time you or me are referred to as ze, hir or zir, Summer is going to call for a mistrial."

My face must have totally revealed the bafflement of my mind.

"They're assuming you're male," Individual Aspen whispered to me.

"I'm not?"

"Yeah, he's male," Eve said, coming up to the table, breathless.

I was so happy to see her at the defense table with us.

"Snores, farts, hustle his balls, eats with his mouth open and thinks stank is attracting. All the male attributes."

At that point, the judge, the same judge I had met with in chambers, Judge Roy Bean, banged his gavel. He still had the same whiskey breath I had picked up in his chamber. The courtroom had a great many spectators, a good number from *The Pompey*. The courtroom smelled like a keg of bourbon had burst open. I saw Gee and he gave me a nod. I nodded back.

The Prosecution was directed to make its preliminary remarks.

I sat there listening. The prosecutor sounded like Clarence Barrel in that old film, *Inherit the Dust Storm*, as well as Adenoid Flinch in *To Kill Some Bird*, probably an annoying parrot. In short, he was spellbinding. I looked around for the guy who played Hamilton, who got shot by Aron Bird, an early Americana annoyance.

I looked at Eve.

"Better start your anus flexibility exercises," she told me. "Your Kegels."

I ignored her and turned to Summer.

"Don't worry," she said to me, "Individual Aspen is hashtag

metooing that Prosecutor right now. It'll go viral in an hour or two. Then the pop vote on *Twitter* will yank him out of here. Or a flash mob will form. The justice of all the People will be served. All authority to the People. We do flash mobs now, not elections."

I wasn't sure. The Prosecutor was an old guy, fluffs of cotton white hair coming out of only one place, namely his ears, several piece antiquated suit, brogues heavily polished. Bow tie. Suspenders. He had a warm, friendly smile, which he laid on the jury and me too. I could smell the whiskey on his breath from where I was sitting.

As he spoke in a *Gone Out the Window* War Between the States drawl, I saw that Summer was checking off items from a legal pad page that was full.

"Are you going to challenge all those?" I asked.

She shook her head.

"We're just going to repeat them. Slowly. Wear the jury out. Repetition and volume. We don't need argument. We made sure we had nomophobiacs on the jury. They've got a twenty second attention span. Six of them are already dozing off and the others are sneaking looks at their phones. They fear losing them. They also have as great a need to tweet as a heroin addict to shoot up."

"They have them?"

"They certainly do. Twelve. Packing guns and cell phones. I mean can an inmate sneak a butter knife out of the mess hall and stab you with it?"

"What?"

Then it was The Defense's turn to present my defense. I could see that the Prosecutor, Mr. Freeman, had left the jury thrilled, although they must have smelled the whiskey on his breath.

Ze rose, I-phone clutched in Ze's right hand. Extra slim fit suit, pointed toe shoes, funky socks, pink hair. High bright beams for eyes. Anywhere in age from 12 to 42. Clean shaven. Ze walked up to the jury box and stood there for long minutes before speaking.

"Black Lives Matter," she said calmly to the jury, who nodded with one neck.

"We are all shells with floating nomenclature played on a chess board without a bottom, Your Honorable. A whale was once a land resident. I, for instance, was a zygote. I quote: a diploid cell resulting from the fusion of two haploid gametes; a fertilized ovum. I am no longer haploid. My client is no longer what he was."

"Is that an opening statement, Counsel?"

"Preliminary to," Ze said. "Now I begin. Can't kill someone when coma has been you," Ze said, then turned and looked at me. "Can't be put on trial if you're too binaried to know you're on trial. Can't say you are the indicted, if you don't know if you've been identified. This is a case of mis-identification. The accused is one of identical twins. Tony and Donny always changed places. It was a Bratwurst family twin thing. You've got the wrong human. So sad."

Ze shook Ze's head, turned from the jury and walked back to the Defense table.

"What the hell is this?" I whispered to Summer. "How could I have been Theo or whatever. Theo is dead. And who's Tony?" Donny?"

"She's tweeting the jury," Summer whispered back. "She'll get to the Likes."

I went total WTF and looked at Eve.

"Don't fucking look at me," was all she said. "All I've got is contempt for the Court. Poor defense. The universal order blew me up with a bomb. I've got only universal contempt."

Ze took a run at the water bottle then went back to the jury.

"The Prosecutor has given you his facts. But he has not given you alternative facts. Mr. Prosecution is very old. He's a grandpa. He's old, analog and twentieth century. He has minus friends on *Facebook*. He doesn't know where the "send" button is. So sad. He claims to give you the truth, but truth isn't truth. It's fake news."

I could see Ze had captured the jury. They were nodding their heads as if they were sucking in every word. Ze took another intermission. Pulled on her water bottle then went back to her mark in front of the jury box. The water bottle reeked of whiskey.

"The Defense has a witness that will prove the accused was somewhere else at the scene of the crime. And if they were at the scene, it was by accident. At that point, the Accused may have accidentally killed the victim. But may I remind Your Honorific that Deuteronomy 19:3 requires that we set aside cities of refuge for those who commit accidental homicide. I ask is anybody sure the victim was dead? Did anyone put a mirror near they nostrils. Run a stake through they heart? Stuff they mouth with garlic? Did anyone do that when the body was first found in a dumpster? The Defense contends that the victim was alive, improperly gender identified as cis when they is clearly neutrois, and that therefore arresting our client for murder is false arrest and we intend to pursue charges against the Government."

I wasn't the only one who had a WTF look on his face. The Clyde Barrel prosecutor had the same look.

"To spare The People the expense of this trial" Ze went on, "we, The Defense, call for a mistrial. This trial is a witch hunt. A hoax. Our client, who is in the middle of a gender re-identification, and therefore of fluid identity, has no peers on this jury. So unfair. Nothing but a witch hunt. This great country deserves better. The Defense therefore calls for a mistrial. Must I remind the jury that we are not here to rescind Obamacare? The Defense rests."

With that, Ze returned to the Defense table where Summer congratulated the Individual on nailing it. She nailed me was what I thought. Nailed me to an electric chair.

I looked at Eve.

"You're going up," she whispered.

Judge Jail had the WTF look on his face as he banged the gavel.

"Counsels to my chambers," was all he said, banging the gavel. We all stood up as he left the courtroom.

"Is this good?" I asked Summer.

"Very good," she told me, nodding.

I watched as she and Ze, followed by the Prosecutor and another guy went into the judge's chambers.

Eve was now seated in Summer's place.

"She'll get you shived in Rikers like she did your bro," she said to me, not overly concerned, judging by the look on her face, at my fate.

We sat there waiting for about ten minutes and then the Judge and the counselors came out of his chambers and resumed their seats.

Ze had her head down and was thumbing her phone pad at light speed. Summer's face was bloodless, and her lower jaw dropped. Her eyes were riveted on the Judge who banged his gavel.

"Firstly, in lieu of mistrial that the Defense has petitioned, I am placing Ms. Raw ... "

"I accuse The Court of gender bias and discrimination!" Ze shouted, jumping up. "I am Individual Aspen."

"Just so," the judge told her. "Bailiffs, please remove Individual Aspen from the courtroom and hold her on contempt charges."

Ze turned, terrified look in Ze's eyes and ran for the door. Ze was stopped by three officers who managed to get hold of Ze, though Ze was kicking and screaming something about Ze's rights, and then Ze was dragged out of the courtroom. I could now hear Summer swearing under her breath. They breath.

"Citizen Rawlee," Judge Freestone went on, "is under arrest for coming before this court without proper attorney credentials as well as for blatant and astounding contempt of the American jurisprudence system. I order that she be examined for severe emotional dysfunction. This Court also finds the lead Defense counsel, Ms Arpeggio ...

"Or should I say Individual Arpeggio?" he said to Summer.

"I got a gender," Summer said, belligerently.

"As we have no lockup for Individuals but only for men and women, having a gender makes life in this Courtroom a great deal easier."

"Whatever," Summer mumbled.

"Ms. Arpeggio, I find you to be an accessory to fraud, contempt of Court, and conspiracy to subvert the justice system. Bailiffs, place Ms. Arpeggio under arrest."

"This court sucks feet, Your Honor," Summer said as they led her out.

Then Judge Freebird looked at me.

"You are either a simple man who has been led astray by his counselors or you are an accessory to the crimes committed this morning in my courtroom."

"He's a naïf, your honor," Eve said. "There's two other idiots he follows around."

"I'm a naïf," I told Judge Freeballing. "But I didn't kill Billy Hashfries."

"Is there a double murder charge, Mr. Prosecutor."

"No, Your Honor. He is referring to the one murder. That of William Hasborough."

"Tell him, you couldn't have cut Billy Hashfries' throat because you can't cut an apple without praying over it," Eve whispered to me.

"I couldn't have cut Billy Hashfries' throats because ... I'm a religious individual ... "

"Avoid that word, Mr. Bratter. It's overdetermined."

"It is?" I said. "What I'm saying is that I wouldn't break the fifth commandment."

"Sixth," Eve said.

"Sixth, either."

"I'm happy to hear that, Mr. Bratter. You will be held at the Metropolitan Detention Center until a public defender is appointed in your case."

"They're warehousing you, Babba," Eve told me. "That place is grimsville, smells of ass, and grits fried in suet is all you'll eat."

I stood up. I would live life ashore once again. That boat reeked of whiskey. I guess because all we did was drink.

"Tell'em you're not going. Make a fuss. Swing your arms. Run for the exit. Nobody left in here big enough to tackle you. Show'em the wolf."

I did what she said. I swatted a couple of cops out of the way and made a run for the exit.

I didn't make it to the goal post. I went down. I looked up and Eve was peering down at me.

"Don't forget when you're in prison that you're in the throes of a gender re-identification process. That should help you make friends."

CHAPTER THIRTY-NINE

"PRE-SALVAGING"

"I want to leave everything to the Octopoi Fund," Eve, seated at the small desk in my cell said to me.

I was sprawled out on the hard horsehair mattress on top of a plywood board with legs and wheels attached. I was doing some fine stitch work on the face of my Individual Ze Aspen hand puppet. I had told Eve that in my opinion Ze had been harshly treated beyond any offenses Ze might have committed. Isn't gender ID part of Know Thyself?

"Foundational," Eve replied.

"I can leave my shit-rock," I said to her. "I still have the patent on that."

"Moran is dealing that away right this second."

"He is? You think he's ignoble, don't you, Eve?"

"Ignoble? Parrot teach you that one? If I believed in souls, I'd say that man doesn't have one."

"Moran says we say we have souls just to hold it over the lower orders."

"Yeah, I don't object to ignoble views. They come with eyesight and hearing but Moran is a cockroach with a vocabulary so I wouldn't take anything he says seriously."

"Williams says Moran has charisma."

"Clearly Williams is what you get when you turn a body inside out. Look, I'm not saying either one of those individuals couldn't be elected president, Babba. Even cockroaches have some charisma in your kitchen when the lights are out. Among their kind."

"I'm out of here," she said and was as good as her word because I blinked and there was no one seated at the desk. There was a book lying on the desk.

I knew she had been here because her fragrance still lingered. Castile soap, I think. I was back to hallucinating. But her visit had been real. Not so with Theo.

I leaned over and picked up the book.

"*The Laundry Bible.*"

I noticed that the bookmark was on page 167. I still couldn't get over how much Theo still read boring stuff. Then again, I couldn't get over running into him here at Fishkill. Correctional. Office of Mental Health ward.

Dennis Moran didn't buy that line of thinking.

According to him everyone gets what they deserved in the end, their fair share of the pie, their end of the take, their end of the thread Odin wove, short or long, their ripe desserts, what was legally coming to them, as the gods fated, and all as God wills, and the Oracle revealed. Fate happened for a reason and so on.

When I mentioned to Nicholas Sweetheart that sometimes I found Moran opaque, a word Eve had used on me more than once, he told me Moran was a contrarian and that was part of his sociopathic nature.

It seems Moran understood the bottom of everything before the top. His mind went sideways down the public highways even when the roads weren't icy. The norm floated in a sea of insanities and impossibilities. Williams had a total diagnosis of his friend, none of which I could get a hold of … opaque is what I'm trying to say here … except Moran broke laws the way monkeys in kitchens broke dishes and untrained pups pissed and shat on clean kitchen floors.

One time when I asked Williams why he hung around with a guy like Moran who he knew was trouble, he told me he was the other half.

"Of what?" I naturally asked.

"You are one of identical twins. You shouldn't have to ask. You and your brother are twin flames emerging from an original single ovoid."

No sense in that.

P.T. Bratter, my pater, had held up a lump of shit and said I came from that. Prime Evil. Pre hysterical. Prime or Deal. I never could see how other people could figure out who you were when you yourself couldn't. I mean where was the point of reference? Them or me?

Thusly, I'm in Fishkill because I'm talking to people who aren't there and to people who are hand size and made of wool.

Moran and Williams haven't been to see me. I think Williams is squatting at the Farnsworth Mansion and Moran? How could he sell off my patent without my signature?

But that doesn't come into the picture until my public defender finesses a plea bargain for the Billy Hashfries murder and I get twenty years, chance of parole in ten. If that was finesse, I wondered what a botched job was?

I had a hand puppet, Mister Grogan, who I stitched with a lawyer's wig, and I think he could have done a better job in defending me. At least, he tells me that.

Everybody who came to see me at the Metropolitan Detention Center said I had gotten a good deal. It seemed like when I first went in, everybody thought this would be good for me, the pain that wouldn't kill me would make me better. The dark night in a bowling alley, a dark, smelly hole out of which I would emerge like a fresh … Kleenex.

Eve, on the other hand, just straight out said, "You're really fucked now."

After some time, Nick Sweetheart did show up. As an inmate. It was like old times, except Moran was still on the loose, in the wind.

Williams was rounded up by the New York State Police who came upon him in the process of loading everything from an estate adjoining my family's.

The load included oak flooring, fireplace stones and marble, crown molding, banisters, paintings, sculptures, drapes, copper pipes, sideboards, chiffoniers, commodes, escritoires, lockers, davenports, safes, tombs, bunkers, seed vaults, vases, all hardware, chandeliers, tapestries, bed frames, cupboards, shelves, kitchen and dining room tables, automatons, spinning wheels, antiques, books, utensils, crockpots, tajines, toasters, microwaves, flat screens, laptops, bar and bar stools, jams, whiskies, sourdough starter and much more.

In my estimation, Williams stole a lot of stuff for a guy who said he didn't live in what he called the Anthropocene. He recited the stuff he had stolen the way Catholics recite the Rosary or Jews the Begats.

Williams had everything he had stolen in his life memorized. To him, if you kept in mind what stuff was, item by item, you would turn from it in disgust and give yourself to Jesus or to trees, ponds, earth, flowers or to Saint Genesius Maritinus, patron saint of plumbers and clowns. He admitted to me that he really liked stuff, nevertheless.

The only explanation I got for such a lust for stuff by a guy who said he lived in an ether real world came from Moran who just told me that what the world had to offer was never too much for him.

"Half the time, Nikcy likes his ease," Moran told me. "The other seven eights, he's in love with The Numinous."

"The new what?"

"His sweetheart. Anyway, it was just a salvage operation. The waters of the Sound will rise, and all those mega magna mansions will wash away. Nicky was pre-salvaging. We're both into pre-salvaging. Why wait? The Anthropocene is over my friend. Get used to it."

I didn't have a clue as to why an obscene aunt, probably his, mattered to me.

A twenty-minute inkblot Rorschach test in which Williams saw only his sweetheart on every inkblot, plus an observation of Williams' conversing with this invisible sweetheart, earned him his place at Fishkill.

I was there because Alpha-Zed had decided to have me declared nuts and a murderer.

I could easily have stopped talking to Mr. Spinalzo and friends, or Eve, who the guards never saw when she and I were conversing. I just think why shrink my world of friends to satisfy those too shrunk to see them?

Williams told me that Moran had gone sideways with Alpha-Zed/ Mob Affiliate and I imagined he had either gotten wrung out in their laundry operation, as the Theo hallucination who was visiting me said had happened to him, or he had just pushed too far with his patent leverage.

"Theo's dead. I talk to him. They tell me that it follows then that I'm nuts."

"You are wrong, sir," Williams told me." I say talk to who wants to talk to you. There are certainly more people dead than alive so isn't it logical to assume you are more liable to run into the dead than the living? And that, further, they would have more to say, having been both alive and dead? Experience, my friend, is priceless. Would you rather oblige these prison guards as to what conversation is, or would you rather converse with FreeDick Knee G, Val Tear, and Gaucho Marx?"

Right then I knew, if I hadn't figured it out before, that, as Eve said, Williams was two points off the beam.

"You should have a positive mind. Think how Fishkill serves a humanitarian purpose. It comforts so many not in here to know that derangement can be so confined to this place. Identified and removed from the world. If madness is here, it can't be there. At the moment, in the Fifties when Hollywood was leading the country into an abyss of derangement, it became necessary defensively to build Businessland. That of, course, is the home of President Walter Raygun. He would not have come to us otherwise."

It felt like my brain was ping ponging back and forth and that if I wasn't nuts entering this place, I would be when I left. If I ever did.

I expressed my state of mind to Williams who said two or three guns under the mattress would make me feel better in the morning. Sanity close at hand was the way he put it.

Eve was a faithful visitor and she kept me alive by just being there, but I didn't see how her explanations of what I already knew helped. She also wanted to get the band back together.

"Let's sum up," Eve told me on one of her visits. "We know Nicky Sweetheart here is being held because he's a visionary with a hot vision, namely, a babe he calls his Sweetheart nobody in this world but him has ever seen. That lady is as real as plastic wrap talking. And you, Babba, are a man sent here by under utiilized forces conspiring against you. Namely, your own mind. In conclusion, you're having a hard time proving you're a fully *compos mentis* heir to billions of dollars smarter people want to get their hands on. And myself? I'm in here because I got funding for us to do a podcast, you and me, right here from Fishkill. We're going to get the band back together right here in this asylum for the criminally insane. The parrot, the hand puppets, you, me and Williams, his Sweetheart as a guest. Moran would be good, but I heard an unidentified, short lunatic was killed in a shootout with State troopers, the FBI and the local constabulary somewhere outside Oshkosh. I'd say it was Moran. They found a trunk full of cash."

When I mentioned Moran's unfortunate end to Williams he just laughed.

"Moran is outside so very much. But never Oshkosh."

...

Theo had been appearing, mostly after lights out to sit and read at my desk. I don't know how he read in the dark but then again how were his eyeballs there to do any reading? Was there seeing after death? Not after death but while dead?

In the mornings, I checked and saw that the bookmark had advanced and sometimes there were comments in the margins. I had no idea you could continue to learn after death. Do the mysteries of laundering follow you to the afterlife? I planned on choosing a more interesting topic in that situation.

Eve knew that Theo was showing up but there was no way I was going to mention this to anyone else. I wasn't talking to him so there was nothing to be heard. I just went back to sleep and let him do his reading. Once again, why dead people need any new knowledge is not for me to ask.

Eve once told me that life provided us with many choices in regard to death, beyond the fact that mortality wasn't a choice. We could be grateful that someone had died for us, or someone had killed someone and then been killed themselves, or that everyone in our lives had enough guns to bring meaning into the lives of everyone.

If my life had had a plot or, beyond that, what Eve called a theme, what she had told me had not made it evident to me or brought it to closure. I did find in one of Cag's tweets explanation that I supposed would have satisfied a parrot's quest for meaning in life:

"My life is in a labyrinth cage where cremains, monsters and lovers, all noisy, do battle and I am at the center, winged but flightless What the hell is going on and why a goodly parrot such as myself should give a fuck is not clear, neither is it clear what's been lost or found, and less clear who has been lost and who has been found."

Eve said the parrot was repeating his parrot cosmogony: You fly through an open window, scream your brains out, drop some turd loads and then fly out the opposite window into an eternal darkness.

I didn't think I was in a danger zone but just something like a radio static zone when bits of sound come at you and you wait, and then other bits of sound and you can't pull it all together. All of that kept me very nervous.

I pulled my flask of Jim Beam rye from under the bunk and took a swallow. I was in a nostalgic mood, remembering the five- or six-words P.T. had spoken to me regarding condoms and white rats.

"What do think my father meant when he told me once to search for what is important but not to listen, remember or repeat any of it. I could then enter The Statistical Norm."

""Let me ask you, Numb Nuts. Does a regular, normal guy that's normal and regular in the way everybody thinks is normal and regular wind up in an asylum for the criminally insane?"

"No. But you know I'm innocent."

"Ignorance is never innocent. Only Liberals believe that.

"You know, Williams told me that there's something like a vestibule of a perfect world I carry inside me and I can't get rid of. And it's you. That's where you come from right now. I can't get rid of you and you can't get rid of me because we started out together. Some place."

"Where you come from wasn't perfect," Eve replied. "It wasn't even anything real. Your father, the crazy scientist, somehow mixed shit rock genetics into your half of the egg."

"That's not what I remember," I told her, shaking my head.

"You don't remember. You're half asleep half the time and the other half you're still sleeping. Kind of like a confused sleeping zombie can't remember when he was alive. And, by the way, half an egg has no fucking memory. It has major ellipsis."

"Well, primordial shit rocks have no genetics."

"There was something alive on that chunk of hemorrhoid from Mars and its crawling inside you."

"Get off it, Solly. You know talking with you is like having someone … I mean you … poking hot coals into my head."

CHAPTER FORTY

"EVE'S STORY"

"Cacography! Study of Shit-hole countries"

"Caesura! Queen of a Shit-hole country."

"Coleworts! Common skin disease in Shit-hole countries."

Cag was on *Twitter* day and night, absorbing a lot of information he found there about the featherless in what they called shithole countries, which the parrot seemed to know instinctively but I could not make any sense out of.

I once mentioned to Eve that maybe I should buy some kind of smart phone, but she said it was too late. Too late for what? Anyway, Cag's turn from holy texts to *Twitter* seemed to me to be a descent. Eve thought if you went from words spoken by a burning bush to words misspelled on a roll of toilet paper, you had dominated Nature. I did wonder about this because my many days at sea had taught me that Nature fit, and we didn't. She, of course, went negative on this. Nothing taught me anything because nothing had nothing to say and because lives that mean nothing learn nothing. On the positive side, she told me that everything does seems like it fits if it's there long enough and the end, when it comes, will be like that. You know, she said, as if it all weren't random.

Then she told me about the bird flying in one window in the morning and out another window at night. Every time she told me this matador or mata something about this bird, I nodded like I knew what the hell she was talking about.

Now, I think she meant Nature fit in a room, like for one day, and then it didn't.

I took a letter I was writing to my Public Defender and wrote down what Cag had said.

"Ice water plunge, voltage to the ballocks, the old upside-down hang and fifty lashes to soles of my feet, spinal tap stretch."

"Where's the C in all that?" I asked him. "I thought you were up to the "C's" already."

"Colbuter!" Cag shouted.

"Shut up or I'll shoot you," Eve told him.

"Theo came by last night and I accidentally told him he was dead."

"How did he take it?"

"Not well at all. He frenzied and ran through the wall. I haven't seen him since. Then again, I wasn't sure I was seeing him when he was here."

"Why the hell did you tell him? Didn't you say he seemed to enjoy just sitting there reading? Why complicate the guy's eternal rest?"

"I guess I wanted to know more about the launderette he ran in Paris."

"Okay. I can't take any more. Sit back and listen to my story for once. Get you out of your own head, where there's not enough room for you."

"I'd love to hear it. You never say anything about yourself. We've got the time now."

"Says the Eternal Lounger. Okay.

She curled up on my cell bed like a feral cat.

"What I remember is that what I always wanted to be when I grew up was not what I was at that moment. If that sounds bad, then you're following along. I didn't know my brain was growing fast, say ten times as fast as yours was at the same age. I was left on a doorstep as a baby but it's also possible I might have been too attention deficit and hyperactive as a child or refractive in toilet training and so I was sent to an orphanage, The Little Sisters of Jesus Mercy for We Have Little Mercy Ourselves Orphanage, called Little Mercy for shot. At that point, I questioned how a newborn could not be a disturbing presence for a solipsist mother. Anywho, I was told that I had a mother and she toured in a carny show as a Little Person, though she was simply petite. A Father, not my father but a Catholic priest, a Jesuit I think, told me all this when I was tall enough to hear.

He said my father was a tall, white, heterosexual, Christian man who followed carnies around and knocked up the talent. "

All I could say was WTF and did she ever meet her father? A question that made Eve close her eyes and mumble.

"Yeah, he hung around and changed my diapers. He washed the dishes and cleaned the toilet. No, Fooker, it wasn't his M.O. to hang around after a one night stand and see if my mother conceived and birthed, at which point he'd jump up and marry her and the three of us would live happily in a small house with a garage and toxic lawn service in Indiana."

I had thought everything was going along nicely but now I decided to shut up and not ask any more questions, but Eve volunteered more of her story. But the way she said "fooker" made me wonder if she was Irish.

"At some point in time, I decided to empower myself and will myself to be about 5" 10". Those were days before we knew The Secret: Wish It and It Will Come was a crock of turd. One day, a Little Sister of Little Mercy comes into the classroom, where I'm perched on the dunce's stool near the blackboard because I used a celestial or a celestial's relative's name in vain whatever that means, and she gives us the results of the `God Made the World in Seven Days IQ' test which I failed the way Hindus, Buddhists and Apaches fail the same test. She gave me the name Little Heathen and prophesied Hell in my future. At that point. I just knew I had to join the Order of Little Sisters with Little Mercy."

"Jeez, I didn't know you were a nun."

"Yeah, I did that before I became a Hollywood actress. Did I ever tell you how many times I spread my legs on casting couches? Didn't I tell you how much help Harry Winesap was in my career?"

"Did you succeed?"

"I fake organism," she retorted. "Ventriloquist is what I worked at. I wanted to be able to do both voices in a conversation. You know to protect my exceptional brain from the constant attacks of stupid minds. It also prepared me to become the first woman President of the United States, which I turned down when I started a radio show, eventually winning a Marconi Radio Award that Mr. Marconi personally handed me the night after I fucked his brains out. No one at that time on the radio could see that I wasn't the requisite norm height."

That info blew me away but as I looked into her eyes, better than the Betty Mavis eyes in that old song, I got nervous. I was falling into it. I seemed to recall that Eve had told me she went to Princeton like I did or had thought she graduated, and I didn't. And that's where she met me. Was what I remember her telling me. Now that wasn't true at all. I could see now that none of this story fit the other story.

"You fly through an open window," she continued, " scream your brains out, drop some turd loads and then fly out the opposite window into an eternal darkness."

I nodded. The old matamucil for life. Now I wondered about the bird. He or she seemed interesting, kind of bold for making that voyage.

"Thusly," Eve continued, "I used my brains to scramble other people's brains at the local Y, I pimped the daughters of the American Convolution; I hedged the hedge off Gordon Geek's balls; I financially advised Goldbloomers & Slacks to become Chinese; I learned how to push a needle in a rich man's eye. Things like that. I made gazillions."

She hesitated and took a swig at the pint.

I didn't know what I said. I was impressed.

I think we were both crying but she wasn't on my cell bed because she wasn't there, and I was the only one crying.

It took me a long time, but I knew then that Evangeline Solly was dead, that she had died in that explosion. How could she not have? Only a fool would have believed that she hadn't died, that the way she had been visiting me was the way Theo visited me. She was dead but she hadn't left me.

CHAPTER FORTY-ONE

"MORAN IS OUT FRONT"

I woke up in the middle of the night and saw Theo looking at me. He was seated in his reading chair.

He didn't look like himself by which I mean he didn't look brave and fearless, the Admiral of all Seas, but worried and frightened. I immediately asked him what was wrong, and he told me in a hushed, stuttering speech that some plot had been formed against him by some Randoms and that he feared a butter knife being stuck into his ribs in the mess hall.

"I don't want to die," he pleaded, as if I could give him a guarantee of that.

"I'll see what I can do," I lied and then he was gone.

I had noticed blood stains on his shirt. I wondered if he was really any good at laundering.

The last time I saw Eve, alive or dead, she set me straight about us being soulmates.

"'Don't pitch that horseshit at me. I wouldn't take it when I was alive, and I won't take it dead. Guts or groins and salivary glands aren't noble enough places to put our celestial yearnings. Too gross and earthy. But the soul now is a bridge to an everlasting spiritual Afterlife, which is in your head. The bridge too. When you go, I go. I'm not a mate. I'm an imprint."

Something about that bothered me and it was this: how could all that thinking come out of my head? It was all Eve's, not mine.

■■■

"I see her too," Williams said and I did a little jump and a quick look around. I didn't see Eve. "I see her clenched like a fist around your heart."

"Jeez," I said, feeling my chest.

"He's dead. I know this poem."

Williams stood up, closing his eyes and reciting:

The fist clenched round my heart
loosens a little, and I gasp
brightness; but it tightens
again. When have I ever not loved
the pain of love? But this has moved
past love to mania. This has the strong
clench of the madman, this is
gripping the ledge of unreason, before
plunging howling into the abyss.
Hold hard then, heart. This way at least you live.

"Love is like a madness," I said, after a while. "That's what Eve told me one time."

"It was written by a man who had a twin, as you do," Williams said.

I didn't know Eve Solly and me were tight like a fist. I guess if I thought like Williams I'd think that.

Williams sighed deeply, still standing.

This has moved
past love to mania.
This has the strong
clench of the madman, this is
gripping the ledge of unreason, before
plunging howling into the abyss.

Then he looked at me.

"This way at least you live."

"Okay."

When Eve showed up a couple of days later and I told her about my conversation with Williams she just reminded me that the guy was deluged, or something like that.

■■■

As soon as I saw the face in the visitors' room, I remembered the name: Brad aka, Broad, our radio show producer in the old days.

He came by to visit me one day because he had just found out that Eve Solly was dead and that I was in a mental asylum. He felt guilty.

He thought things would have ended better all-round if he hadn't cancelled our show. I saw right off that Eve's death and my insanity had no meaning except regarding what might have been his part, which was small. I don't mind people being something big in their own lives. I guess it's natural. But I feel it's a kind of personal perversion for them to think my life's on hold until they get around to me.

We were seated in the visitors' lounge. Cag was on my shoulder and then took to the carpet and began to walk around looking for whatever birds look for on a carpet in a mental asylum.

Broad's attention was drawn to the bird and when I told him Cag not only spoke but compiled lists, like "The Parrots' Book of Begats" and "Vocabulary for Avian Success." She had been working on a dictionary and gotten up to the letter "F." She also did evangelical rants that could put the fear of the Lord in you and get you to accept Jesus as your personal savior. She did a weekly Revival service for about a hundred or so inmates. This was a better crowd of folks than those she tweeted with on her phone.

Broad had a "WTF" look on his face but I could also see the same glimmer that PT Barnum had when somebody pitched a 40-inch grown man. Of course, I did wonder why he had forgotten about the parrot but then again maybe he hadn't left a place for her in his personal memory.

I told him I had all Cag had done thus far on my Dictaphone. I pulled it out of my pocket.

"I carry it around. I never know when she's going to start work again."

I played him several minutes' worth of evangelical.

"From now on you will have wars and some sores…

"I lie down and sleep. I wake again. I lie down and… "

"All Ye! Get out of here quick … "

Broad was astounded. He said he was seeing a glimmer of hope in his life, which made me think that the parrot might have been a great evangelical orator.

Broad then told me things hadn't been going so well with him and that in fact if he didn't come up with a new show for our old spot, he thought he'd be out on his ear.

"Does the parrot answer questions? I mean can he do call in?"

"She," I said. "Probably. Might need a delay to block out stuff. She's kind of … I mean, no social filter. Misreputable."

"Like Eve," Brad sad, nodding. "She'll be missed."

It was then I told him that I still talked to Eve and, yeah, she still could take out a military advance with a couple of choice words.

I could see in his eyes that he was conjuring up something. Would I be willing to do the old *Shut Up!* radio show? Me, Cag and transmissions of Eve Solly's voice in my head. I figured he was at the end of his rope, not far from winding up in Fishkill, down on his rent, girlfriend gone, mountains of debts, somebody toying with his emotions, stretching his last nerve, pushing all the wrong buttons, last chance to grab the ring, on his way out that window into the darkness and so I said, "Why not?"

He'd get it organized.

"See if you can get some of my hand puppets in here," I said. "I'll give you a list of names."

He gave me a funny look but then recovered.

"I'll get it all sorted out," he told me and then he was gone.

And he did.

...

Eventually she would go away.

I would watch her walk away. I would keep watching her asleep, awake. She knew how to rock those heels without interfering with the switch of her very tight ass. I thought about being her man again. I also thought about what I was going to tell her if I saw her again, and I would be someplace where we both would be. It couldn't be dark. The sun had to be there. We were in the room. We hadn't flown out. And I would tell her what I was thinking.

...

What if humans hadn't moved on but had just stayed there at those closed gates and waited for a chance to get back inside? Half fallen into ... into dysphoria and half godly, like Achilles? Not ever in daylight or darkness but always a mystifying twilight.

How to penetrate the mystery?

I was waiting for Eve to tell me.

...

Time passed. I lost hair, weight, some eyesight, some hearing. I drank less and ate less. Cag died but I could still hear her last words:

"I told you to get the hell out of here!"

Theo came by less and less. He seemed never to have gotten over the shock that he was dead.

I listened to Mr. Spinalzo and Mr. Patawala in the mornings tutoring me on fractions and Hindi. In the afternoons, I met with Nicholas Williams who strangely had not aged one bit. He was as devoted to his sweetheart as ever. I envied that enthusiasm. My own energy seemed sapped. It was as if mine had existed in the mysterium of a twilight I had never pretended to understand or command. *Nascent, rudimentary, formless, amorphous,* Eve had scrawled on the wall of my cell

Eve. I no longer see her. She no longer visits me, but the name is luminous. Numinous is the word I remember.

I slept through hours I had before always been awake. Now, these days when I struggle to open my eyes, I see Williams standing outside my cell. Time for breakfast.

Another morning. But different. I can barely see him through eyes that I am having a hard time opening. He's holding the cell door open and smiling. Why is it open?

"Let's go."

"What? Where?"

"Moran is out front."

...

Eve's words at my memorial service surprised me. No sarcasm, no obvious false narratives, no attempt to implant false memories.

"You stood your ground, Babba. More exactly, you lay in your bed or that smelly overstuffed chair. Everything and everyone swam around you. Lots of stuff offered. None taken. All ambition denied. Even Nihilists couldn't recruit you. You were the nothing truer than the nothing they knew. You had an algorithm of one choice: absence. You didn't do anything with dividends but sewed the words in capitals on the shirts and blouses of your hand puppets. Long passage to mature wisdom on calm waters? Starved and sober pathway to Heaven? Naw. You fell through an open window, stumbled across the desert of Nada, the Banquet Hall of Happiness and the Vale of Ass wipes, Hucksters and Cretins, threw up more times than I can remember, and fell out the opposite window. You never reached for anything further than the distance a knife and fork took you."

I couldn't help at this point in the oralogy to ask if Eve had liked anything about me?

"Babba, for me, you've always been refreshing. In need of a daily airing out like an old blanket but existentially refreshing."

I told her I never knew that.

"I stand my ground without the excuses, rationales, memes and mythologies offered me. In you, I saw the same thing. That's our glue. My body put me on the outside. And my mind did too. I fought to be there because it was natural to me. No substitutes. No cheap flights out. No agents of change. No gurus. I made no apologies. I made no confessions. I held to no -isms. I took it all of what I am to the wire. Intact. I stood my ground. Like you."

"I'm sorry you got blown up for me."

"Me, too. But you put all my quarks together in your mind."

"I did do that?"

"We're doing that right now."

ABOUT THE AUTHOR

Joseph Phillip Natoli was born and graduated in egg creams, the Dodgers, Steeplechase boardwalk and stickball Brooklyn, now has a website www.josephnatoli.com, is a contributing writer for *Counterpunch*, oil paints on self-stretched canvas boats or houses. *Between Dog & Wolf and On a Lee Shore* complete a trilogy, the *New Utrecht Avenue trilogy*, begun with *Get Ready to Run*. Some characters die, some reappear, and some do both.